# Devil
# Dealing

D1450395

## IAN PATRICK

**Cover designed by RGS**

# DEDICATION

*To my wife and sons for love, support and glorious music.*
*To honorable men and women in uniform.*
*To my mother, who reads crime thrillers more avidly than anyone I know.*

.

## OTHER BOOKS BY IAN PATRICK

GUN DEALING
PLAIN DEALING
DEATH DEALING

# CONTENTS

# PREFACE

This crime thriller is the first in a series of four stand-alone books. Each can be read as an independent self-contained volume. Or they can be read in sequence or out of sequence as four related episodes in which the central themes and major characters reappear in other episodes, the intention being to provide an overall organic and cohesive narrative for the quartet. .

The four individual volumes explore moral and ethical choices made by police in their day-to-day confrontation with rampant and brutal crime in contemporary South Africa. The texts are fictional but based on field research and the author's physical exploration of the local environment, including actual locations where different events take place. Interviews were conducted with detectives and forensics experts both currently active and retired, and with local observers and participants, including victims of crime. The action aims for authenticity and plausibility, and strives to be resonant of conditions on the ground. The research included detective-guided tours of front-line scenes in the war against crime, and of police facilities, protocols and procedures. Actual events are reflected alongside fictive events, although all characters are fictional.

In the thoroughly absorbing task of writing this work and its sequels over a few years, I owe an inestimable debt to many people. Some of them prefer to remain anonymous. Others have graciously allowed me to name them. To all of them I offer enormous thanks and gratitude.

First and foremost in the ranks of people to whom I am grateful are my wife and two sons. As much as I value reading, and however indebted I am to the craftspeople of literature throughout history who have instilled in me a love of words, I cannot find language that will sufficiently express my gratitude to them. They have tolerated with great patience my frequent retreats into the silent joys of research and creative writing.

The detective who took me into KwaMashu in April 2015 to study some of his *work on the front line*, as he described it, had no idea that he would be taking me into the teeth of a dramatic xenophobic storm on that particular day. He allowed me to sit with him while we watched drug-dealers at work.

He explained in meticulous detail exactly what was going down before my eyes, and how the team of children (for that's what they were) played their individual roles in a sophisticated series of drug trades. We watched as the various role-players passed money and contraband on the street, as cars and motorcycles and pedestrians slipped past the youthful traders and quick sleight-of-hand saw packages and money being exchanged, unnoticed by most of the people passing in the road.

After taking me to different locations to watch the kinds of crime that permeate society on many street-corners, it was time for the detective to return me to base. As he did so, we ran into a horde of people caught in the throes of massive protest. Violent action hit the streets and the country reeled in shock at what became media headlines for the following week about xenophobic violence. The detective ensured that I was returned safely to my base in Durban, and I wrote that night into the early hours of the morning, trying to capture the flavour of what I had seen that day. I begged my detective to allow me to identify him and thank him for his work, but he declined. Nevertheless, although he felt more comfortable remaining anonymous in this prefatory statement, he kindly allowed me to re-name after him one of my characters who appears in the sequel to this volume. I am pleased to pay homage to this extraordinarily helpful detective in this way, and I thank him for his time, dedication, interest, and unwavering commitment in the mammoth task of South African police work.

I am grateful to many people for their willingness to correct my misconceptions, and to enable me to adjust some of the nuances in my writing in the interests of ensuring more authentic depiction of the day-to-day work of the police. Any remaining mistakes are entirely mine.

I am indebted to Gerrit Smit for very helpful detailed conversations about police procedure and protocol. This ranged from day-to-day interactions among police both in the field and in the station office, to procedures and protocols and actions and behaviour at crime scenes. In particular he gave me wonderfully detailed descriptions covering the work of police divers (who feature primarily in another sequel to this volume).

My thanks go also to Captain Saigal Singh. The enormous wealth of his experience as both a detective and a forensics specialist were particularly exciting for me after I had studied different courses on forensics and crime scene management. Having him hold up a mirror of extraordinary reality to what I had until then only studied academically, was most helpful.

Penny Katz was helpful beyond any call of duty. Apart from referring me to front-line detectives she gave me insights into aspects of crime and policing that have proved enriching beyond what I had imagined possible.

To interview victims of crime, and to go some small way toward understanding the pain and loss and trauma involved, has greatly affected my approach to research and writing. My personal experience of family trauma as a result of crime plays only a background role in my writing, but Penny allowed me insight into facets of this experience that I greatly value.

Some potential interviewees chose to decline my requests for interviews, and of course I entirely respect their choices in this regard. In one or two other cases, after initial readiness to participate the contact went cold and emails and phone-calls were simply ignored. I suspect that this was not unrelated to me mentioning that I would also be covering police corruption in my work. But even in those cases willing and helpful comments were received from people working in the very same offices as those who ignored my calls and emails.

I extend grateful thanks, therefore, to many people, ranging from police Brigadiers to Detectives and Constables both retired and currently active, from victims of crime to forensic investigators, and from my family to friends and colleagues. Many of them don't know exactly how helpful they have been to me even in brief communications or by referring me to other sources. Hennie Heymans, a retired policeman in Pretoria, has done extraordinary work in preserving the historical record on policing in South Africa, and he answered my questions promptly and with extensive knowledge of the past.

For any shallowness, superficiality or mistakes that might remain in my text, I apologise to these sources. I can only offer the excuse that the act of writing transports me into realms of satisfaction and joy. Not a day goes by during which I do not marvel at my good fortune in being able to create characters both evil and understandable. I live each day with them, exploring their thoughts and actions, enjoying their deviousness, their energy, their joyfulness, and the excitement of their lives.

I derive great pleasure from coaxing my characters out of the shadows and refining and polishing them in an attempt to reflect authenticity and plausibility. Some of them move me emotionally, and some of them are devilishly evasive and lying villains. But they all fascinate me and I still carry them in my head. I want to know what makes them tick, and I want to know their counterparts in real life. I have gone out into the field to find my fictitious characters because I insist on plausibility and authenticity in fiction. Otherwise how will we learn about our lives?

**Ian Patrick, August 2015**

# PROLOGUE

*The eyes were the objects that attracted much of the whispered discussion about his looks.*

*It was not just that the eyeballs bulged more prominently than most, though that feature in itself produced discomfort in anyone meeting him for the first time. No, it was rather the knotted red – almost purple – arterial networks bursting out of the yellow sclera, and appearing distinctly separated from the corneas by very dark limbal rings, that produced most of the discussion.*

*'His eyes are evil,' they whispered.*

*What was it about them? No-one could accurately describe them, or put their finger on what it was about them that so unnerved the observer.*

*They were like deep wells. The opaque dark brown of the irises was so near in colour to the black coal of the centre that the effect was of pupils unnaturally large and permanently dilated. When he glanced at you, it was as if he was staring at you. When he stared at you it was as if you were in the presence of the devil. So they said…*

*The eyes were the last things the young freckle-faced Afrikaner saw as the life drained out of him.*

# 1 MONDAY

**01.35.**

He sat naked in the thick bush, facing the sea; eyes fixed straight ahead on the everlasting nothing. The clamour of insects and frogs, heightened by his arrival, settled into an incessant low hum with counterpointed croaks. He leaned back against the arthritic tree. The glint of moonlight in the black centre of each of his eyes worried even the most adventurous of nocturnal creatures peering through the foliage at him. They might have thought, or they might have sensed, that his eyes were evil.

The only evidence of the sea in the implacable blackness of the night was the crashing of waves two hundred metres away, and the jagged moon-path on the water lurching from the horizon, searching for him. To right and left, far out, he saw pinprick lights of ships at anchor. They crawled up the south coast and down the north coast, waiting their turn to disgorge cargoes known and unknown at Durban's overworked wharves.

He inhaled deep into his lungs the toxic mix of the *nyaope* joint held lightly between a thumb and two fingers. The pungent fumes seemed to him to work their magic in two ways. With each inhalation he felt intense and indescribable hatred of everything that came to mind. At the same time he felt physically empowered, as if the drug infused him with unimaginable strength. As if he could fearlessly take on any adversary that might confront him. Such was the power of *nyaope*.

He sat in cold contemplation, waiting for the salt water to drip and dry away before he would put back on the clothes he had earlier draped over the bushes.

Six hundred metres away to his right a drunken sixty-something man, a portly British tourist, stumbled toward him over the soft beach sand broken in parts by succulent ground creepers. Stumbled in drunken expectation on the arm of a young prostitute. Slouched toward a messy death that would involve less than a minute of traumatic pain. A death that would preclude the much longer, much slower, agony that would have been his if the as yet undiagnosed cancer in his spine had had its chance to mature.

The man in the bush was not yet aware of the oncoming couple. Memory fixed his eyes on the horizon. And beyond, a million miles away. As he stretched back against the tree his tortured memory mustered twenty-three years of parental beatings - real and imagined - and countless incidents in which he was spurned, cajoled, teased, reprimanded, assaulted and raped. The acts had been perpetrated by parents, an uncle, a once-favourite teacher, friends, unknown thugs and assailants, the police, and - most recently - other prisoners.

He had shrewdly suppressed this painful history at his early-release hearing, exactly eight months after the assault on the banker. The assault that had put him behind bars and had reduced him to no more than a plaything. A dustbin. An ashtray. A receptacle for the filth of other much stronger men.

And now it was less than seven days since he had been set free. On each of those seven days he had made his way to the beach before midnight. At different points up and down the coast he had found a new spot each night, depending on the relative solitude of each place. A thicket of bush within a short distance of the breaking surf was the prerequisite.

He had washed himself in the sea each night, forcing the salt water into every orifice as if to scrub and scour the invasive filth from his body. Not just the filth that had been forced into him over many years, but the humiliation and the anguish and the violence that had been perpetrated upon his body and upon his psyche. He screamed in furious humiliation each night under the water, hearing the burbling of his voice under crashing waves, and he emerged from the surf each night with the hate burning stronger in his veins, and throbbing through his temples as he thought constantly of revenge. He sat in the bushes for an hour or more after each submersion, drying off and thinking deep, dark and violent thoughts as the salt crusted on his almost ebony skin.

He thought back to his life before being imprisoned the last time. Sent straight to the *tronk* for fracturing the skull of a man wearing a suit. For no discernible reason, they had said, other than that he had worn a suit.

He had experienced his first-ever *nyaope* fix just hours before that hit on the banker. He had felt strange. Supremely strong. Confident. Happy. He had discovered a new world. The man in the suit had pricked his bubble by spurning him. Not just spurning him, but abusively shouting at him and humiliating him. Right there, in the passageway of the hospital where he used to transport patients on trolleys to whatever floor was required. In front of everyone the man had said those things to him. *Those things.*

He had waited for the moment. He had followed the man at a distance. And then he had pounced.

*They catch me for smacking one banker. And just because I was with amaphoyisa before, they say they going to make a big example of me. So they send me downstairs for eight months. Eish! For a simple one smack across the head. They send a man to jail for that. Then they do those things to me. Those things. They do that to me!*

His desperate thoughts were ruptured by the sound of a high-pitched giggle, less than fifty metres away. He reacted instantly, flicked the joint into the bush, scrambled to his feet and reached for his clothes.

*

The tourist's young companion had fallen to her knees on the sand in front of her victim. She was laughing as she ripped off his belt and flung it aside. The tourist's first reaction was to laugh lasciviously, unsteady on his feet but maintaining his balance even as his trousers fell to his knees. Then he paused, and his confidence evaporated as he suddenly appreciated the reality of his situation. His wife of more than a quarter-century in Dorset. His two children in different universities in Scotland and Wales. His office colleagues. His boss. What was he doing with a young woman, younger than his own daughter, on a beach in South Africa after midnight? The bravura evaporated. The bravura that had been fuelled four hours ago by his sudden good fortune at the Blackjack table, followed by the cheers and applause he had received at the bar afterward, when all drinks had been for his account. Round after round. And now suddenly he was alone with this woman. This stranger.

'No, *lissen*, love. I don't think we can do this, OK? I'm too drunk, you see...'

'Is what? You say what? You say you want me, you pay big money. You pay me money, now, or I'm calling the police. I call my boyfriend.'

'No way, lovely. No way. No way you gonna get money from me, you little tart...'

'You white pig. You don't mess with me. Rape! Help! He raping me!'

"Wait! Wait, you f... No, wait! *Lissen*, love, OK! I'll pay. Wait a minute, lovely. *Cm'ere*! *Cummon*, then. Here you go, I got...'

Suddenly she screamed. A higher pitched scream he had never heard in his entire life. It reached all the way from Durban to Dorset and it turned him instantly more sober than he had been for hours. He tried desperately to clamp her mouth with his big meaty paws. This made it worse. She bit him and then started scratching and kicking. Her screams rose in pitch. He lunged at her and stumbled in the process. She was on him in an instant, tearing his jacket and ripping his wallet out of its inner breast pocket. She grabbed at it. He grabbed at it. She came away with a fistful of cash. Shocked at the realisation, she started stumbling away across the soft beach-sand and tangled ground creepers toward the lights of Battery Beach Road in the distance. The tourist tried to follow, then dropped his wallet, stumbled, and fell flat on his face. The woman melted into the night.

The fat man turned over onto his knees, cursing, reaching out, feeling for his wallet and the remaining cash. As he grabbed frantically for the wallet, he became aware of a new adversary.

Now clothed, the man had walked slowly from the bush during the course of the fracas, and had waited for the right moment. As the woman ran off, he positioned himself two or three paces from the tourist, his left foot on the wallet. As the terrified drunk looked up, he saw the eyes of the man, reflecting back to him two tiny circles of moonlight. He froze for a moment as he looked at the eyes. Then he pleaded, softly.

'I'm sorry, mate. So sorry. My wallet. She tried to… can I just have my wallet…'

'Is mine.'

'What? Sorry, I…'

'Is mine. You think you can take our women? For fifty rands? One hundred?'

'No, sorry, sorry. Yes, of course. Look, here, I don't want any trouble. Are you the boyfriend she spoke about? *Lissen*, mate, I'll give you five hundred. I'll …'

'You don't give. You don't take. Me, I take. Is mine.'

The malevolence that had been bubbling up inside, sitting in the bush, did not now emanate in fury or passion. A great icy calm descended upon him as he looked at the snivelling tourist. He felt the power of the *nyaope* coursing through his blood. He felt invincible. He levelled the pistol at the fat man's chest. Cold-moon grey glinted off the weapon. There was no mistaking it.

'No, please! No, what're you doing? You can't… I have a wife and ch…'

He pulled the trigger twice, quickly, and the fat man jerked. Extraordinary pain shot through his shoulder as both bullets shattered bone. One found the left clavicle and the other the scapula. The victim screamed and fell backward, but as his attacker bent forward to put another bullet into his throat, every remaining particle in his will to survive gathered to enable him to lunge out at the weapon and kick it from the assassin's grasp. The blow connected perfectly, but it was too late to prevent a third bullet going into the fat man's face just next to his right eye. The pistol traced an arc high into the darkness. The assailant, in a frenzy, stumbled a few paces in the assumed direction of the weapon and fell to his knees in the dark, hands flying furiously back and forth over the beach-sand, trying to find the gun. Hopeless. The moon gave away nothing concealed in the shadows of the wind-driven ripples and gullies of soft sand.

He cursed in frustration as he felt all around him. His arms and fingers stretched over the sand where he calculated the weapon might have fallen. Nothing. In the distance he heard a police siren. He scrambled back to the dying man and got to his feet. Every violent act that had been perpetrated upon himself over twenty-three years welled into his eyes as he kicked at the man's head once, twice, three times, then paused, as he felt something underfoot. The wallet. He reached down and picked it up. He paused. Then a fourth kick, this time aimed at the man's chest. The blow shattered two ribs, one of them penetrating the right lung.

The assailant walked away from the scene, across the beach to the distant lights of Snell Parade, clutching the wallet, but cursing at the loss of his weapon.

## 04.49.

Ryder always surfaced a few seconds before the alarm. For as long as he could remember he'd never been roused by the sound of the buzzer. Just the anticipation of it was enough.

'Simple fear of being frightened,' she had once suggested, when he told her he'd been that way since junior school. 'You're just psyching yourself to wake up a few seconds before you're forced awake. Why not dispense with the clock? You clearly don't need it.'

He'd replied that he needed it. Just in case. Otherwise he wouldn't get to sleep, worrying about whether he would oversleep.

'I give up,' she'd said.

He hit the button just before it could trigger. Maybe it wouldn't actually buzz. Maybe the alarm had died months ago and he had been wasting time setting the damn thing every night. So what?

He yawned noisily as he sat up, pushed the duvet back, swivelled, and planted his feet together on the floor. She stirred. He switched on the reading light and scratched his head all over, vigorously, eight fingertips digging roughly into his scalp. Got up stiffly from the bed. Balanced himself in the perpendicular for a moment and stretched until he clicked something, somewhere near L4. She turned away from the light and pulled the duvet over her head with a soft irritated grunt.

He dragged himself, feeling like an eighty-year old, to the shower, kicking off shorts and pulling off socks, one-legged, on the way. She insisted that if he used heel balm last thing at night, he had to wear socks to bed. To protect the handmade flat weave kilim that covered the floor next to their bed. It had been there since they had bought it for a small fortune on the Marmaris honeymoon more than fifteen years ago. Its warm terracotta, red and orange diamonds now still as clear and as bright as they had been on purchase. She was frugal but she knew quality when she saw it.

He flicked the bathroom switch and flinched at the bright white light, then grabbed a towel off the rail and hung it on the outside of the shower door while turning on the hot. Two minutes to wait before it would gush at top scalding temperature, during which he brushed his teeth, more vigorously than he needed to. Then in and under, shaking wildly like an Afghan hound under a hose.

'Ten minutes needed in there, minimum,' he had said on occasion to friends. 'Mainly because my hair just does its own thing if I go a single day without washing it.' Fiona sometimes corrected this. 'More like twenty minutes,' she would say, 'along with some loud tone-deaf singing, which usually gets me downstairs to do the coffee.'

He gurgled and bellowed, off-key, while water gushed into his mouth and moulded his hair flat and submissive on his skull, hat size seven and seven-eighths, if he ever was to wear a hat. He didn't have the lyrics in the right order, but his passion for JJ Cale's *Don't Wait* was such that he simply steamrolled on through the half-remembered verse by substituting the forgotten words with sounds ranging from *boom* to *da-da* in an effort to maintain some semblance of the rhythm.

Whenever he got the words wrong, he simply switched to other half-remembered snippets. Volume and passion and imagined guitar, held too low to be anything more than a manufactured memory of some rock festival, made up for inaccurate lyrics.

He emerged, pink and steaming and half the age he had been when he entered the cubicle. Can't do it any other way, he thought. What is it with me? Like a train's run over me when I wake up. Like a forty-something again after a bit of soap and steam. Weird.

He towelled his hair violently. Thrust his face into the mirror to check what was there that shouldn't be there. Alert blue eyes stared back. Dark brown on top was ready for taming by the hairbrush, but sideburns were showing too much grey. Shouldn't that happen only when I'm fifty? Ed had told him the week before that he was using that *just for men* stuff: got it from some guys called Combe International, he had said. But Ed was ten years older. OK for him to *touch up first grey* – he was trying to find a third wife. He needs to do something, I suppose, to nail down one of the particular thirty-something types he seems to be chasing all the time. Randy bastard. Needs a Fiona in his life. A forty-something. Shoulda had some kids and a dog a dozen years ago. Like me. Needs a guitar now. Like me. And an intelligent woman. Yep. Like me.

The bed was empty when he emerged from the bathroom, shaved and smelling of nothing more imaginative than Brut under the arms and Old Spice on his muscular neck and chiselled jaw. And hair now obediently in place. The main light was on, the reading lights were off, and the bed was made. She clearly hadn't much enjoyed his rendition. She didn't care much for J.J. Cale at the best of times. She just doesn't get him, he thought.

He opened his wardrobe, rifled through the shirts, paused, decided to throw on the old favourites: black denim jeans and khaki long-sleeve. Both clean and threadbare from a hundred washes.

He strapped the holster under his left armpit and slid the Vektor SP1 into it. Old friend, he thought. After some serious skirmishes over the years he derived comfort from the SP1's double-stack magazine, short-recoil locked-breeches and double-action trigger. He gave it the briefest of reassuring pats, as if it was the pet Chihuahua his son's girlfriend always carried in her shirt. Ready for the new day. He reached for the dark-brown leather jacket.

Fiona called. 'Jeremy!!! Coffeeeee!!'


## 05.25.

The security guard was asleep as usual, head down on folded arms. His desk faced the two massive glass-paned doors ten paces away. A four-digit code punched in from outside by a returning tenant would unlock them. So would the press of a button from someone on one of the dozen floors above, responding to an appropriate visitor's intercom request. Fronting the doors on the street side, the two aluminium trellis-gates were closed but not locked. They were never locked, unless the guard had to leave his post for a short while.

Beyond the gates and the dual carriageway carrying the occasional freight truck, lay the black murkiness of the bay. It was flecked with the first encroachment of dull morning grey. Yachts in the special enclave in the harbour rocked gently on the turning tide. Four shapes silhouetted against the grey passed quickly, heading toward the exit from the wharf and then swiftly, silently across the carriageway to the buildings opposite. To the trellis-gates.

He had barely stirred at the sound of the gates being thrust back, but started to lift his head as the glass doors clicked open in response to the four digits punched into the box. The four men were upon him before he could get to his feet to hit the panic button. The first one smacked him with the flat of the panga blade across his left temple and he went down immediately, twisting one hundred and eighty degrees from the blow and sprawling face down across the chequered tile floor. The second one grabbed him by the collar and twisted him around, face up. As he started to scream the third jammed a pistol-barrel into his mouth, tearing the bottom lip and cracking a molar. The fourth, also with a panga, hacked open the door to the flimsy wooden cupboard and flung the contents out onto the floor. Four or five bunches of keys, a spare visitor-book, pen, pencils, pale yellow baked-enamel coffee mug, teaspoon and a bottle of water all skidded across the surface toward the terrified hostage.

The man with the pistol bent close to him, hissing into his face:

'Number 82. Keys. Now. Or you die.'

The guard gagged in terror, rasping sounds trapped in his throat, pointing at the nearest of the bunches of keys, three feet in front of his right foot. The pistol man pulled the weapon roughly from his mouth, wreaking more damage to teeth and lips. He reached for the bunch of keys and thrust them into the old man's face.

'Show me. Now! Number 82. Which one?'

The guard whined as he took the bunch and isolated no. 82 with its yellow tag from the rest of the keys, each with its own coloured tag. The gunman snatched it back and walked swiftly with the two panga-men to the elevator, while the fourth dragged the guard to his feet and pushed him down into the chair.

The whites of the old man's bulging eyes were arctic against his dark wrinkled skin. They reflected fear that he had never imagined possible. He trembled violently and cried like a child as blood trickled from his mouth over his white beard.

His tormentor smiled. His brown eyes were rheumy and bloodshot. The old guard thought that the young man's eyes seemed to be those of a much older man. The eyes seemed to be an extension of a brain that had been slowly fried away by noxious weeds mixed with potent chemicals.

'Today, *madala*, maybe you die,' the young man said. 'Maybe today.'

## 05.57.

The two detectives chuckled together next to the urn as the third, deadpan except for a slight smirk, poured his own cup of thick black coffee. The two Afrikaners could never comprehend how their two *Engelsmanne* colleagues – especially this one in front of them – managed to muster up an endless supply of jokes, each seeming to start with *This guy, he walks into a pub*. And almost all of the stories – from this one, they thought, but not so much from his partner – were built on sexual innuendo.

'*Sies, jong!* You're a filthy man, Trewhella. No wonder you've had so many divorces.'

'*Ja, boet*. How do your women react to filth like that?'

'Never been a problem, as far as I can see. You gotta laugh, guys. Don't bore the women. Make 'em laugh. Trust me. Get them chuckling. Makes them cuddly. Which reminds me. This feller. Walks into a pub…'

The sergeant ripped open the inner door, phone in hand, and bellowed out at them:

'Koeks! Dipps! Captain needs you to go over to Addington Hospital. Right away. Shoot-out last night. Something about the bush near Suncoast casino. Pillay will meet you there. She called it in. She's with the first responder. She says she needs help urgently because he's got no clue. He's already stuffed up the cordon, she says.'

'OK, Piet. Let's go, Dipps. See you, Trewhella. Hold that story for us, OK?'

'Cheers, guys. I'll wait for Ryder and practice it on him. If he doesn't find it funny, you will.'

Koekemoer and Dippenaar grabbed their polystyrene cups and slammed the door behind them as they strode out to the cars. Sergeant Cronje retreated back to the inner office.

Trewhella pulled a chair up with his foot while stirring his coffee. He sat down to look at yesterday's *Tribune*. He didn't get past the back page. A colour photo of a model, twenty-five-ish, he surmised, kissing a chocolate flake that was stuck into a vanilla soft-serve cone. Nice, he thought. Just like wife number one, all those years ago. But before he could read the commentary the sergeant was back at the door, repeating his earlier performance, but more urgently, this time yelling at a much higher pitch:

'Ed! Robbery and shooting. Now! At The Grove, Margaret Mncadi Avenue. Opposite the Yacht Club! Uniforms are there but they called in to...'

'OK, Piet! I know the place. I'm gone.'

'Ryder's only due at 6.30, but...'

'Don't worry, I'll get hold of him. You set up some backup just in case, Piet. I'll call in if I need it.'

'OK. Will do.'

'If I miss Ryder, send him along as soon as he gets in...'

He spilled half the coffee on his way out while shouting all of this and by the time he reached his car he cursed and threw away what was left. He tore out of the parking area, kicking up white vapour as the souped-up police car lurched out into the empty street, skidded round the corner into Stalwart Simelane Street and burned its way up the road like a sewing machine about to burst.

**06.15.**

Ryder eased the Camry down the driveway. Following her plea on behalf of the neighbours as she kissed him goodbye, he waited till he was at the corner before turning on the CD player.

The main selling point for his purchase of the 2009 vehicle had been its six-speaker stereo with auxiliary input. The dealer had made a big thing about the five-speed transmission and seven airbags and anti-lock brakes and electronic stability and traction control and cruise control and power windows and locks and sport-tuned suspension, but Ryder had already made up his mind when he heard the impact of the speakers. Fiona had gone straight to the sound system and turned it on, *knowing that it would play the key part in Jeremy's choice*, as she had told friends. She had been right. The rest of the stuff was no more than OK, in his view. *The car's great*, Ryder had said to the salesman.

He turned up the volume to full only after scanning for the right lyrics from *Don't Wait*, the ones he hadn't been able to bring to focus in the shower. He found them when he was already well down the old main road.

Banging out the beat on the steering wheel, as he glided from the King Cetshwayo highway onto the N3, and bellowing aloud in an attempt to keep with the words, he missed the first three rings on the iPhone. He picked up halfway through the fourth, and heard Ed screaming:

'Jeremy! Get over here! Two down at The Grove. Eighth floor, apartment block, Margaret Mncadi, right opposite the Yacht Club. Where are you?'

'Three minutes, Ed. Maybe four. Coming up to Toll Gate.'

Ryder grounded the pedal and the V6 responded instantly. The Camry bolted forward, thrusting him back into the cool leather. He crested the rise under the bridge with a clear freeway down to the city, as Trewhella yelled:

'Make it three! This is bad stuff! Gang of four. Security guard also badly smashed up. Uniforms are looking after him downstairs. Guard says they ran across the road to the harbour area. And - shit - I can see them from way up here! They've been into the main boat area and are now heading down to Wilson's Wharf. On foot, walking fast. Not running. Carnage up here, Jeremy. Really bad shit! Old couple. Waste the bastards if you have half a chance. They're really bad news. I'll join you at the Wharf. I'm leaving the scene now!'

Ryder hit one hundred and eighty kilometres an hour on the straight as he bellowed into the phone:

'What are they packing?'

'Can't tell. Big blades, definitely. Maybe pangas. And from the wounds and what the security guard shouted at me it looks like at least two 9-mm as well. I'm still way up here, waiting for the damn lift. I'll have to cross the Embankment to the yachts. Then down the road to Wilson's.'

'I'll be there! Wait for me!'

'No! I can't wait. I'll be on foot. Don't pick me up. Go straight past me down to the restaurants. Maybe they don't know it's a dead end. Scare the shit outta them with everything you got on wheels. They'll duck from you and probably come straight back up the drag to me and I'll nail them. Getting into the lift now - losing signal!'

'Got it!

He opened the window, placed the magnetised blue light on the roof, and left the end of the freeway through the red light, spinning a right turn with all four tyres slipping, then grabbing, then slipping again before finding traction then screeching and depositing rubber through the intersection. He caught the next four lights – *or was it five*, he thought – on the green at one hundred and twenty, slowed down a fraction while pulling hard left as he skidded onto the old Victoria Embankment, then lurched forward again with his foot flat. Another twenty seconds and he had got there in way less than three minutes.

As he skidded up to the entrance to the bay area on his right he glimpsed Ed over the low wall, sprinting down the road to Wilson's. He spun the wheel, clattered over the railway lines with siren bellowing and blues flashing and within seconds he had surged past his partner, who waved him on and hunched forward as he ran, eyes straining to see any shapes ahead that might be outlined against the bay. The dawn was still slow enough to provide dim cover for Ed. If Ryder's partner was right and they chose to backtrack away from the car, they would run right back into him.

As Ryder's car careened over the rail tracks all four of them had broken into a sprint. They were still a couple of hundred paces from the restaurants and shops ahead, and would have to cross a car park to make it to the darkened buildings. No time. Best to duck in at the sea wall, they decided, and take cover in the rocks before the headlights swept over them.

Bad decision. There was not enough light on the bay for them to be more than dimly discernible shapes, but Ryder gunned the car past them without slowing, as if he had missed seeing them altogether, then suddenly spun the car one hundred and twenty degrees just inside the entrance to the car-park, with the headlights aimed out over the edge of the bay behind them, now turning all four of them into perfect silhouettes for Trewhella.

Turkey shoot, thought Trewhella. Jeremy's lined them up perfectly for me. He kept low on his approach as he heard Ryder's warning shout piercing through the dawn:

'Police! Stand up and put your hands on your head! Do not, I repeat, do not...'

A shot rang out. Ryder heard the slug sink into the Camry, somewhere front and left. Ed had been right about the weapons. Probably 9 mm. Sounded like the old standard-issue Vektors in the unit.

Three of them, including the shooter, broke cover and ran back, away from Ryder and the car, just as Trewhella had hoped, back the way they had come in. Meanwhile the second weapon came into play as the fourth man, holding back, raised his right arm toward Ryder and put another bullet harmlessly into the Camry's front fender. Definitely sounds like the Z88 thought Ryder, cool as ice. He calibrated the moment as he moved swiftly to his left, away from the car, and raised his own weapon calmly at the silhouetted shooter. The Vektor Z88 double action was patterned after the M92 Beretta. Denel had started delivery of these to the South African police years ago. Ryder reckoned that judging from their aim these guys were strangers to the weapons. They had probably recently stolen them.

They certainly couldn't have had much practice with them, judging from the poor aim behind the first shot. And this guy had probably never experienced a real contest between a Z88 and the SP1. That was about to change.

The other three ran straight into his partner. Trewhella was not the talking type in these situations. They were running away from a cop, and now toward him. They had fired a shot at a detective. Arguably the best detective in the province. His buddy had warned them, and they had replied with a second bullet. That was enough. Trewhella pumped two into the shooter's head with his first effort, two-handed, rock steady, as calm as if he was back on the range putting holes in a paper target. Then he switched aim very slightly to put three into the chest of the second guy who was already raising his hands in surrender even before his crony's body had hit the ground.

'Too late, arsehole,' the detective muttered.

It was as if the second target had run into an oncoming bus. He flew back with bits of his ribs and breastbone floating outward in a pink cloud from the effect of three bullets entering within a radius of no more than four inches before following the rest of the corpse to the ground.

The third man stopped in his tracks, frozen in terror, hands raised high above his head and screaming something incomprehensible, which sounded like a plea not to shoot him. Trewhella considered blowing his head apart anyway, to save on the paper work, but then decided they might need at least one of them to interrogate about the carnage upstairs. So he put a single bullet into the right shoulder instead. If the guy bled out and didn't survive for questions, tough. Not Trewhella's problem.

He walked over to Ryder, leaving the third man screaming on the ground. Trewhella had heard the single shot from the SP1, and he knew that Ryder had a simple rule in action like this. Don't pull that trigger unless you're going to waste someone. And in this case the bullet had gone into the fourth guy's throat, severed the spinal column, and continued on its way taking lumps of gristle with it. Very messy.

Ryder was already on his iPhone, calling Piet Cronje to check with the War Room and find out about sending in the cleaners. He turned to Trewhella as he hung up on the call.

'Two vics down upstairs, you said?'

'At least two. I couldn't check it out properly. Once I saw the scene I thought we had a chance if we acted quickly, so I called you. Couldn't get hold of you till I was up there in the middle of it. No signal in the lifts.'

'Check this out. Vektor Z88. Check the stamp. Ours.'

They both bent over the grounded Vektor, lying next to Ryder's victim. Without touching it Trewhella could see the identifying numbers.

'Stolen from our own guys?

'Maybe bought.'

'Why don't you check the other weapon, Jeremy? I'll go and ask the wounded arsehole where they got it.'

'OK. Careful with him: we need him to sing.'

'I'm never careful with guys like this. You know that.'

'I can but hope.'

'You hope on, buddy.'

As Ryder moved to the other grounded weapon, Trewhella walked back to the whimpering wounded. Turned him from a whimperer to a screaming banshee by putting his foot on the shattered shoulder, using considerable force.

'Where'd you get the gun? Hey?'

The man screamed in agony as the detective started rolling his shoulder back and forth under his boot.

'You want more of this? Hey? The gun! Where did you steal the gun?'

The man passed out. Silence.

'Stuff him. I'll get it out of him later.'

He walked over to Ryder who was squatting over the second weapon.

'Also one of ours? What does the stamp say?'

'Yep. Vektor Z88. Same thing. Check this stamp. Also one of ours. Captain is going to be very interested. Two Z88s, both from his own unit.'

As Trewhella squatted, peering from different angles at the weapon while being careful not to touch it, Ryder walked back over to the man he had put down.

'Check this out. Panga with blood. Still carrying it. You say the two upstairs were cut, Ed?'

'Bad. Really bad, Jeremy. Old guy's skull hacked deep. Ancient guy. Must be eighty or more. One blow. He didn't have a chance, man. Old woman, too. Her abdomen just sick-making, man. Hacked repeatedly.

You're looking at the murder weapon right there. Why they then also had to pump bullets into them beats the hell out of me. Judging from the bloods they were hacked first, dead very quickly, then shot afterward just for good measure. They took three or four slugs each, so these guys were out of control, man. Why they let the security guard survive I don't know.'

'Let's go talk to him.'

'OK. Then breakfast.'

'You sick-head.'

## 08.15.

The entrance to The Grove was all flashing blue and red lights as they finally left the building. The photographers had done their bit, at both scenes: upstairs and on the wharf. The first responder was in a panic, being scolded by everyone about the inadequacy of his two cordons. Someone from Forensic Services was shouting that this was her second incident this morning and the second time someone had screwed up the cordons. The bodies on the wharf were still getting the full treatment, but forensics were satisfied with their first scan upstairs, had done a thorough Bluestar spray, lifted what they needed, and were moving out from there to join their colleagues on the wharf. Tenants were gathered on the pavement, others still peering out of windows from the floors above. Some journo was asking the locals various questions about crime in the area. Traffic was grinding to a halt as the rubber-neckers were at it, with those behind leaning on their hooters until they, too, got their chance to rubber-neck. Then they got the same hooter treatment from those further behind.

Trewhella and Ryder had interrogated the security guard in the entrance area while a paramedic was repairing him. He had been brilliant, thought Ryder. Impressive detail. And he had loved the old lady upstairs, he said, crying as if he had lost his own mother.

'Ninety-five years old, boss. Good lady. Very kind. Every day she is walking, she is going to the shops. Very strong lady. My *gogo*, boss. My *gogo*. She gives me Christmas presents every year. And money for my family.'

They learned from him that the old guy upstairs with her hadn't lived there. Just visiting. Overnight stay.

'Old man was her friend, boss. He comes sometimes. Sometimes staying one night only. He lives on other side, Aliwal Street. He eighty. Madam she ninety-five. She strong. Him not so strong.'

Ed smirked as they left the building.

'Hope I can still get it on like the old guy did when I'm his age. But not with ninety-five-year-olds.'

'You are a very sick man.'

The guard had been able to give them more than they had hoped. No, he had never seen the four men before. *Tsotsis*, they were. *Nyaope, all of them, they take it.* He knew what *nyaope* did to the young men. No, nothing different had happened around the building for weeks. It appeared that the old girl's routine had been as predictable as sunrise.

'Every day she is walking eight o'clock. Morning. Every day she gets the newspaper. For the crossword, boss. She is not reading the other stuff. All politics, she say. Bad thing, she say.'

Once a month the old man had visited. At the end of the month. *Gogo* always baked scones or sausage rolls for his visit, and gave the guards some when he had gone, the next day. She went to the casino twice every week.

'Suncoast Casino, boss. Tuesday and Thursday, always. One time, long time back, she was going to the Wild Coast Casino with the bus. But she was saying never again, too far, bad machines and no luck.'

Twice every week. Tuesdays and Thursdays. But never with the old man. No, there had been no other visitors. Sometimes her son would pick her up in the car. Maybe once a month. Sometimes twice. The son never went upstairs to fetch her. She met him downstairs each time.

Useful detail. Clear enough picture, thought Ryder. Only one gap. Motive. Why butcher an old couple? No cash on the three bodies on the wharf, or on the wounded guy. No sign of wealth in the apartment upstairs. The perps had searched the flat. Made a mess of it. Definitely looking for something. But no safe. No money, other than three or four coins, still in the old woman's purse. What were they looking for? No alcohol. Healthy living. Lots of vegetables and fruit. No red meat. Lots of paperback thrillers. The TV armchair well used. Spent her time watching soaps, doubtless.

*Why her? Ninety-five years, man. What for?*

The old guy was probably just there on the wrong night. They hacked him down with one blow, then they pumped bullets into him. It was her they had wanted. Her key they had demanded from the guard. They took longer with her. Maybe making demands first. She didn't give them what they demanded. So they cut her to pieces. Then the bullets. Maybe in frustration, because she was already dead when they shot her.

Why kill her?

**09.25.**

Captain Nyawula had agreed that they should handle the case together. They had decided to go to the son's place in two cars so that they could split for follow-up stuff afterwards. Trewhella to go to Addington Hospital to question the guy with the shoulder - Cronje had called to tell them that the wounded man had been taken there with serious loss of blood - and Ryder to get to forensics and then probably back to The Grove to question tenants further.

They had agreed that Trewhella would do most of the talking when they met the son. The opening of this session passed more easily than Ryder had anticipated. After the initial trauma of the news and the questions and the reassurances - Ed surprising Jeremy with unusual sensitivity, including an offer of personal contact at any time if there were further questions - Ed got some breakfast out of it from the maid. Lillian always hovered, according to the son, in the hope that guests would ask for proof of her employer's proud boast about her cooking. Trewhella accepted - after the obligatory *no thanks, much as I would like to, but we're on duty* - which the son saw through immediately, instructing Lillian accordingly. Ryder declined. Except for the coffee. Jeremy Ryder never declined coffee.

The son had gradually calmed down after the initial shock, and eventually they were able to go through some fairly detailed family history for ten to fifteen minutes. Nothing there of particular interest. During the course of delving into this history they had moved out onto the deck, overlooking not only the other high-security palaces in the neighbourhood but also with a view all the way to the Indian Ocean some ten kilometres away. Lillian had laid one place for brunch at the table on the patio. The son stood with Ryder, looking out into the distance as they talked. Ryder sipped the rich coffee – better coffee than he could remember ever having had – as he listened to the brief history laced with anecdotes, taking it all in, mostly in silence. Trewhella sat next to them, shovelling down the scrambled eggs, bacon, pork sausage, grilled tomato, baked beans, fried banana and mushrooms.

There was another son abroad, and the brother would handle that side of things. Some tough days ahead for the family, thought Ryder.

He reinforced everything the guard had said about the old woman. His mother was amazing. Everyone talked admiringly about the ninety-five-year-old who looked like a seventy-year-old. She was well known in the area around The Grove. She was completely independent, very strong, with all her marbles in place. The son derived some comfort in illustrating with a couple of examples.

'She was a complete whizz-kid on the machines at Suncoast Casino. Well, according to her, that is. I never heard her say that she'd had a losing day on the machines. Always a winner, it seemed. I would always take her claims with a pinch of salt, of course. Having said that, though, a buddy of mine once called me from the casino and told me how he had recognized her - he always went on a Thursday and she was always there, he said - and how she was cleaning up at the slot machines even as we spoke. The management were handing her an envelope, and he said that people were applauding her and saying they always saw her there and that she always got terribly excited when she won anything, which was frequently the case. So she certainly wasn't a loser. She probably broke better than even over the years she's been going to the place.'

He invited Trewhella to go and help himself to more bacon and eggs in the kitchen. The detective needed no prompting and within seconds came the sound of him laughing and teasing Lillian, as the son continued with Ryder.

'Trouble is, my friend also told me that she was attracting attention to herself and she needed to be careful of mugging as she left the place. So I gave her a serious talking-to next time I called her. The other thing is – oh – did you find the money under the carpet?'

'What?'

'She always put her winnings under the carpet.'

'Carpet? Where?'

'In the corner of her lounge. Under the easel. Where she paints. Under the carpet. She put her gambling money, as she called it, under the carpet. Didn't want to draw from the bank in order to gamble. A principle of hers.'

'How much are we talking?'

'Don't know. She told me it was five or six thousand. Just *emergency money*, she said. I left her to it. Didn't you check? Under the carpet, man!'

## 11.45.

Ryder pushed up the volume to the max for his favourite Fleetwood. He thudded huge dangerous slaps onto the steering wheel with both hands matching the escalating percussive rhythm, while he bellowed atonally, pleading for the imagined recipient of his singing not to say that she loved him, but just to tell him, instead, that she wanted him…

He pushed the needle up to one hundred and forty kilometres as the song climaxed, then settled back into his seat, resting both hands as the beat faded away and he held steady at cruising speed as he drove under the old Toll Gate bridge for the second time that morning, back to The Grove.

Enjoying the feel of the Camry, he raised an imaginary glass in a toast to his Captain. Nyawula had pulled some strings to get Ryder onto the private car scheme, normally open only to much more senior ranks than himself. But Nyawula knew who his top detective was, and he intended to treat him accordingly.

## 11.50.

There were four men in the room, one seated behind the small desk in the only chair in the place capable of bearing his weight, and the others standing together, more or less in line, in front of him. The man in the black leather and stainless-steel chair was ominously still, staring at two of the others. Even seated he loomed large in the room, his three hundred and fifty pound body compressed into five feet and one inch of height. His hairdo, a slicked-down, carefully side-parted black bob, suggested ice-cold control and precision but also something atavistic waiting to burst out in uncontrolled fury. His fleshy pink neck bubbled out of the triple-X collar, held tightly closed by a double-knotted red and violet silk tie.

There was a long silence. The air-conditioning unit was barely audible as it cooled and refreshed the room. Other sounds - the whirring CPU fan of the HP desktop, the muffled hum of the Xerox Phaser 7100V Printer, the ticking of the cheap desk clock mounted on a slab of inch-thick glass - all seemed to be deadened by the lush thick carpet.

Two of the three, standing shoulder to shoulder, were wary, unsure of their next moves, ready to appease at any opportunity. The third, as if to distinguish himself from them, stood a pace apart but, like them, with his hands clasped lightly behind his back. He was about six feet in height, carrying two hundred and twenty pounds, and the white linen jacket pulled tightly across the chest, shoulders and biceps suggested that he was no stranger to heavy gym equipment. His pale blue eyes gave nothing away, as he stood, waiting. The seated man addressed him first, three simple words growling up from his diaphragm through the enormous torso and emanating as a rasp from the back of his throat.

'Tell me, Tony.'

The man he addressed couldn't help thinking yet again that the voice was so harsh and falsely phonated that it had to signify strained vocal chords, the consequence of a voice incorrectly pitched from early childhood. If cancer had a sound, thought Tony, then this voice was that sound. It was the worst case of ventricular dysphonia he had ever encountered. The vocal chords, doubtless oppressed by nodules, were producing sound through torturous misuse of the larynx and insufficient air from a diaphragm too oppressed by weight to muster the necessary energy for a properly supported voice.

'The info was good, Vic,' he replied. 'They watched her over a period of five weeks. They nailed her routine exactly. She would arrive at 10.00 am almost every Tuesday and Thursday. Then she would wrap up at 12.30 and go across to John Dory's for fish and chips and a glass of white wine. She never - not once - ate anything else. Then she would leave at almost exactly 2.00 pm each and every time. They watched her hail taxis, and followed her back to her apartment block a couple of times.'

Vic didn't look at Tony through any of this. He kept his eyes on the other two. Tony had paused. Vic gestured - a simple beckoning from the second and third fingers of his right hand - that Tony should continue.

'On two key occasions after she had big wins on the machines, they even tracked her all the way home and right up to her flat on the eighth floor: once on pretext of checking elevator doors and another time making as if they were checking passageway lights in the building. Both times, the guys were right behind her and checked the numbers she punched in for the main door, and both times they were able to follow her all the way up and see her unlock her security gate and go in, leaving the door wide open but locking the gate behind her ...'

One of the two underlings, overweight, perspiring, and nervous, wilting under Vic's inscrutable stare, added his piece.

'That was me, the second time, Vic. I mean the overhead lights. I checked the passage light right in front of her door just after she went in, one Tuesday. I got past the security guy no problem, just walking in behind her, holding a clipboard and carrying a toolbox. Told him I had been sent by the agents after a complaint. I told the old bird, too, in the lift, that I was there to fix lights, so when we got to her flat she didn't even bother to close the door while I started checking her passage light just outside her security gate. She just locked the gate behind her and left the door open. I saw her take her handbag straight into her lounge and she pulled the envelope out right there, twenty feet in front of me as if she forgot I was there. That was the day she won twenty-five thousand rands. I had watched her wrap up things at the cashier's when she cashed out, and followed her all the way, and Jannie picked me up in the car and we followed the taxi, and he waited downstairs to watch while I went up...anyway, she left the envelope on the table in the lounge and made herself some coffee. As if I wasn't there. She was talking to herself, like…'

His partner, thin, young, freckled, highly strung, speaking rapidly and with a thick Afrikaans accent, interjected, apprehensively.

'... and like Dirk says, Vic, that was the day I was watching there by the front of the building, Vic. Tony, you know? There where I showed you? All afternoon, Vic. I watched Dirk leave after he did the lights thing and the old *ouma* didn't come out the rest of the day. I watched all the time until the banks were shut and she didn't come out. The next day I was back *vroeg* in the morning and she did her normal newspaper walk then went straight back to the flat. Never came out again. The day after that one, Vic, I followed her on the newspaper thing again and then followed her when she did the 9.30 taxi to the casino. She definitely didn't visit any bank after winning the 25k. And she only played with a few *hunnertrand* notes that day, so she definitely left the 25k in the flat...'

Dirk nudged his partner:

' - tell them about the day you were at her door, Jannie.'

Jannie continued:

'*Ja*, that's right, Vic. I was there on the other day Tony mentioned. The guard thought I was checking the lift, you know? Same thing for me: I had a *watchamacallit* - a clipboard and box of tools, and I was in. I saw her go into her flat, and leave the door wide open but lock the gate, you know, and she put her bag straight there on the table in the next room where I could see and she just pulled out the envelope and *sommer* started counting *hunnertrand* and *twohunnertrand* notes without even caring about me being there.'

Tony added his bit to clarify:

'That was the day she went home with 14k, Vic. A Thursday. Cashed out, all stuffed into an envelope. I was with the guys that day and all three of us watched her do it at the cashier's counter then saw her put it into her bag. Then Jannie tracked her all the way back home and did the elevator thing, while Dirk watched the front of the building this time. Same thing after Jannie left, right, Dirk?'

'Same thing, Tony. I watched Jannie leave and watched the rest of the day and the next day and she definitely didn't visit any bank.'

Vic drummed the fingers of his right hand on the glass top, scowling. Then he got up from the chair and rasped.

'OK, guys, let me have a word with Tony. Don't go far. Hang around downstairs near the tables where Tony can get hold of you. Get yourselves a drink at the bar.'

Jannie and Dirk were visibly relieved. They muttered their thanks and left Tony alone with Vic. Vic leaned his enormous bulk back against the edge of the desk, chewing his bottom lip and thinking. Tony waited.

'You say it was Jannie that contracted the four black guys for the job this morning?'

'Yup.'

'Where did he find them?'

'He told me they were the same guys - well, two of them anyway - that he had used before. For the hit last year on that guy who reneged on payments for the confiscated slot machines. Remember him?'

'How could I forget?'

'They worked fine that time, Jannie says. He organised two guns for them through a contact, a disgruntled ex-cop who'd stolen a few pistols and sold two of them to Jannie dirt cheap, especially for that hit. Jannie said it had gone well that time so this time he just called the same two guys. They still had the guns. They'd been part-payment for that first job.'

'So Jannie never met the other two from this morning's hit?'

'No, Jannie's two just went ahead on their own and got their two buddies in on the act. Apparently Jannie didn't know there would be four of them.'

'Arsehole.'

'Yup.'

'I want you to watch Jannie, Tony.'

'OK, Vic.'

'And what's the case with Dirk? Seems nervous as all hell.'

'Doesn't like fouling up, that's all.'

'Watch him.'

'OK, Vic.'

'Any chance of the fourth bugger in hospital leading the trail back here?'

'Don't think so, Vic. None of us knows him or has had any contact with him. Jannie's two guys were two of the three guys wasted by the cops this morning. There's no trail back to Jannie. He himself never met this fourth guy.'

'All the same… can we get anyone into the hospital before they move that guy to the cells?'

'You want him taken out?'

'It would make me sleep easier.'

'I'll get onto it, Vic.'


## Noon.

Ryder sat there, cross-legged on the floor, with the carpet peeled back from the wall and the easel leaning against the opposite wall, where he had moved it to get at the carpet. One hundred and eighty-four thousand rands. It had been spread out in piles of no more than ten notes each, to avoid creating lumps in the carpet. Spread over more than half the area covered by the carpet.

Because Ed had gone on to the hospital, he had called Piet Cronje to send someone else to meet him at the apartment. He had wanted a witness if there was going to be cash. Piet had come himself, and had arranged for a photographer, too. No-one else had been available from the team, so Piet had issued instructions to the intern who had arrived mid-morning after a training workshop. He left her panic-stricken to look after the office and to call him if she needed to.

Cronje had never seen so much cash in one place.

'Fok.'

'Not bad, hey? A year's salary for you, Piet.'

'Nooit! Much more, Jeremy, man. Jislaaik!'

'Let's bundle it up and get it signed off.'

Ryder sat, contemplative, as Cronje gathered up the notes and the photographer recorded as much as she could from every possible angle. This is what the bastards were looking for, thought Ryder. How had they known? If the old woman was this careful, she wasn't likely to blab about it to anyone. How had they known which key to grab from the guard? How had they got the code for the lock on the front door? How would they know about the old woman's secret stash?

He reached for the iPhone on the first vibration and before the first ring.

'Yep?'

It was Trewhella.

'Our survivor is talking.'

'Good, Ed. Did you remove fingernails, or what? I would have thought that Addington Hospital would allow you to see him only with witnesses present. Did you charm the nurses?'

'Just the opposite, buddy. I arrived while his legal-aid appointed friend was out taking a pee. As I walked in and the guy recognised me he almost crawled up the wall. When the Spiderman walk didn't work he tried to jump into the nurse's arms to escape me. Tore all his dressings and covered her in blood. She was only too pleased to leave me alone with him while she ran off to scrub down in case of HIV. Actually, I really enjoyed my time alone with him.'

'Don't tell me you used some Trewhella stuff on him.'

'You think so poorly of me, partner. What *can* you be insinuating? No, he actually turned out to be a very obliging young man. But they might have to re-set the shoulder.'

'*Jeez*, Ed, you gotta be careful, man. What did you learn from the guy?'

'Well, he told me that the four of them had got a good supply of *nyaope* off a dealer in a boat moored at the yacht club a few hours before they hit on the old couple. Tried to explain their  actions as drunken behaviour attributable to *nyaope*.'

'*Nyaope?*'

Cronje looked up enquiringly and Ryder brought him into the conversation.

'Ed tells me the guy in Addington is talking, Piet. Apparently he and his cronies bought some *nyaope* off a boat right there in the harbour before they hit the old couple. What else did you learn from the guy, Ed?'

'Well, you were right about the guns, Jeremy. His dead buddies had a contact who paid a cop for the two guns. They were part of our own supply at the station. Remember our beloved Constable Thabethe? Sacked last year? Him. Looks like the Captain called it right about that bastard. Hated him from day one. Told me he didn't trust Thabethe as far as he could throw him. Couldn't pin it on him, but was convinced that the four guns we lost last year had something to do with Thabethe. Nyawula gets these things right. That's why he made Captain. He's got a nose for shitheads. Despite being such an irritating bloody academic. What you got?'

'Guess how much the old lady had stowed away under her easel?'

**12.20.**

Dippenaar and Koekemoer stood in the passageway outside the general ward, each with a polystyrene cup of coffee. Pillay sat, slumped and yawning, in the only chair in the passageway. She was short. Very short. This had prompted a perception in many that she was probably quite vulnerable on the streets. That perception was faulty.

Sergeant Navaneetham Pillay had topped her Police Training College group in hand-to-hand combat. She could up-end a two hundred pound six-foot adversary in the blink of an eye. She had biceps that bore testimony to many victories in arm-wrestling contests with devastated new male recruits. By popular consent she still held the one hundred metre sprint record at Durban Indian Girls High School, though this was contested in the record books. More than ten years ago, at the athletics day in question, her time had been disallowed by the official time-keeper 'because of wind conditions.' But her coach, the teachers, and her classmates rejected that official decision. For them, and for her, the time stood. She was the champion. Unofficial, but the genuine champ. She had a name-sake - *same spelling and all,* as she would frequently say - who was more famous than her. Working for the United Nations, her friends often said. But Navi was the one that was the real legend because of the hundred metre unofficial record.

'Tired, Navi? Drinking all night again, Sergeant?'

'I wish, Dipps. Since I briefed you guys this morning I've done nothing but paper. Forms and questionnaires, *yissus!* Trauma data collection form for this, form 308 for that, blank copies of form bloody 297 missing. Special permission for surgeon's report to be filed over here. FPS report to go over to that office. *Form 308 is being phased out, didn't you know? Well, then, why the hell don't we have the new forms? Don't know. Better use Form 308 until we hear from someone else up the line.* I didn't join up for this shit, man. You and Koeks have it easy. You just have to shoot the bastards and leave me to play the clean-up woman. I have to go and collect all the rubbish.'

Dippenaar and Koekemoer chuckled. Pillay continued.

'Remember the days when the cops would just shoot, call the cleaners, and write a sentence on the file when they were next back in the office? Gone, man. Now it's about the guys getting off because a form 308 wasn't completed. No, your honour, I didn't do the form because I'm the woman who put four bullets into him. Yes, your honour, I knew the bullets in his arsehole must have been from my gun. Why, your honour? Because it was me that shot him in the arsehole, your honour. I saw the bullets go in and saw him crap himself as they went in. Yes, your honour. No, your honour. And what about the rights of the woman he raped and killed, your honour?'

Yes, your honour. No, your honour, I don't have a law degree. That was the other Pillay. The famous one. Yes, your honour, you go ahead and set him free, your honour, and next time I'll do a form 308. But next time I'll make sure I put six bullets into his head, your honour. Then we can all spend more time reading more forms. Then...'

She was interrupted by a small, wiry, nervous man with dandruff and a perpetually open mouth who emerged from the ward, carrying an ancient leather briefcase in his left hand and two sheets of paper in his right. He addressed himself to Pillay, who remained seated.

'Thank you, Detective Pather...'

'Pillay.'

'I beg yours?'

'Pillay. Not Pather. I'm Sergeant Pillay. And thanks for the promotion.'

'Oh, sorry, I thought...'

'That's OK. I look just like her. She's a cousin of mine. We all look alike, you know. I got lots of cousins. Want a new car? I got a cousin can fix you up, quick.'

'Thank you. Yes. Thank you. And thank you for completing form 308. I was able to get the information processed quickly.'

'And?'

'There were three bullets in the body. We'll only have accurate information after a full autopsy, but it is likely that all the bullets came from the same weapon that was found twenty feet from the body, on the beach next to the bush. A Vektor Z88 9mm. The surgeon says he didn't have a chance of saving the man. The bullet to the face was the fatal one, and bounced around a bit, you see... anyway the autopsy will tell us more. And ballistics... But in the meantime you asked about the bullets, so I...these copies are for you.'

'Thank you.'

Pillay took the two pages proffered, and the small man coughed, nodded his goodbyes, and walked down the passageway, pretending not to notice the suppressed chuckles from Koekemoer.

'So much for complaints about form 308. Hey, Pillay, or Pather, or Naidoo, or whatever your name is, what can you tell me about...'

Pillay wasn't laughing. She looked up from what she was reading in the forms held firmly in her grasp.

'Hey, guys. The weapon from the bush on the beach. Last night. The Z88.'

Dippenaar was first to respond.

'What? What about it?'

'It was one of ours. Last few digits on the number stamp reminds me of my cell-phone, so I remember it well. One of those four guns we lost last year. When Constable Thabethe left. Remember? That creepy bastard with the eyes. Captain Nyawula got rid of him, and a few months later he went to jail. Last night's weapon was one of ours. One of Thabethe's haul.'

## 14.15.

Trewhella and Ryder stood on the pavement outside The Grove. Trewhella stuffed the last piece of the chicken burger into his mouth as Ryder spoke.

'I don't know how you can eat that after that brunch this morning.'

'Five hours ago. Late breakfast, late lunch. Just a snack before dinner.'

'We're not going to get any more out of the tenants. Not one of them knew anything about how much cash the old bird had stashed. The hit came from someone outside.'

Ryder's iPhone sang.

'Yep? Yes, Piet. Yes, he's with me. We've been interviewing tenants in The Grove. What? Both of us? When? 4.30. OK. What's it about? This morning? Also at Addington Hospital? Ed was down there too, on The Grove case. They must have been within spitting distance of each other. What? Serious? Whew. OK. Tell the Captain we'll be there.'

He hung up. Trewhella raised his eyebrows and waited.

'Captain Nyawula wants us at 4.30. Interesting development.'

'What?'

'You told me this morning that Dippenaar, Koekemoer and Pillay were on a case at Addington?'

'Yep. So?'

'They were also handling a homicide with gunshot wounds. No panga in this one. But three bullets. 9 mm.'

'So?'

'Like ours. From a Z88. Like the ones we retrieved from the scene this morning.'

'Go on. Keep me waiting.'

'A Vektor Z88.'

'So? Dime a dozen.'

'One of the Vektors that disappeared from the station last year.'

'Shit.'

'Just like our two Vektors, this morning.'

'Shit.'


## 15.10.

Tony walked silently and purposefully down the corridor in Addington Hospital, past the newly re-furbished A&E holding area. He knew exactly which ward he was aiming for. He carried a shoe-box size package, with the kind of gift wrapping that only a department-store gift wrapper can produce. Perfectly cut and folded, pastel colours, bland, but with a pretty gaudy ribbon. Only Tony knew that inside the box lay no more than a common wire-cut clay brick, standard size 225mm, wrapped in ample newspaper to prevent slipping and sliding in the box while creating a good sense of weight. The gift wrapper in the Musgrave Centre hadn't needed to know what was inside the box. She provided the free service for all customers wanting the wrapping, because that was what she was employed to do, and to be pleasant about doing it.

The box itself would soon be deposited by Tony on the top of the little cupboard next to the patient in the recovery ward. It would by then have fulfilled its small part in the larger masquerade of the kindly gift-bearing visitor. It would be opened only later that evening by investigating officers. Until then, the brick would rest on the cupboard, a silent witness to the approaching act of violence.

Tony wouldn't ever read the report that would describe in careful detail the results of the action that he was about to undertake. For him, the action itself would be simple, direct, and in harmony with his world view. It had worked six or seven times for him in the past. But that action would be broken down into much more detail in the autopsy report that would in time come to be written by an appointed forensic pathologist

The report, when written, would describe death as 'asphyxia due to ligature strangulation.' It would note that the deceased's eyes had irises that were brown and corneas that were cloudy, and that petechial haemorrhaging was present in the conjunctival surfaces of the eyes. It would be noted that body temperature, rigor and livor mortis, and stomach contents would combine to place the time of death at between 15.00 and 16.00. The local distributions of bruising in head and neck would be recorded as 'presumptive of violent strangulation,' and further confirmation would be adduced from the ligature marks on the neck, left, behind, and front, along with evidence of bruising or ecchymosis, haemorrhaging in the strap muscles, and in the tissues around the trachea and larynx. The ligature marks alone would not be recorded as diagnostic, but would be taken into account along with other signs of mechanical violence having been applied to the neck, resulting in fracture of the hyoid bone, the thyroid and the cricoid cartilages, along with extensive bruising of the muscles and the visible skin impressions.

All of these would help with the conclusion that the man who had been admitted to hospital early that morning with a shoulder shattered by a policeman's bullet had later in the day been garrotted in his hospital bed by a person or persons unknown.

Tony entered the ward. He walked silently over to the patient, lying asleep, drugged with pain-killers, to all appearances peaceful. He placed the gift on top of the cupboard and silently drew the curtains, enclosing the bed on three sides. He turned the dial on the radio to increase the volume on the thudding Hard Trance techno-rave that some nurse had probably turned down, earlier, for the sanity of both herself and other patients in her area.

Then he pulled the rope and leather contraption from the pocket on the inside of his jacket.

### 16.25.

Captain Sibongiseni Nyawula had achieved his rank through years of meticulous service, following formal studies in which he had been the star student. Starting at the very bottom in the post-apartheid era South African Police Service, he had gained a reputation for impeccable commitment to the service of law and order. He was highly regarded by his superiors and among those over whom he presided in his particular team. Within the broader unit, he elicited respect from new-era detectives and grudging approval from old-era detectives. With the exception of Major Swanepoel, for some unfathomable reason. He was the one perpetual thorn in Nyawula's side. Maybe because Swanepoel was such a short-arse, thought the Captain. Short man syndrome. Coupled with a bit of good old-era racism.

Six feet tall, slightly stooped, and carrying no excess weight, Nyawula gave the appearance, before speaking, of someone who might have a thin, reedy voice and tentative demeanour, probably accompanied by the limpest of handshakes if ever he were to offer a hand in greeting. The truth was somewhat different. Those who proffered the hand in greeting would experience a bone-crunching grip that would be prelude to an unnervingly warm gaze, as Nyawula's dark brown eyes would fix boldly and comfortably in search of a truthful exchange, the focus of his eyes momentarily excluding any and every thing that existed outside the field of such a greeting. This physical exchange was accompanied by the most surprising of deep, resonant, and assured voices, occasionally accompanied by an extraordinarily infectious smile which betrayed arctic-white teeth perfectly straight but never touched by orthodontists. When Nyawula spoke, others listened. As a consequence, he was always brief, focused, and unwaveringly clear.

He leaned back against the front of the standard-issue desk in his office, addressing those who had gathered, each of them seated in the charcoal-coloured plastic chairs that had been brought in from the outer office for the meeting and, in two cases, had been dragged back from their normal position facing the front of his own desk. Nyawula spoke, quietly.

'We lost four of the old Vektor Z88s last year. You'll remember we said goodbye to one Constable Skhura Thabethe at around the same time, but that we couldn't pin anything on him. Later on he went to jail for an assault on a businessman, so he clammed up and the trail on those four weapons went cold. It looks like Mr Thabethe is back in business. He was released from prison a week ago. Strange coincidence: three of the weapons turned up today. Two of them from Ryder and Trewhella's case at The Grove. The third from last night's homicide in the bush near Suncoast Casino. Sergeant Pillay?'

'Thanks, Captain. Detectives Dippenaar and Koekemoer and myself have checked with ballistics. Dipps has pulled some strings there, and they ran the stuff very quickly for us, and they also ran the info on the guns involved in the other action with Detectives Ryder and Trewhella. Full report only tomorrow, but we know enough to say that these are three of the four guns that disappeared with Thabethe last year.'

'I don't have to tell you, colleagues, that if we trace this back to anyone else in this station apart from Thabethe, more than heads will roll. In the meantime, I want Thabethe found and I want him in front of me. That bastard slipped through my fingers last year. It's not going to happen again. Now I know that everyone here is thinking that the major task for the week is Thursday night's party at the stadium. End-of-year function, they call it. I call it a waste of police time. A chance for lower ranks to impress higher ranks. A chance for higher ranks to pretend to lower ranks that they're interested in their career progression. Well let me tell you that you won't impress me with what you wear or how you behave on Thursday night. What will impress me is getting Thabethe by the end of the week. Navi, I want you to get into the township and trace him. I want to stand in front of the little shit. Dipps, I want you sitting on ballistics. Koeks, can you dig up all the stuff we had on Thabethe for that disciplinary hearing? Let me have it as soon as you can tomorrow.'

Pillay, Dippenaar and Koekemoer all nodded and grunted their assent, as Nyawula turned his attention to Trewhella.

'I understand that you got some information from the survivor of this morning's shoot-out at Wilson's Wharf?'

'Sure did, Captain. Saw him in hospital just before lunch-time. He confirmed that they had bought two guns from someone who had contact with Thabethe.'

'Very helpful of him to tell you that. I suppose you applied no pressure?'

'Me? No, Captain. I was a bit persistent in my questioning, I admit, but...'

'No chance of some clever lawyer arguing that you applied force on the guy to get him to tell you stuff that wasn't true?'

'No, Captain. No chance. The guy told me willingly.'

'Willingly? Willingly. I've had a report from the hospital that the guy's nurse doesn't think the guy was so willing. Are you sure you didn't engage in some rough stuff with him? Are you aware that in his condition enough stress could see a blood clot break free and do some damage? And if that happens then you might be held liable? In fact, if he were to die as a result of such a blood clot scenario, you could even be up for a murder charge?'

Trewhella was spared immediate further embarrassment by the ringing of the phone on Nyawula's desk. The Captain nodded at Cronje.

'Get that, please, Sergeant Cronje.'

Cronje got up and took the call, speaking *sotto voce* into the receiver.

'Captain Nyawula's office. Yes. Sorry, he can't. Yes...'

Meanwhile Ryder decided it was time to bail out his partner.

'Captain, I wondered whether... I was just thinking .... Maybe Ed and I could go back to the hospital - both of us together, I mean - and see the guy again and put together some more information on their movements last night, how they chose the old woman, and stuff like that...we'd invite him to have his State-appointed guy present, of course, while we questioned him...'

'I think that would be a good idea, Jeremy. I want to suggest that you do that sooner rather than later. This evening, if you can, before knocking off, so that if Navi brings in Thabethe tomorrow morning we have something more from this other guy.'

Cronje interrupted, putting down the phone.

'Captain, sorry, I – '

'What is it, Piet?'

'That was a call from... some information from... Addington Hospital are telling us that...'

'What, man? What is it?'

'The guy from Wilson's Wharf. With the shoulder. The guy Ed saw today in the hospital.'

'What about him?'

'He's dead, sir.'

Trewhella choked on his coffee. The others were in varying states of jaw-droppingness. Nyawula froze, staring at Cronje for more information. It came immediately.

'The guy died a few hours after Ed saw him. I mean, they're saying – well they just told me that the guy was murdered in his bed in the hospital. Sometime this afternoon after 3.00 pm. He was strangled. Some white guy in a suit. Brought a present, wrapped up, and left it on the table. Saw the nurse as he left and told her that the guy was asleep so he was just leaving the gift for him to get when he woke up. The nurse apparently just looked in at the door but didn't bother to check the patient until later...'

Trewhella relaxed, visibly. The others tensed, visibly.

Nyawula looked at Trewhella. Then at Ryder.

'Better get down to Addington. Let me know what you get.'


**17.30.**

Tony stood alone in front of Vic, who sat in the chair behind the desk.

'So tell me.'

'The guy in Addington is safe, Vic.'

'Safe?'

'He won't be talking. To anyone. Ever.'

'OK, Tony. Thanks. Do I need to know any more?'

'No, Vic. I think that's it.'

Vic paused, looking at Tony, drumming his fingers on the desk.

'I have one thing for you, Tony.'

'What's that, Vic?'

'The cops have traced the two weapons from this morning at The Grove.'

Tony stared at him. Vic continued.

'You said this morning, Tony, that there was no trail back to Jannie because three of his guys had been put down and out by the cops at The Grove. Now you've sorted out the fourth guy in Addington, but he might already have said enough to lead the cops back to Jannie's other contacts. My own information is that there's still a connection via the weapons. You told me Jannie had got two guns for the hit last year on the guy who reneged on our deal. Bought them from a cop, you said?'

'Yes, Vic. Some guy who was pissed off with his unit and was sacked and took some police weapons with him then sold a couple of them to Jannie.'

Vic drummed his fingers on the table, looking at Tony.

'Get me Jannie.'

'OK, Vic.'


**18.20.**

Ryder and Trewhella sat in the latter's car outside the hospital. Trewhella was still shaken. Ryder spoke first.

'Drop me off at my car, will you, Ed. Let's think through this tonight, but I reckon we need to join up with Pillay tomorrow morning and get after Thabethe. Looks like he's the link to a lot of this stuff.'

'OK. Did you see Nyawula, every time Thabethe's name was

mentioned? He really wants the guy badly.'

'As you said this morning, Nyawula's got a nose for shitheads. I wonder what other stuff he's got on the guy?'

'It helps to have the captain wanting something so badly. Maybe he'll turn a blind eye to the Trewhella method, for once. Looks like all roads lead to Thabethe.'

'Sure looks like it. I think there's some bigger stuff behind it, though. Nyawula is under pressure from the guys above him.'

'Like that Major Swanepoel prick.'

'So I hear. But remember, Ed, that report a couple of years ago about the no-nonsense policy on lost firearms? Thirteen thousand SAPS firearms lost or stolen in five years, or something like that?'

'Yeah. And this province was one of the worst. I remember Nyawula exploded when we heard that ninety-eight weapons were stolen from Inanda and they removed the station commander and put the exhibit clerk in jail for twenty years. I s'pose he just doesn't want to see that stuff happen closer to home, and for his own unit to get that kind of publicity.'

'Yep. But the big statistic that always bugged Nyawula was that soon after he started here some politico pointed out in parliament that KwaZulu-Natal had lost an average of five weapons per station. I remember that five lost weapons per station became this crazy benchmark that stations were being measured against and Nyawula felt we were doing incredibly well against that. But when Thabethe walked off with four, our own average was blown out of the water.'

'Which then gave the Major something to go on about. I remember the word from above being that the focus now had to be on firearms, that Nyawula should take people off other so-called petty cases. Drove Nyawula up the wall, the guy interfering like that.'

'Which is why he wants to put the Thabethe thing behind him.'

'OK, Jeremy, buddy. Let me get you back to your car.'

'OK. Thanks. And let's join Pillay in the hunt for Thabethe tomorrow.'


**18.40.**

Vic sat in the chair behind the desk. Tony and Jannie stood before him, Tony to one side and Jannie directly in front. Vic paused, staring at Jannie.

'Tony tells me you never provided a weapon for the guy in Addington.'

'No, Vic. He was brought in by the other two *ouens*…'

'I know all that. All I want to know is the nature of the contact you had with the two guys that your two idiots brought into the game without your knowledge.'

Jannie was too terrified to follow the possible implications of Vic's words, so Tony prodded.

'Tell Vic how you got the weapons, last year.'

Jannie responded to the lifeline, words bubbling out more rapidly than his brain could structure them.

'There was this *bantoe*, Vic. Called Thabethe. A *kêrel*. Or, should I say, ex-*kêrel*. He was really the *moer in* with his unit. His Captain. Said his Captain was causing grief for him and he was wanting to *trek* so they couldn't find him. Had stolen some guns and was offering them dirt cheap, like. It was when we were planning to *bliksem* that guy in the bush at the beach last year. He had let you down *moerse* on some business, Tony told us, and Tony wanted us to *donner* him. I mean you wanted him out, Vic. Tony told us. So we got two guns from this Thabethe *ou*, and…'

'Where's Thabethe now?'

'Ah - I dunno, Vic, I - ah - I could find him for you. He hangs around a shebeen that I know. He was always there by the shebeen in the old days. Before he was bust, I mean. If he's not in jail he'll be there. I'll trace him.'

'You do just that. Tonight. Tomorrow. As soon as. Report back to Tony. I want Thabethe wasted. And I want no trail back here, got it? This is a big week for us.'

'Wasted? Thabethe? Yes, OK. Sure. Definitely, Vic. For sure. Don't worry, Vic…'

'I'm not worrying. Are you?'

'No, Vic.'

'Good. Tony, brief him downstairs. A word with you, first.'

Tony nodded at Jannie who retreated quickly, assuring Vic on the way:

'Don't worry, Vic. Thabethe will disappear. I promise… the *oke*…OK, thanks, Vic. I'll get on it tonight. Like I say, I know where he hangs out. I'll wait for you down there by the bar, Tony, is that OK?'

Tony nodded and Jannie left. Vic waited for the door to close, then looked at Tony.

'After he's done Thabethe, I need you to do something. I need you to look after Jannie.'

'Sure, Vic. I think it's time. He's not coping, is he?'

'No, he's not. How will Dirk take it?'

'I'll make sure there's no problem with Dirk. I think he sees it coming anyway. Dirk's OK. Doesn't like foul-ups. He's reliable.'

'So you said.'

'I'll wait for Jannie to sort out Thabethe, first, shall I?'

'Yes. Thabethe's the problem. For now. Let me know as soon as he's down. Then we can take care of Jannie. I don't think we want Jannie around when we hit the big stuff on Saturday.'

'OK.'

'We don't need him, Tony. We need to wind up the muggings, right now. They're becoming a distraction. They're a side-line. We've done well enough out of them, but they pale into insignificance next to the warehouses. That stuff has been growing. Big time. And Saturday brings it all home. We need to walk away from the small stuff now, before it bites us and we lose out on the big stuff.'

'I agree.'

'It's a matter of supply and demand, Tony. At the moment, there are guys out there willing to pay top bucks to get the machines for their operations. There's big demand in this province, and we've long been in a position to supply. Simple economics. In addition, Dirk has proved himself useful on that side of things. Jannie's the one who gets off on the muggings. The little prick has annoyed me ever since he lost that Desert Eagle you gave him. Little bastard didn't deserve a weapon like that.'

'You're right, Vic. Pissed me off, too. It was a beautiful weapon. He went around flashing it in front of everyone down there in Umlazi, attracting attention to himself. I was the hell in when he told me he'd lost it. It was part of a neat little trio that I had got for the three of us, all titanium gold. Special import. Dirk and I have always taken great care with our own, and we were the *moer* in with Jannie when he lost his.'

'The little shit irritates me big time. He doesn't see the bigger picture. Gets off on screwing the little guys and picking up a bit of cash here and there by picking their pockets. Dirk strikes me as being more interested in the bigger stuff.'

'I think you're right, Vic.'

'OK. So let's pull right back from the muggings. The killing of this old bird in The Grove was unnecessary. Messy. I don't like mess. And there are more and more idiots getting in on that stuff. '

'Agreed, Vic. I've seen it myself. You can stand at the taxi rank downstairs and you can pick out the guys - not even our own guys - watching the winners go home after a good day at the machines, and following them. More and more people hitting on careless pensioners.'

'S'what I mean. It's getting too risky. The management will also have the cops watching that stuff soon. And they'll begin to train their cameras on it, too. I think we should pull out before that market gets too exposed, and concentrate on the bigger stuff.'

'OK. I'll get after Jannie, then, shall I, once he's done this Thabethe guy?'

'You do that.'

'Will do, Vic.'

As Tony left, Vic pulled out his iPhone.

## 22.15

Skhura Thabethe let go of the branch and dropped to the ground. He stood in the dark, his back against the tree, eyes scanning left and right for any potential witness to his stash. The moon was brighter than it had been the previous night. He looked up at it, then at the place above him where three branches created a natural hollow for the bundle he had secured. Then he looked around again, eyes alert.

The eyes were the objects that attracted much of the whispered discussion about his looks. It was not just that the eyeballs bulged more prominently than most, though that feature in itself produced discomfort in anyone meeting him for the first time. No, it was rather the knotted red – almost purple – arterial networks bursting out of the yellow sclera, and appearing distinctly separated from the corneas by very dark limbal rings, that produced most of the discussion.

'His eyes are evil,' they whispered.

What was it about them? No-one could accurately describe them, or put their finger on what it was about them that so unnerved the observer.

They were like deep wells. The opaque dark brown of the irises was so near in colour to the black coal of the centre that the effect was of pupils unnaturally large and permanently dilated. When he glanced at you, it was as

38

if he was staring at you. When he stared at you it was as if you were in the presence of the devil. So they said.

As he leaned back against the tree he fumed at the loss of the weapon on the beach last night. The money he had retrieved from the tourist was probably less than that bitch had got out of him. Just over two thousand rands he had retrieved from the wallet. She had probably got at least double that. Should have followed her instead of wasting time with the fat man. The mugging hadn't been worth the loss of the gun. He could have sold it for much more than he had stolen from the guy.

Now he had only one pistol left, and soon – maybe even tomorrow – that one would go, too. If the white boy wanted it. Asking for him again. Early tonight, at Nomivi's. *Left me message. Told Spikes he wants to see Skhura first thing tomorrow. Got money for Skhura. Hayi! I don't trust that one. Aikona! He wants another one gun. This time he pays double, big time, this time.*

He slid down on his haunches, back still against the tree, and closed his eyes. Tomorrow morning, early. Then he would have some *real* cash. Then it would be time to start again. A new life. Tomorrow.

# 2 TUESDAY

**04.49.**

Fiona had beaten him to it. She was in the shower. The button on the alarm had already been hit. He could hear her singing Handel above the sound of the gushing water, not at all considerately in respect of the neighbours - she was enacting a full chorus, after all - but very much in tune. How come he can't match that kind of singing? And she's completely untrained.

He sat on the edge of the bed for a few seconds, marvelling at her. He could see her in the shower, fully exposed through the wide-open bathroom door, soaping herself all over as she sang, eyes closed to avoid the shampoo.

His whole approach to starting the day was about to change markedly from the norm. The eighty-year-old of yesterday disappeared instantly as he removed socks and shorts and crept into the bathroom just as she was losing herself, dramatically, in the third sequence of repetitions.

*'All we like sheep!*

*All we like sheep!*

*All we like...'*

She screamed as he gently cupped a breast in each hand from behind. Then immediately chuckled and turned to face him, eyes still closed against the shampoo.

'I hope that's you! Bastard!'

He didn't answer but gently crushed her body into his chest as he found her lips with his. Then she came up for air and continued, eyes still closed.

'Mmmmm! It is you after all. I suppose I'm going to have to start all over and shower again in a few minutes?'

'Looks like it.'

'Mmmmm. Feels like it, too.'

'Mmmm. Here or in the bed?'

'Here.'

## 06.50.

Tony sat in his car and hit number seven on speed dial. After three rings Vic answered.

'Vic, I got something for you.'

'Speak to me.'

'Jannie found out last night that Thabethe is out of jail, and around. He left a message for the guy last night at his favourite hangout and thinks he'll see him today, early. He knows what to do.'

'Good. And after that, you'll get Dirk on the job?'

'Yes. I'll take him through it later today. Maybe we can aim for the end of the week, and plan it carefully. First, though, I want to bring him up to speed on the deliveries coming in this week. I want to make sure he realises how big the stuff is, without giving him all the details, and that if he plays his cards right he could score. That way, when we come to telling him we're going to offload Jannie, he'll have something to think through.'

'OK. I'm OK with that. Meanwhile, I got something for you. I found out that the cops are also after Thabethe, big time. Sounds like he's important to their current investigations. I'd prefer that bastard down and out rather than in prison, where he might sing.'

'Definitely. Leave it to us.'

'OK. See to it. Anything else?'

'That's all for now, Vic.'

'OK. Stay in touch.'

Vic hung up. Tony sat for a moment, in deep contemplation. His fingers drummed out a beat on the steering wheel. He clenched teeth together and nodded his head in affirmation of the decision he had come to. Then he reached for the ignition and switched on.

He enjoyed the cool plush leather of the Mercedes as he pulled out into the traffic.

**06.55.**

Ryder and Trewhella were chuckling at the discomfiture of the two Afrikaners.

'*Sies*, Trewhella. You get worse every day, man.'

'*Ja*, Jeremy. How do you put up with this *oke*? He'll pollute your brain.'

'Actually, I think he's quite erudite. I'm trying to persuade him to write this stuff down. In England a guy like him could make just one half-hour video and retire. I thought maybe we could persuade the Captain to let Ed do some of his stand-up routines at the function on Thursday night. Should have the General and the Brigadier and the Colonels and the Majors rolling in the aisles.'

'It would be a pleasure, Jeremy. You ask the Captain for me. Tell him I have some good one-liners that'll appeal to all those Chinese businessmen who're going to get awards. Tell him I have a good routine on corruption among police commissioners. There's this National Commissioner of Police, guys, she's great, but with one chink in her armour, and...'

The four were rocking on their chairs, each nursing a polystyrene cup. Ryder brought them back on track.

'OK, Ed. Can it, buddy. Maybe we can find you a microphone on Thursday night. For now, though, Dipps, how fast can you get the stuff on ballistics?'

'I'll have it by two this afternoon. Made a couple of calls last night.'

'And Koeks? What time are you seeing the Captain about Thabethe's disciplinary record?'

'He told me to team up with Dipps and when we've got the ballistics stuff and the disciplinary stuff we should both see him, together. So I suppose around three o'clock. Piet's helping me out by pulling together the disciplinary records. He's got a filing cabinet that has everything. He's like a *blerrie eekhoring*, that guy. Can tell you anything about anyone. Keeps copies of everything that anyone ever said. Probably has Afrikaans translations of Trewhella's sick jokes.'

Cronje entered from the inner office, carrying a file. Trewhella chuckled.

'Good timing, Piet, your buddy's just been nasty about you. Koekemoer just described you as a very whoring something-or-other.'

'*Wat*?'

'I'm telling you. Says you're a whoring sonofabitch who can't be trusted.'

'Bullshit, man, Trewhella. I said Piet was like an *eekhoring*. Nothing wrong with a squirrel, Piet. I meant that you can be trusted to find anything. Like you keep records of everything and - is that Thabethe's disciplinary record?'

'*Ja*. January year before last. The full record.'

'Thanks, Piet. Don't listen to the *Engelsman*. I owe you, man.'

'Give him a nut.'

'Bugger off, Ed. Dipps, let me know when you have the ballistics. I just want to run over this file. Piet, can I use your desk?'

'*Ja*, fine, Koeks. I'm just going out for a smoke. Take the calls for me, hey?'

Koekemoer muttered assent as he went into the adjacent office, while Cronje poured some coffee and then left the room for the car park.

'You're right about Piet, Dipps. Walking file cabinet. How long have you known him?'

'*Ag*, Jeremy, must be eleven or twelve years now. He was also here a *helluva* long time before I came along.'

Koekemoer's voice called out from the next room.

'I arrived here fourteen years ago and he was already here, guys. I remember him telling me that he was here just before 1994 and all that. When you were still there in England, Ed, and we were writing a constitution. Did you limeys get jealous of us or what? A country governed by a constitution instead of by some *ou toppies* still living in castles?'

Trewhella called back to him.

'To tell you the truth, Koeks, yes I did, I had thought until then that you guys were all going the way of Bosnia, and I was pretty impressed that you didn't.'

Koekemoer appeared back in the doorway.

'*Ja. Struesbob*, hey, Ed? And then the next year we messed you up at rugby good and proper. Is that what made you come out here? To learn how to play *rugger*?'

'Wrong again, *Koeksister*. You never beat us in that world cup. We didn't even get to play you guys. Lucky for you.'

There were instant protests from Dippenaar and Koekemoer at this.

'I wouldn't push this too far, Ed. I think you're on a loser here,' said

Ryder.

Dippenaar jumped in with alacrity.

'*Ag* rubbish, man, Ed. You *Engelse ouens* were too *poep* scared to play us, man. You threw in the towel against New Zealand just so that you wouldn't have to play us. Forty-five to the All Blacks, twenty-nine to the *Engelsmanne.* You let in six tries from them. Six! *Sies, jong!* It was terrible. My old high school could have done better than you guys.'

'Yes, well, OK, that was a bad day at the office for us. Jonah Lomu decided to turn up for New Zealand on that day. But then he decided to take a holiday when he played you guys. Or maybe he had food poisoning - so I hear - when he played against you.'

Trewhella's comment led to outrage and an uproar with all of them talking at once. Which was loud enough to bring Cronje back inside.

'*Yissus, ouens,*' said Cronje. 'The *okes* in the car park think there's a murder going on here. Cool it, OK?'

'*Die Engelse praat kak,* Piet,' said Koekemoer. 'Trewhella says that the only reason Jonah Lomu didn't score against the *bokke* in 1995 was that he had food poisoning.'

'*Ag kak, man!*' was Cronje's simple reply.

'I have to admit, guys,' Ryder contributed, 'I had a friend in Jo'burg who told me his ten-year-old son had nightmares after that game. Apparently thought every night that Jonah Lomu was under his bed.'

'*Ag,* no, Jeremy, man,' Cronje replied. 'The *Engelse ouens* were just scared of the guy. That Mike Catt guy was *poep* scared. When we played them in the final Lomu had nothing, because our guys weren't scared to tackle him. They showed everyone how to contain the bastard as long as you weren't scared of getting a little bit hurt.'

'*Dis reg,* Piet!,' Dippenaar added, rubbing it in. 'Ed, you guys were twenty-five-nil down after twenty-five minutes against New Zealand, man. You were a disgrace to world rugby.'

'OK, so we had a bad day in the first half. But all anyone remembers is Lomu. What people forget is that in that game – I don't know whether any of you realise this – we actually won the second half twenty-six to twenty.'

Screams of laughter from everyone else. Including Ryder. He wasn't going to support his partner on this one. Trewhella threw in the towel.

'OK, OK. I know when I'm out-numbered. But you have to admit, then, that we turned the tables in 2003...'

Cackles of laughter again, with Koekemoer leaping in immediately.

'No, Ed. Let's not talk about 2003. Let's rather talk about 2007! Isn't that what brought you out to work in South Africa? To learn how the real *manne* play rugby? Or was it because we handled our economy better than you guys with your sub-prime mortgages and stuff. Is that why you came out here to work?'

Lots of back-slapping and mirth. Trewhella gave up altogether and decided on a change of tactic by starting up on Dippenaar again.

'Hey, Dipps. This guy called Dippenaar goes into a toilet...'

Dippenaar stood up, drained his cup and threw it expertly into the waste-paper bin in the corner.

'*Fok jou*, Ed:

*Kaatjie, Kaatjie*

*Kekkelbek,*

*Val van die trap*

*En breek jou nek.*

I'm going to chase the guys on those ballistics reports.'

And he left for the car park. Before Trewhella could comment, Ryder stood up.

'Let's go, Ed. Navi said she'd be outside Nomivi's Tavern at 8.00 am, following up a lead on Thabethe. Let's join her.'

'Sure. They do breakfast there?'

'Come on, man. You and your pork belly. We've got time to pick up a McDonald's on the way if you like. Or just a coffee, and we can get something to eat after we see Navi. Let's go. Your car. You can drop me off here later.'

## 07.15

The *nyaope* cocktail was generally thought to combine dagga, rat poison, heroin and – it was long erroneously claimed by some users - antiretrovirals, especially the drug efavirenz. The rumours about the ARVs had persisted for some time even after laboratory analyses of different batches of the drug had found no traces of ARVs, and even after evidence had been presented that the heavy molecular weight of efavirenz made it almost impossible to vaporise and therefore impossible to smoke. Nevertheless, rumours about the ARVs in *whoonga* persisted. They added to the mystique attached to some of the more violent actions reported in the media.

*Nyaope* had emerged from around 2000 in Tshwane neighbourhoods in Soshanguve and by 2007 it was particularly well known in Atteridgeville, Mamelodi and elsewhere. But by 2010 Durban had become the informal capital for the drug. Jannie had known that he would find Thabethe in or around Nomivi's shebeen, an area where he had supplied *nyaope* for some time before he had been bust. Bust not for supplying, but for the vicious assault on the banker.

Learning that Thabethe had made parole only a week ago, Jannie had been in no doubt, the previous night, that Skhura would be keen to meet with him, especially if the message to be conveyed mentioned money. The *ou* must be looking for a way to get back on his feet, Jannie thought. So the message he left was that the Afrikaner guy Jannie wanted another one of the things he had bought last time, and he needed it quick so he would pay well for it. Right outside Nomivi's. *7.30 tomorrow morning. Please get the message to him. Tell him it's urgent.*

As it turned out, Nomivi's was open early that morning, but only for a special cleaning. After the *gemors* from the previous night, according to the cleaners. *One heck of a mess after the birthday party last night, so they asked us to come sharp-sharp at 7.00 to do the big clean.*

The two of them sat in a corner of the tavern, no drinks. Nothing available at that time. Just talk, while two women mopped and swept on the other side of the gloomy room. One of the women glanced nervously at the man with the eyes. She had never liked him.

Thabethe's bloodshot eyes were fixed on the young freckle-faced Afrikaner in a stare that Jannie knew only too well. Had he already had some *whoonga* of his own, this early?

'*Yissus*, Skhura, man, I can't pay that much. I'm *swak, ek sê*. That's more than both guns you sold me last year. And Z88s are being replaced, anyway: they're old and cheap.'

'*Hau!* What you think, white boy? Is inflation. You think I'm sitting in jail with no inflation? I must eat. You not wanting guns, then you can use the bicycle spoke, like me. Cheaper. You not wanting to pay me, you *fokoff! Tchai!*'

'OK. *Jeez.* OK, man. Take it easy. Just *lissen* for a minute. I'm working with these guys. I meet them each time at Suncoast Casino. They pulling big money. Not from the casinos, you know, because that's all, like, controlled, you know, but from some other stuff involving gambling. Like, I mean, really big money. I'm talking *hunnerts* of thousands. There could be big money for you if you want to work with me and Dirk. You remember that *oke* Dirk? You met him once, right here. The fat guy. My friend. Here, check this, this photo: me and Dirk in the Drakensberg, man, after we scored big time *geld* with these guys. Remember him? You see the big smile there? Hell, man, he was happy that time, 'cos we were paid big bucks. They handed over our money right there by Suncoast. Cash, man. We both working for these guys, and when we score they give us big money. That time we went to the mountains for a *lekker* holiday. These guys pay us well. And we going to get more big money soon. So if you give me the gun now for the same price as the last one, then next time ...'

'*Hayi! Fokoff, man!* What you think? You think me, I'm stupid? You think I'm waiting for next year for you to win casino? You win casino money you can come then and look for me here, at Nomivi. Then, not now. Now, you give me money or I *fokoff* and no gun for you. Give me. Now, or I am going.'

Jannie realised there was no room for bargaining any further. He pulled the wad of bills from his right trouser pocket as he spoke, and put it together on his lap, under the table, with the wad he pulled from his left pocket. He had calculated that he might bargain Thabethe down to about half the amount he carried on him, so he had kept half in reserve. He was wrong.

'OK, man. Here's the *geld*. But for that price I want bullets, too, hey?'

'I got fifteen bullets for you. Sixteen. One extra. For testing. I know you. You like to test, huh? Sixteen bullets. No more. Is all I got.'

Jannie cast his gaze around the darkened room before sliding the thick wad of cash across to him, along the length of his thigh. Thabethe snatched it and flicked through the two bundles, each held together with a thick rubber band. Jannie waited. Then, after the counting, Thabethe leaned across to him, fixing him with that stare that bothered Jannie so much.

'You wait one minute. Then you follow. I give you the gun across the street. Around the corner. Big tree. You stay one minute now, or I *fokoff* and you are not seeing me.'

Before Jannie could protest, he was up and making for the door. Jannie cursed, but waited. He knew that Thabethe would drop the deal instantly if he didn't follow instructions. And maybe it was better, anyway. Not here. Outside. Once he had checked that the gun was still good, his first target was going to be this black bastard. *Those eyes. I swear he's mal, man. I'll feel better when he's vrek.* He paused another few seconds, then slid out from behind the table and followed Thabethe.

Jannie saw him turn the corner at the end of the street. He followed briskly, glancing around for any possible spectators. There was only an old woman walking in the same direction on the opposite side of the street with two kids – probably her grandkids – all three showing no interest in either him or Thabethe because of the more interesting sight of the grey cat that sat, imperiously, on the bonnet of a rusting Toyota Carina that was catching the warm morning sun. As he rounded the corner he saw Thabethe leaning against the tree, partly behind it and to one side. The side furthest from the street. Jannie joined him, looking around to see if anyone was watching. There was no-one in sight.

Thabethe motioned him closer to the tree then he crouched momentarily, jumped, and with his left hand clutched a thin branch some ten feet from the ground, at the same time placing his left foot in a knot-hole about half-way up the trunk. Then he reached up with his right hand to the natural hollow created by three converging branches, and pulled the Z88, wrapped in dirty oilcloth, from its sanctuary.

He passed the weapon to Jannie, who expertly checked it. Jannie knew that more than a hundred thousand of these had been through the SAPS but once it had been announced that they would soon be phased out in favour of the SP1 it had become harder to find replacement parts for any unauthorised Z88s. So any weapon that wasn't functioning properly was a serious liability in any of the actions that he and Dirk would be planning on behalf of Vic and Tony. Including the business he had to attend to today. The fact that in his experience the Z88 was also prone to jams if not properly maintained made it doubly important that he check the weapon carefully.

Jannie had lost his Desert Eagle two years ago. Mark XIX with the Picatinny rail polished lovingly to highlight the titanium gold. It had been Tony who introduced both him and Dirk to it some time before that. *Get rid of the Beretta, guys, Tony had said. The Deagle is gas-operated. Polygonal rifling cuts back on the wear on the barrel. Easy to clean. Accurate like you can't believe. Good for two-hand stuff. Here you are. Both of you. One for me, one for each of you. I picked up these three beauties in one pack. Three brothers, in matching titanium gold. Came off the production line together. Six-inch barrels. Just under eleven inches, the whole thing. You'll love it.*

He did. For some months. Then he had lost it. In that action in Umlazi. Tony had been incandescent when he heard. Dirk still had his own. And Tony still had his, too.

Jannie's experience with the Z88 since losing his favoured weapon had not been good. It felt alien in his hand, and the slide was never easy, pretty soon showing the orange stuff that preceded rust. Like those that Skhura had sold him last year, which those idiots had lost yesterday at Wilson's Wharf. They were not like the Desert Eagle. Anyway, this one seemed OK. Typical SAPS stock. Seemed good to go. He paused a moment. Thabethe was watching him, closely. He looked up at Thabethe and asked:

'OK to fire a test round here?'

Thabethe nodded perfunctorily and reached a hand into each of his right and left trouser pockets. With his right hand he withdrew a small cardboard box, while in his left hand he held a solitary bullet. He handed the box to Jannie and snatched the gun back from him as he said:

'Here. One bullet, to test. You keep the box for later.'

As Jannie pocketed the carton, once again looking over his shoulder to see if there was anyone in sight, Thabethe deftly loaded the single bullet, flipped the weapon around and, holding it by the barrel, handed it back to him. Then he stepped back against the tree.

Jannie paused. Looked at the weapon in his right hand. Looked again, quickly, over his shoulder, then smirked as he raised the weapon, pointing it at Thabethe. No comment. No time to be funny or clever. Someone might come. Time to blow away the devil himself. And take back the money, into the bargain. He looked into the black wells of Thabethe's eyes, paused only very briefly, and pulled the trigger.

The dull empty click was possibly the most paralysing sound Jannie had ever heard. It was infinitely more devastating to him than the loud metallic click of a cell-door that he knew so well and hated so much.

Before he could recover from the shock Thabethe was in his face, his evil eyes now only four inches from his own. Jannie felt a cold - inexplicably cold - sharp pain under the tip of his sternum. The cold seemed to penetrate upwards, and upwards, slowly, terrifyingly, as Thabethe rasped words over foul breath.

'One bad bullet. SHAME. No FIRE? You FUCK with me, white boy, you DIE. I tell you use bicycle spoke, better than gun. You SEE?'

He gave five powerful, inexorable thrusts, one on each stressed word then, finally, he stepped back and surveyed his handiwork.

'Nice, hey? *Wena uclever!* You like? *Fok jou, skelm.*'

The long sharpened spoke protruded only a couple of inches from the lower part of Jannie's torso. It was embedded all the way up from beneath the sternum, through the lung, finally penetrating the striated muscle in the upper third of the oesophagus with its rich blood supply and vascular drainage. Jannie's mouth quickly filled with blood. The gun fell from his limp hand. He stared at Thabethe. *Those eyes. Those black, evil eyes, they —*

Thabethe moved in again, quickly, before he collapsed, and held him up against the tree for a few more seconds as the life ebbed from him. Then he withdrew the spoke and let the body fall, slowly, guiding Jannie so that he ended up partly behind the tree, out of sight of the street. He looked around, quickly, then bent over the corpse. First to wipe the bicycle spoke on Jannie's shirt. Second to retrieve the gun and the carton of bullets from his pocket. As he stood up, he saw the photo of Jannie and Dirk protruding from the dead man's shirt pocket. He paused a moment, thought, then bent down and took the photo. Then he walked away, swiftly, the carton in his left trouser pocket, the gun tucked into his belt in the small of his back, and the spoke carried point down, flush against his right leg.

He was almost at the end of the street when the grandmother and the two children came into view around the corner.

## 08.05.

Pillay had been interviewing neighbours, looking for whatever clues might help her in the search for Thabethe. It didn't take long for five of the older women, gathered together over a few strands of meshed chicken-wire that served as the front garden fence of one of them, to link Thabethe to the local *nyaope* problem. Pillay rapidly learned that the drug was the single most important topic of conversation among the parents and grandparents in this particular street, and that it was inextricably tied into talk in the greater neighbourhood about devil-worship. Various brutal murders elsewhere in the country, in addition to high-profile cases that had made it into the newspapers more than a year previously, were resuscitated by one of them, who reminded the others and set them all off again, fuelling the gossip.

'That very old woman, there near Jo'burg, it was her own grandson —'

' - for her pension money…'

' - no, because of the drugs, I'm telling you. *Nyaope*!'

'*Tcha*! The devil! Satan!'

'*Ja*! Like that child in Benoni with the axe. Fourteen years old!'

'*Hayi*! Man! They steal for money because there's no jobs. Then they use *nyaope. Whoonga!* Then they lose their mind. Then they kill for more. Is the drugs, I'm telling you!'

Pillay had driven around the streets for the better part of an hour, stopping to chat to whoever was interested in talking to a cop. The story was the same. The Nigerians. The Zimbabweans. The Malawians. The reason for the xenophobia, and the attacks on foreigners. The young ones. The drugs. *Nyaope.* And Skhura Thabethe.

She arrived at Nomivi's tavern to see a commotion at the end of the street. As she got out of the car a group of people started shouting at her, beckoning her to come toward them. A distressed older woman with two young children clutching onto her dress was crying and being comforted by two other women.

People were on their cell-phones, describing to friends or loved ones or colleagues what they were seeing, proud to be part of the first group of people on the scene, which they would elaborate and embroider later that day in discussions with friends and families over drinks and meals. By then their stories would escalate to include phrases like you *can't believe how much blood there was* and *I tell you, I seen dead people before but this one was scary, man* and *they say it was a bicycle spoke or something like that, but I'm telling you, I think it was some ritual killing or something* and *I heard it was, like, you know, Satanism – they say that the blood had been taken out of him in a tube...*

For now, the callers were just calling in the news, without the dramatic colouring. The elaborations would follow later. As Pillay ran toward the group one of the callers whispered into his Samsung Galaxy:

'I'll call you back. The cops are here. Want to watch this,' and he stepped in front of Pillay. 'There, officer, just around the corner, behind the tree, there. Terrible, man. The old woman found him. Do you want me to call the ambulance or something?'

Pillay ignored the man and rushed forward. As she was about to turn the corner she became aware of the blue lights and siren flashing behind her. At a glance she recognised Trewhella's car with two shapes in the front.

'Tell those policemen to come up here,' she shouted at the man with the phone. He was only too pleased to do so. It would flesh out his story later that day: *The police asked me to help, like, so I was, you know, the adrenalin was pumping but I thought it was my duty, you know.*

Trewhella and Ryder, pausing briefly in front of Nomivi's, saw the commotion at the end of the street and the man waving frantically at them. Trewhella floored the pedal. They lurched forward another hundred metres.

**08.30.**

Tony and Dirk sat across from each other at the innermost table in the

Musgrave Centre Mugg & Bean. Dirk had the South African Farm Breakfast: fried eggs, grilled tomato, boerewors – without the salsa – hashbrown, back bacon, toast. Tony had plain black coffee.

'Are we cool, Dirk?'

'Yes, Tony. You can count on me. For sure.'

'And after you've sorted that out I want you to clean the Montpelier Road house, too. We don't know what else the idiot told that Trewhella cop in Addington before we got to him. In fact, I might even take Trewhella down if I can. He's getting too close. And his partner, too.'

'*Jeez*, Tony. Taking down a cop. I don't know...'

'Don't you worry about that, Dirk. Leave that to me. For now, I want you to go over the place and remove any papers, old envelopes from the post, phone numbers that might have been scribbled down by either you or Jannie on scraps of paper, or on walls, behind pictures, that kind of thing. We want the place clean. No connections. No trace back to anyone or anything. We still want to use the house. Got some big stuff coming for dispatch to Gauteng and the Cape. We need the place. If they start looking at it we'll have to move more things to the Overport place.'

Dirk shifted his weight uncomfortably, but continued spooning the food into his mouth. Tony observed him with some disgust for a moment, then stood up and threw a hundred-rand note on the table.

'Let me know when the house is clean, Dirk. Get over there as soon as you can.

'OK, Tony. Thanks, man, I – hey I just want you to know...'

'Don't worry, Dirk. We'll look after you. Big money coming through on the deliveries. You'll get your share. Play it cool, that's all.'

Tony left. Dirk stared at his plate for a moment, then continued eating.

### 09.45

Forensics had got there in record time, so after the initial scan of the body and the surrounding area Pillay and the two detectives had left them to it and driven in Trewhella's car the hundred metres back to Nomivi's in the vain hope of some coffee. The cleaners were still at it, so they hung around outside instead.

They had found on the body of the freckle-faced boy nothing apart from an empty wallet with a driving licence, a Suncoast Casino gold card, a branded *Chinese Skull Knuckle Duster*, and a seven-inch dagger inclusive of a three-inch blade, double edged and very sharp, with a black Micarta handle, highly polished.

Pillay had not recognised the particular brand of knuckle-duster despite having taken many of the weapons off suspects over the years. And the dagger was fairly unique, too. High quality.

'Let's go and find some coffee, somewhere, guys,' said Ed.

'You mean bacon and eggs, buddy? Coffee sounds good, though. Want to join us, Navi?'

'Thanks, Jeremy, but I'll leave you guys to it. I want to get back to check on some stuff I was told by the neighbours around here about the *nyaope* deals going down in the last few days.

'OK. We'll grab some coffee and when forensics have finished we'll follow up on this young guy, and see where he comes from. Nothing but the licence to go on so far.'

'And the knuckle-duster. And the dagger,' said Pillay.

'Sure,' Ryder replied. He paused, looking at her. Sharp, she was. And getting sharper by the day. 'Them too. We'll look into those, too. Let us know what you get from the neighbours, Navi.'

The three of them parted, the two men burning away down the street in Trewhella's car and Pillay pausing a moment, watching them go, before walking to her car. As she opened the driver's door and got in, a battered green Mazda 323 SL Sedan that had seen many better days crawled around the corner from the same direction as the departing detectives, and more slowly than any normal vehicle would travel in the normal course of business.

Pillay sat for a moment, and watched. The driver peered into the gloom of Nomivi's as he passed, not noticing Pillay in her car, the sun bouncing off her windscreen in a way that obscured any clear vision of the car's interior. He went slowly half-way up the street and then came to a halt. Pillay thought it was because he could see the edge of one of the forensics vehicles at the end of the street, alongside the remaining cop car, one of them still with its blue lights flashing. The driver did a three-point turn in the Mazda and started slowly back toward the tavern.

Strange, thought Pillay. Someone seeing a flashing blue light at the end of the street and having no interest in seeing what was up. She watched in stillness, her interest in the Mazda now piqued.

She watched Dirk stop outside the tavern, get out, and walk to the door.

He entered and she could see him in the gloom of the interior speaking to the Nomivi cleaners. She noted down the registration of the Mazda and decided to wait and watch. Three or four minutes later Dirk came out, and before going to his car he walked to a point just beyond it where he could look up the street to see what was happening with the blue lights. He paused then got into the Mazda and drove off.

Pillay went into the tavern to speak to the cleaning staff.

## 10.30.

Ryder and Trewhella sat in Nino's in the Old Mutual Centre, the debris of the latter's Piccolo breakfast in front of him, a pen and notepad in front of Ryder, and both of them nursing a drink. Trewhella a cup of tea and Ryder a mug of coffee.

'You gonna die of cholesterol, Ed.'

'At least I'll have used my taste-buds to their max. You're gonna die of caffeine.'

'At least I'll be awake when it happens.'

They both slurped at their drinks.

'Navi's gotta get promotion, soon, I reckon.'

'No doubt. She's very focused,' said Ryder.

'Focused? Focused? Listen, buddy, I don't care what focus she has. What I mean is that in a scrap I'd be happy to have her watching my back. She's got balls. She's as tough as nails. I observed one of her kickboxing classes with the new recruits. They crapped themselves. After a while no volunteers stepped forward to help her with her demonstrations.'

'So I heard. I also hear she gets the top marks from recruits when they assess their induction trainers at the end of the week.'

'Probably shit scared that she'll come looking for them if they give her a bad mark. And shit scared that she'll catch them easily, too. Apparently she can do the hundred metres in about eleven seconds.'

'No kidding. I heard that too.'

They mused in silence for a moment. Then Trewhella continued.

'Seriously, though, Navi is one of the guys one can trust not to go rotten. That stuff in Cato Manor, with the OCU guys and all that twisted media exposure, was frightening, man. For a time there no-one knew who were the good guys and who were the bad ones. It bugs me every time I see some new so-called scoop on corruption among cops. First reaction is to say wow! amazing! well at least they nailed some of the bad guys. Then you hear the other side of the story and it's just the opposite.'

'Yup. Then you find out who was bribing who, and who didn't have political connections, and the rest of it.'

'Drives me up the wall, man. You just don't know who your real friends are! Good cops being paraded as scum by journalists looking to establish their careers. Bad cops operating under the radar and never getting the publicity. I hope I never have to go through that. I crapped myself yesterday when Nyawula got the news that that prick in Addington had died. I really thought I was in for an IPID interrogation.'

'Which reminds me, Ed. Piet tells me you and I will have our IPID forms to do on the guys at Wilson's Wharf.'

'More admin crap. You face these creeps with guns and they can take you out and there are funeral notices and flowers and tears for a couple of days, then it all fades away. Cops and autumn leaves blowing away into history. But a cop takes one of them out and we have forms and enquiries and court cases for months on end, and journalists asking why did the cops have to shoot them. How long was that Cato Manor guy suspended before they threw out all charges against him?'

'Two years, I think.'

'That's what I mean, man...'

'OK, Ed. Look, yeah, I agree, and all. No question. It's a big problem. But I think with guys like Nyawula we have a chance of getting on top of this.'

'Yeah. He's one of the good guys, for sure. When I started in Joburg I was a bit horrified at what the guys got up to. There were some amazing cops up there who were as sharp as anything I saw in the UK. But there were also some really shady guys, too. Like some cops I knew in the UK. Have to admit, the Captain is a breath of fresh air. Young and smart. And razor-sharp.'

'Sure is. You know, I have a friend who was his tutor in college.'

'Get away.'

'No, serious. He told me that Nyawula was the top student all the way through. Apparently wrote a thesis or research report for one of his assignments that this tutor marked at one hundred per cent. Which he had never done in his career before, he told me.'

'Really? How do you get a hundred per cent for an essay? I thought that was reserved for God.'

'Apparently it was a thesis on the management of policing in the country.'

'Exciting stuff. I'd rather watch England play one-day cricket. Not for me, buddy.'

'No, I'm sure not. Anyway, this tutor said it showed amazing insights into the history. Stuff that he had never even begun to think about. He said what was really refreshing about it was that it never lapsed into the old lame arguments about apartheid-era versus new era policing, you know? My buddy said that reading Nyawula's writing was like reading a true detective at work.'

'How's that?'

'I remember the phrase he used. He said most dissertations and research reports he had ever read did the normal thing. Stated a hypothesis and then set out to prove it. In other words, most of his students set out to prove something they had already decided on. That's a bit simplistic, but...'

'So how was Nyawula different, then?'

'Well, according to this guy, Nyawula did something else. Instead of setting out to find what he was looking for, he set out to search for what he might find. He thought that made Nyawula quite special.'

'You got me, buddy. What does all that academic crap mean?'

'Well, he saw Nyawula as a genuine sleuth. Like a forensics guy, he said. Nyawula would follow the evidence wherever it took him. Didn't make hasty judgements. So in this history thing that he wrote, he apparently worked his way like a true detective through the key features of policing systems pre- and post-94, and made an eloquent case for the future management of crime investigation.'

'Hmmm. An eloquent voice in the midst of chaos and re-structuring and knee-jerk changes and promotions and demotions and suspensions. And with political interference all the way. Not hard to be a sane voice in the midst of all that crap.'

'Maybe. But there's no question that Nyawula is a guy one can take seriously. Meanwhile there are other fat-cats from the past who are still part of the old system and they still manage not only to cling on and survive, but actually prosper.'

'That's for sure. Some of the top brass I've met are like museum exhibits. Bet we see lots of them on Thursday night at the Stadium.'

'Yeah. Well, Ed, maybe one day Nyawula will be National Commissioner. We can only hope.'

'If he survives. There are big bad guys out there with big bad money. Very tempting.'

'Not to you, I hope?'

'Not to me, matey. The only temptations I have in my life all wear skirts.'

'That much, Ed, I already know. Fiona and I have been looking around for counsellors for you.'

'That's great, buddy. As long as the counsellors wear skirts, I'm OK with that.'

'Let's go.'

'OK. Let's go and look for what we might find.'


## 11.30.

Dirk was shaken to the core. Ashen-faced. They stood next to his Mazda, outside the Spar, Dirk still clutching the two bags laden with goods he had bought. Tony removed his hand from the younger man's shoulder, took the bags from him and put them in the car as he spoke.

'Take it easy, Dirk. Vic thinks it must have been Thabethe. But that makes it even more important that we wipe out that bastard before he causes any more trouble for us.'

'*Jeez*, Tony. I think I was right there, man. Just after it happened. Just down the street, man. I saw the commotion at the end of the street and thought: cops, better stay clear. So I went back to Nomivi's to see what I could find. Shit, man. Maybe I could have saved Jannie. Maybe I could have got the guy. How does Vic know who did it? Did he ...'

'No good thinking about that now, Dirk. What I said earlier still applies. We still need to track Thabethe but it's now even more important to get rid of anything that can connect him with Jannie. Clean the place from top to bottom. We want nothing left there that leads back to us. Vic wants you over there right now. Do it, Dirk. Don't leave anything that gives them a trail back to us. You get it, Dirk?'

'Yes, Tony. Yes, man. I got it. *Jeez*, man, what am I going to tell Jannie's mom? She's not going to handle this, man.'

'That comes later, Dirk. You'll sort something out there. And Vic will arrange some money for her. Big money. From the big deals coming in right now. But for now, we want Montpelier Road cleaned out. I'll be across later. I have to get on to something for Vic. And I'll also let you know when we have the new place ready. Vic wants it somewhere in the vicinity. He's looking at that Argyle Road house, remember, the one that we saw?'

'Yes, Tony, I remember. I found it first, you remember? Vic liked it.'

'That's the one. Vic wants to go for it now. The Overport place is also getting a bit too hot, so we'll be pulling out of both there and Montpelier. We'll let you know when we set up in the new place, then we'll move everything there. OK. Get going, Dirk. Don't worry, man, we'll get Thabethe.'

Tony watched as Dirk collapsed in the car behind the wheel. As he crashed the gears and took off, Tony thought that Jannie's passing was probably the best thing that could have happened. If Thabethe had done Jannie, in a way it was a relief. He didn't think that Dirk would have been able to handle Vic's own plans for freckle-face. And maybe the killing of Jannie would spur Dirk on to nail Thabethe.

Tony watched the Mazda turn the corner, thought for a moment, then walked toward his own car.

## 12.10.

Pillay was on the line to Ryder.

'The women in Nomivi's told me that freckle-face was well known in the area. Used to meet some interesting locals there. And get this. He used to be a buddy of someone we once knew.'

'Thabethe!'

'Got it in one. But even more important than that.'

'What?'

'Freckles met Thabethe there early this morning. As the cleaners opened, they were there.'

'*Jeez*! And what went down?'

'They couldn't - or wouldn't - say. Normal evasive stuff. They never pay attention to the customers, and stuff like that. I get the feeling they're scared of someone in charge, or someone who hangs out around there.

They kept on looking over their shoulders, as if someone might come along and see them talking to me, you know? But anyway, listen, I've got something else, Jeremy.'

'Yeah? What?'

'Just as you and Ed pulled off, some creep arrived in a battered old Mazda. White guy, fat, mid-twenties, looking very much as if he was hoping to find someone hanging around Nomivi's. Strange time of the morning to do that, wouldn't you say? The place is supposed to be for night-birds, not breakfast. He was kerb-crawling past the place like there was a 10 miles an hour speed limit. Then, as soon as he saw forensics and blue lights up the road he turned around suddenly and came back. But he stopped and then went inside to talk to the cleaning women. He didn't see me, but I watched the creep every step of the way. He was definitely up to some shit.'

'What'd he tell the staff?'

'Like I said. They wouldn't tell. Told me some rubbish like he was just looking for his friend. But they did tell me they had seen him before, in there. They thought he might have been around a couple of times about a year ago.'

'Another friend of Thabethe's.'

'Maybe. Anyway, Jeremy, I've traced the Mazda and I have an address for Mr kerb-crawler. Do I need to wait for backup? I'd like to chase this right away. I've got a feeling we can get to Thabethe with this guy.'

'Captain will give you a hard time if you try it on your own. Where is it? Ed and I can meet you there.'

'I'm sitting just up from his place right now. He's in. I've just seen him walk in with two heavy bags from the Spar. I'm parked opposite 276 Montpelier Road. The guy is in a ground-floor flat twenty paces away from me.'

'We'll be there in fifteen.'

'Can I at least start asking a few questions about his car, roadworthy certificate, and stuff like that? See if he gives anything away?'

'OK. Captain won't be happy, but go ahead. We'll try and get there in ten. We'll come in two cars. I have to get to a meeting with K and D afterwards.'

Ryder hung up. Pillay crossed the road.

Within minutes she was sitting inside on the tall bar-stool, her notepad on the counter, looking around the apartment while she waited. She had watched carefully for any give-away signals as Dirk opened the door. But he had given away nothing. Having declined coffee from him, she waited for him to return from the bedroom behind her with his ID documents and roadworthy papers. He had told her without hesitation that there must be some mistake because he had a copy of the certificate and the other papers for his car that he would gladly show her.

How would she move the conversation from the vehicle to Nomivi's? Should she wait for Ryder and Trewhella? Should she get into anything deeper before she had back-up? The questions were answered for her as he came out of the bedroom.

Pillay was taken completely by surprise. Dirk's right arm snaked around her neck, and for a second she didn't react. But all the training that had put her at the top of her martial arts team kicked in after that second, as did her long experience as an instructor in the female kick-boxing section. The SAPS Kwazulu Natal team's top medals haul at the 2013 Martial Arts Championships had been in large measure due to her work as both competitor and instructor, and ever since then she had been revered as an exponent of the art.

Instead of trying to twist out of his stranglehold, the movement he was expecting from her, she used both thumbs on his elbow, which Dirk had positioned conveniently for her just under her chin, along with that elbow's exposed ulnar nerve. The ulnar is the largest nerve in the human body unprotected by muscle and bone. Pillay's two thumbs jabbed savagely, simultaneously, into the medial epicondyle and produced a high-pitched atavistic scream of pain from Dirk, with an instant paralysis of his arm.

As he froze in searing agony Pillay spun from his grip anti-clockwise, knocking over the barstool, then she corrected for an instant and stepped backward onto her left foot to shift her weight in preparation for the massive blow from her right boot. She aimed at a spot two inches above his left knee, kicking downward and following through with her full weight, in effect stomping on the lower thigh.

The blow locked his knee backward for a moment before she followed through with her full weight, giving him what she frequently described to her martial arts students as *the cartilage treatment*, producing massive simultaneous medial and lateral crushing of the meniscus. She stepped immediately to her right to collect her weight and complete the damage, this time preparing for a kick to the same knee, thinking for a second about the words she had used to her students to accompany the diagram she always put on the board for this particular lesson: *to tear the medial collateral ligament and to rupture the posterior cruciate ligament with an ugly and unpleasant popping sound, and produce instant patellar dislocation.* With such a blow Dirk would be in a wheelchair for a very long time if he survived any further action from Pillay, and if he survived to old age the pain from his crippled leg would bring her face daily into his thoughts for the next half-century.

For now, however, Dirk was spared the second kick, because he had collapsed instantly from the first blow, and lay screaming and helpless at her feet.

Pillay rolled him over onto his front and cuffed him behind, brutally, producing more agonised screams. Then she searched him quickly for weapons and within seconds had removed his Desert Eagle. Six-inch barrel. Titanium gold. This guy's for real, thought Pillay, as she tucked the weapon into her belt and continued the search.

Next came a wallet with no more than a hundred rands, a couple of bank cards, receipts, a Suncoast Casino gold card, a Chinese Skull Knuckle Duster. Then a seven-inch dagger, blade about three inches, double edged and very sharp. With the handle in black Micarta. Polished.

Pillay paused, contemplated for a moment, and stood up. Then she put the weapons on the counter and rolled him over again.

'Let's talk,' Pillay said. 'You and me.'

## 13.05.

Ryder and Trewhella sat at the bar-counter. Pillay chose not to use the third bar-stool, which had survived the fracas with no more damage than a split in one of its four pine legs. She stood leaning against the wall. Before them on the counter lay Dirk's Desert Eagle, the dagger, the knuckle-duster, cash and bank cards, the casino card, and receipts. Dirk lay groaning in agony in the corner where she had dragged him. Their comments were entirely for his benefit.

'He told me he doesn't know freckle-face. Strange that they have exactly the same supplier in daggers and knuckle-dusters. Don't you think, Ed?'

'Very strange, Navi. I knew a feller once. Chinese guy. Supplied lovely knuckle-dusters from Shenzhen. Just like this. And would you believe it, exactly like the one we found this morning on Freckles. I knew another feller once. Not Chinese. Had a lovely line in seven-inch daggers with double-edge blades and black Micarta handles. Just like this. And would you believe it, just like the one we found this morning on Freckles. I knew another feller once, also not Chinese... hey, does this guy have any coffee? Hey fatso? Got any coffee?'

'*Fok jou! Engelse...*'

Trewhella moved quickly and positioned his foot above Dirk's shattered knee. Before either Ryder or Pillay could stop him, he thrust down without actually making contact and Dirk screamed:

'OK! OK! Stop, man! I know him! I know him!'

Pillay and Ryder stopped dead in their tracks and left it to Trewhella.

'Yes? You know him now, do you? What's your connection to Freckles? You work with him? Who pays you?'

Within minutes Dirk had spilled his guts: Jannie, his connection to Thabethe, the stolen Vektor Z88s. Thabethe had also supplied the knives and the knuckle-dusters. Last year. No, he said in reply to Pillay's question, not his gun. That was his own, the Desert Eagle, from someone else. Yes, it was an impressive weapon. He had liked the look of it. Titanium gold. Bought from a friend a few years ago. No, he wasn't in touch with the friend any longer. He dared not mention Tony, who had warned him with icy seriousness that no trail involving the weapons should ever go back to him. *Under any circumstances. Ever.*

Dirk omitted Tony and Vic altogether from his sobbed narrative. He knew that whatever fate lay in store for him with the cops, it would be better than crossing Tony or Vic. He would take his chances with the cops on illegal carrying.

Ryder pulled his two colleagues outside for a quick exchange.

'Good stuff, Navi. Nyawula's going to be pleased with this. It's the breakthrough he's been wanting.'

'Time for that promotion, Sergeant Pillay?' chuckled Ed.

'Pity it's not up to you, Ed,' she replied.

'Navi, can you get this creep back to the unit and have him processed? Along with his impressive titanium gold Deagle. Then try and get what else you can on him. I've got a 2.00 pm with KoeksnDips to check their stuff on ballistics and the info on Thabethe before they see the Captain. Ed, can you spend a bit of time and scour this place for anything you can find? Maybe he's hidden a phone number or some other useful stuff somewhere in the place. Seems to me like this guy's got handlers. He doesn't have the *suss* to do this stuff on his own.'

'Sure thing, Jeremy. I'll take the place apart and see what I can get. Maybe start in his fridge.'

'Why am I not surprised? I'll get back here at about four-thirty if you want to wait for me.'

Pillay and Ryder punched fists with Trewhella as they left, each in their own vehicles, Pillay having firstly locked Dirk in the back seat of hers.

As they pulled away, neither of them saw the sole figure behind the wheel of the black Mercedes-Benz 2.1 Sport parked in the shade twenty metres up the road, watching.

As the two cars disappeared from view, Tony stepped out and shut the door of the Mercedes gently behind him before crossing the road.

Trewhella did not start in the fridge. For once. He had only said it in jest. He removed his jacket, holster and weapon, and placed them on the counter. Then he set about checking each room again. This time the floors and walls would also come under scrutiny for hollow spaces. There was something in this place that someone was trying to hide, that's for sure, he thought. He checked the kitchen thoroughly, tapping on walls and the bases of cupboards, checking behind pictures hanging on the walls, and standing on one of the bar-stools at one point to get a closer look at a stained area on the ceiling.

'Come to daddy. Come out wherever you are,' he muttered to himself, and got more and more absorbed in what he was doing. He moved to the living-room area and up-ended an armchair, then felt underneath and peered through the gap in the imitation-leather that had started to peel away in one corner. He examined it closely then concluded there was nothing to warrant further study. He moved to the sofa and did much the same. Then he checked the television set. He whistled quietly as he worked, occasionally murmuring to himself.

After fifteen minutes he moved through to the bedroom. He felt a draft run through the apartment, and was about to step back out to check for an open window somewhere, when something caught his eye.

'Hullo. Interesting. Let's have a look at you then.'

He had noticed the flapped-over corner of the carpet in the corner of the room, next to the wardrobe, and walked over to it, chatting to himself.

'Careless, I would say. Wouldn't you? Me? Yes, you. Let's have a look at you, then. Who, me? Yes, you. I'll tell on you, I will. Will you, now?'

He squatted down and flipped back the carpet.

'Hullo! 'Ullo, 'ullo, 'ullo then, me 'earties! What do we 'ave 'ere, then?'

He pressed down on a loose board, about eighteen inches long, and the opposite end tilted up. He sat down, cross-legged, and had a closer look. He pressed down again and the far end of the board tilted up a fraction further. He got a finger-nail into the end of the board and lifted.

Fitting into a gap only slightly wider than itself was a long narrow red box. Trewhella expelled breath not so much in a whistle as in a stream of sibilant air that ended up approximating the sound of a whistle.

'Oh, yeah! Jeremy's going to love this. What a nice little prezzy to find.'

He pulled the box out of its cavity, and opened it, still cross-legged on the ground.

'What do we have here, then?'

'Nothing that belongs to you, Detective.'

Trewhella spun around, starting to get onto his knees, knowing that his weapon was in the next room but instinctively knowing that if he could get to his feet he might have a chance...

There was no chance. None at all. Tony had the Desert Eagle trained on him. Another titanium gold. Just like the one Pillay had taken from fatso. Trewhella knew, as he saw the gun, that he had no chance. He froze, on his knees, staring at the adversary. Tony stepped back. Two paces. And stared straight back at Trewhella, his finger on the trigger.

**15.00.**

Dippenaar and Koekemoer stood, leaning against a wall each. Ryder sat in one of the chairs, turned around, bronco-style, in the middle of the room, the file held up in his right hand.

'This is brilliant, Dipps. This puts all three weapons in the frame. And takes all these perps back to one common source. One Skhura Thabethe. Captain's gonna be thrilled.'

'You think, Jeremy? I don't know. I think he's gonna go – if you'll forgive the pun – ballistic.'

'I agree with Dipps,' said Koekemoer, waving the other, much thicker, file, 'and when he looks at Thabethe's disciplinary file, too, he'll just explode. The stuff in here is frightening, *mense*. Thabethe should have been nailed within a month of starting as a cop, but he was a slippery bastard, I tell you. He lasted too long before he was caught. The stuff in here will freak out the Captain. This slimy *oke* was probably ripping us off long before his first disciplinary. The stuff he was pulling from the moment he was appointed is just amazing. How do guys like this get away with it?'

Ryder stood, taking the proffered file from Koekemoer and passing the other back to Dippenaar. He opened the disciplinary file on the desk, and started paging through it. He shook his head in disbelief as he saw report after report verifying Koekemoer's comments.

'As you say, Koeks. What a slimeball. No wonder the Captain wanted him so badly.'

'You see where they even wonder whether he had a hand in the loss of those ammo boxes? They couldn't prove anything. No-one would talk, by the looks of it, so nothing happened there, but *yissus* Jeremy it looks bad, hey?'

'It looks as if no-one would *ever* talk against the guy, Koeks. Maybe he scared the shit out of them, or something.'

Sergeant Cronje opened the door and entered from the inner room.

'OK, guys. The Captain says he's ready. You can come through.'

Ryder felt that the Captain was probably going to throw a frothy and then turn his energy to nailing this guy. Maybe things were finally starting to pull together. Dippenaar was right. It wasn't going to be a pleasant reaction from Nyawula. But he, too, would start seeing the light at the end of the tunnel. Thabethe's days were numbered.

### 16.35.

Thabethe sat in the back in a corner of the taxi. The 12-seater carried only three other passengers, all up near the front. He flicked through the two bundles of cash. The Afrikaner boy's money coupled with the money from the English guy on the beach on Sunday night. It was more money than he had held in his grasp for nearly two years. He felt alive again. Anything was possible. But he'd be careful. He'd keep his wits about him. He would gamble a bit, just to get the feel of the place. More important was to watch and learn. What had the young Afrikaner said? *I'm working with these guys...I meet them at Suncoast Casino...They pulling big money. Not from the casinos ... other stuff involving gambling ...You remember Dirk? You met him once, right here. The fat guy. My friend...*

Thabethe pulled out the photograph. He remembered. The fat guy with the Afrikaner boy. At Nomivi's, that time. The features came back into focus. Yes, he would know him if they met again. He needed to find out more about these guys pulling big money. He'd watch out for the fat friend. Make some enquiries. Find him. Find out more about the big money.

The taxi pulled in at Suncoast Casino and Thabethe got out.

Within twenty minutes he was wondering why he had never thought of this previously. He had watched, walked around, watched, and even bought a day card and experimented with the slot machines. On one occasion he even won something. He had been shocked when he hit the button and suddenly the crazy music blared up and he had gone from less than fifty up to eight hundred and thirty credits, whatever that meant. He didn't fully understand the rules, except that he knew that something had happened in his favour. The old man next to him, with one tooth in his head, explained to him that he had just won eight hundred rands. He couldn't understand the guy's explanation of why this had happened, so he turned away from him and carried on hitting the button. He watched his eight hundred and thirty credits go to zero in less than five minutes. He gave up his seat and moved on.

He asked further questions of a few of the old women playing the machines, who seemed to know exactly what they were doing. Then he watched some more, and wandered around the place. He watched gloomy irritated people pressing the button time and time again and winning nothing. He watched old women stuffing cash into their bags, into their shirts, into their trousers, as others watched enviously. He followed one old man, a very big winner, out to the taxis and watched him get in. Easy pickings, he thought, as he watched the taxi drive away. Then he realised.

The guy he had shot on Sunday night, next to the bush at the beach. No more than a few hundred yards away from where he was now. He must have walked from here, from the casino. Drunk on his winnings at the machines or at the tables. The guy was far gone. Could hardly stand. The cash he had carried must have been his winnings from this place. Hundred-rand and two-hundred-rand notes. And that casino card. The idiot had stumbled out of the casino, or out of some bar somewhere, and had decided to celebrate with a woman on the beach. Fool.

Thabethe hadn't put it together until this moment. This place was pissing money. Money for the owners, for the managers, and for a few lucky patrons. Patrons who got so excited about their winnings that they dropped their guard, and became the very best kind of mugging target.

He walked out of the main entrance and made his way toward Battery Beach Road, and from there down to the beach. He wasn't going to go anywhere near the scene of Sunday night's action. He could see it at a distance, and he could see that there were some people inspecting the place where the guy had died. Forensics. They were sifting through the sand. One was writing things on a pad. Another was typing things into a laptop. Another one was extending the police tape-barrier.

Thabethe retreated. If they hadn't found the gun already they soon would. He cursed as he remembered his stupidity. He was now down to the last of the four weapons that he had stolen last year.

He went back toward the casino complex, thinking of the possibilities. He would have to come back in a day or two and scout the place again at night. Work out the best spot for a mugging. Avoid the beach. No sense in repeating that. The cops might watch the place for a while. Rather catch another victim somewhere else. Maybe even follow a couple of the winners, get into the same taxi, and wait to see where they stepped off. Follow them home, perhaps. Find the right spot. Relieve them of their winnings. Easy pickings.

But for now, back into the casino. Also ask some questions. Find this Dirk guy, and follow the big money. The muggings could provide what he needed. But the young Afrikaner talked big money, not little money. Find the fat friend and see what the big money is all about.

## 17.30.

Ryder had pulled in for petrol and to take a leak. He was agitated. Everything was running behind schedule. The Captain had behaved exactly as Dippenaar had predicted. Wanted Thabethe's head, and wanted it now. Threw orders around the room and had everyone jumping. Expected everything to happen immediately.

Fiona was going to give him a hard time when he told her he'd be late again. On top of everything he'd told Ed that he would meet up with him, supposedly an hour ago.

One thing had been particularly useful, though. In the middle of Dippenaar's discussion with Nyawula about the ballistics stuff, Ryder had had the sudden thought that it might be useful to check the ballistics on that other shooting in the bush last year, also near the casino. Nyawula had jumped at that. Good connection, he had said. Ballistics would of course have got around to matching their findings to past homicides in due course, because that was a matter of routine. That's what they did. But just as well to get on to it right away, instead of letting it follow the normal course of events. If that homicide was found to link to Sunday night's one in the bush next to the beach, then we have another piece of the puzzle. If the same Z88 had been used in both shootings, then something might be happening on an on-going basis down at the casino. Something that we should know more about. He put Dippenaar onto that. Told him to get back to ballistics and check last year's records.

As Ryder returned to his car, the call came in. He looked at the screen of the iPhone and took the call, irritated. What could Piet possibly want from him now? He'd seen him just twenty minutes ago.

'Jeremy?'

'Yes, Piet. What?'

'I'm sorry, Jeremy. The Captain wanted me to tell you. He's just gone tearing off, himself, with Pillay, who just arrived...'

'What? What's wrong, Piet?'

'*Yissus*, man. I don't know how – Jeremy, I can't...'

'Talk to me, Piet.'

Ryder froze as Piet's babble spewed out into his ear. He felt the pulse of every heartbeat pounding against his eardrums. It was as if every sinew in his body would snap, and the puppet-strings that had kept him upright would simply go soft, leaving him in a collapsed heap on the floor. A great, terrible weariness gripped him as he mumbled back.

'I'll go right over. Call my wife, please, Piet. Tell her. Everything. Tell her I'll get home when I can.'

'Leave it to me, Jeremy. Take it easy, OK?'

Ryder cut the call, and stumbled in a daze to his Camry. A part of him had just died.


## 17.40.

Vic and Tony stood, Vic leaning back on the edge of his desk and Tony standing relaxed, hands in pockets, before him. Vic's throaty rasp seemed to Tony even more constricted than usual. He had never seen Vic this ill at ease. He seemed really agitated.

'You sure the place is clean, Tony? This is big time. They're gonna come after us with everything they've got.'

'I know, Vic. I had to go for it, because he had found the red box. If it hadn't been for that, I could have played it differently. Even if we had no way of telling what Dirk might have told the three of them before they took him away. But because the guy had found the stuff I had to go for it. Only problem is there was no time to burn the place, because passers-by started looking in through windows and shit. They must have heard something. I had to get out quick. But I can guarantee it's clean. I don't think they can track anything back to us.'

'From your lips to God's ears. We're stuffed if you're wrong.'

'I'm not wrong. Montpelier Road is clean. No trace of us. And like you said, we'll use Overport until Argyle Road is ready.'

'Argyle is ready. I got the go-ahead just before you came in. It's good to go, right from now. They're cleaning it tomorrow morning first thing. We can start using it from late tomorrow."

'That's good news. Then we're safe.'

'Safe, maybe, from any trackback. But they're gonna put a lot more men on us now.'

'And that damn woman cop, too.'

'The Indian? Yeah.'

'Tamil, I think.'

'What?'

'She's Tamil.'

'Whatever. Watch her. She worries me, whatever the hell she is. She's always popping up around the other detectives. Like the bloody Scarlet Pimpernel. I think she fancies herself as a kind of reserve player to Ryder and Trewhella, and to those other two Afrikaners. Watch out for her.'

'I will. I hope I get a chance to take her out. She's a big problem.'

'Only if you have to. Let things cool a bit. Let's set up the new place and get the hell out of the other places. Including Overport, once Argyle Road is set up. We'll keep the safe in Overport until we've built one in Argyle.'

'Will do. I'll stash the box behind the wall in Overport tomorrow morning when I handle the payment for the last dispatch there, and from now on we'll just give the Montpelier house a wide berth. They'll be finding out around now. Then the place will be crawling with cops. But they won't find anything there.'

'OK. Thanks, Tony. Good work. I think. I'll see what I can find out tonight. Let's touch base tomorrow morning around ten-thirty before your business at Overport in case I need to brief you on anything I might learn tonight.'

'Thanks, Vic.'


**17.50.**

Thabethe sat at the bar watching the slot-machine players, and finished the beer. He had been waiting for the service at the bar to experience a lull in the action, and it came. He caught the barman's attention, motioned for another of the same, and when the beer arrived he held up the crumpled photo of the two Afrikaners.

A pause as the old man contemplated – not the answer to the question, but whether he should be speaking to this young man with the strange eyes. He decided it would be less trouble for him to simply tell the young man and hope that would be the end of it. He didn't feel comfortable being on the receiving end of a stare like that.

Yes, he remembered both the men. No question. They were always hanging around. *They would often go through those doors, there, see, over there...* No, he didn't know where those doors went, but...

He paused in mid-sentence. Thabethe looked at him.

'Is what? What you say?'

'That man, coming there now, walking past the lady with the blue dress.'

'Yes? Is what?'

'Those two men, in the photo, sometimes they come out walking with that man over there.'

Thabethe snatched back the photograph, threw a fifty rand note on the table, left his beer and, keeping his distance, followed Tony through the crowds in the casino.

## 17.55.

Ryder bent again over Trewhella's twisted, empty corpse. Empty. Empty not because of the pints that had bled out through the evil hole in the forehead to congeal, black-red, across the living-room carpet. Empty because of total absence. Abandoned. Discarded. A shell.

He had seen many corpses, but he had never thought that death would ever show itself quite like this. It had sucked the entire history from this previously warm and much-loved body. It had left behind a mere husk, as dry and brittle as cracked autumn leaves with no further purpose. The formerly bright and mischievous two blue marble eyes now stared blankly up at him, half covered by translucent eyelids. There was nothing behind them. They sat there in their sockets, with no connection to a living brain. Mere absence, total and complete and desolate. What lay before Ryder was no longer his partner. There were no more jokes. No more innuendoes. The end of laughter.

He stepped backward, taking care to avoid any interference with what would now become the unit's top crime scene. He had no desire to touch the thing that lay before him. The countless movie scenes he had observed – many of them in the presence of this same movie-loving rogue and best friend – in which the dead loved one was scooped up into frenzied arms, accompanied by sobs and tears and anguished moans, were as far from this numbing reality as he could possibly imagine.

As he straightened his weary spine to achieve his full six feet and two inches of stiff angular height he felt the troublesome L4 in his lower back complain yet again. The dull pain added to his desperate weariness. Utter fatigue. A numbing lack of any emotion at all. It was as if the emptiness of the corpse had attached itself to him. He felt decades older than his forty years as he turned, dry-eyed and ice-cold, to leave the scene for the impossible task of breaking the news to others, to friends and relatives and former lovers and ex-wives and colleagues who hadn't already heard...

It was going to be a long, tough night.

The forensics people made way for him, respectfully, as he walked back in a haze through the apartment to the front door, removing the gloves and the rest of the PPE kit they had handed him upon his arrival. They muttered their condolences as he passed them the objects. As he reached the front door, the crowds were being pulled back behind the barricades across the street and for thirty yards on both sides, up and down.

The barricades were opened, temporarily, with the approach of more blue lights. Three more cars. Four. Five. Among those that screeched to a halt, spewing both uniforms and plain-clothes, he noticed Koekemoer, Dippenaar, Cronje, Cronje's intern, and various others from the unit. Then Captain Nyawula pulled up, with Pillay driving. They got out of Pillay's car, saw Ryder, and waited for him to walk over to them.

# 3 WEDNESDAY

**07.55.**

Fiona had killed the alarm after Ryder finally went to sleep, at around 3.00 am. Half a bottle of Laphroaig had helped. He had gone ice cold, silent, and completely immobile as he fell asleep in her arms. She had never seen that before.

He had had some bad experiences over the years. Seen quite a few cops take a hit, some of them people to whom he had been very close. One, like Frikkie van der Westhuizen, had been such a good buddy, before Ed came along. Frikkie had survived for eight days with sixteen stab wounds in him, before he finally passed. Ryder had handled that with no apparent emotion. But she knew him well. Knew what was going on inside him at the time. She had been a tower of strength to him. She knew that. He knew it. It was only at the funeral that he'd choked up a bit when speaking over Frikkie's grave. He came through that, but he had then been obsessed with finding Frikkie's killer, working round the clock and presiding over the team that eventually nailed him. It was only when they put the guy away for thirty-five years that Ryder seemed to reach some kind of acceptance.

Before that, there had been Ntshaveni, up in Johannesburg. Best buddies with Jeremy, but for such a short time. Ntshaveni and his wife had been frequent guests at their home, and the children had played together, and the two detectives had cracked many high-profile cases together. They had been through so much in such a short time before Ntshaveni was killed in a hail of bullets. Ryder had then pursued the four thugs relentlessly and had personally taken down each and every one of them, almost as if he was driven to pay back a debt to Ntshaveni's three children. He had not rested until three of the perpetrators were behind bars, each of them for a minimum of thirty years, and the fourth was six feet under, where he belonged. The Ryders had then followed up and made a massive contribution to the education of Ntshaveni's children, and made a point of seeing them and their mother whenever they were up in Johannesburg.

Ed's death was different. This was a game-changer. Fiona thought that this time something had given way inside Ryder. He had seldom spoken to her directly about the politics behind the work. Apart from the usual office gossip and the occasional despairing comment following a media scoop on the latest police corruption scandal. Last night was different. What he'd babbled out through his drunken haze, before he finally passed out, had scared her. The corruption. The bribes. The senior guys who were faceless but seemed to determine so much of what happened on the ground. The cases that made it through days and nights and weeks and months of painstaking detective work and then blew up because of clever defence lawyers or overworked State Advocates or because of some unknown instruction from above. Or because of some bribe, and the resultant disappearance of crucial papers or evidence.

Then the other dimension. The IPID investigations. Jeremy was the cleanest cop around, she thought, and he attracted clean cops to work with him. He was all for IPID inquiries. Let the public see that there was no simple whitewashing of actions by the cops. No problem. When an investigation looks necessary, then go for it. But what had begun to bug him recently was the sense that whenever IPID was called in someone up the food chain, thinking of their political profile rather than the case in hand, went miles too far, finding all cops guilty until proven innocent. Shouting about their suspicions in the media. Making themselves look like they were the real corruption-busters when, in fact, they were just milking the publicity. *Major and Colonel Clean: we fight the good fight.* Until the actual evidence, and the cops are exonerated. Then no apology. No climb-down. No *sorry, I jumped the gun.* Silence. That one didn't work for them, so there'll be another chance to proclaim their leadership in the fight against corruption.

*Whose side were these guys on?*

Ed's death seemed to have pulled a cork out of the bottle as Jeremy spewed forth with all of this. She had held him in her arms, rocking him back and forth, as he went silent, and still, and eventually drifted off.

This was the first weekday in the nearly two decades they had been together that she knew him to sleep through daybreak. He had always got up with the light, Monday to Friday. Even after long nights. Always an early riser. That had proved very useful in this particular period, while Nyawula was experimenting with his team with new office hours: *Early start, early finish. Let's try it for a month, guys.* They had all been up for trying it, and were currently halfway through the experiment. Another one of the many innovations that Nyawula had introduced. His popularity was growing within the unit.

But it made no difference to Jeremy, she thought. Something always got him up with the dawn. Except not on weekends. Funny, that. How come the light never got to him on weekends? Weird. But always on a weekday, no matter what.

Except this time. Not today. She was the one to wake up first. She moved stealthily and slipped out of the bed. She took his iPhone with her, knowing that it wouldn't be long before the calls started coming in. Condolences. Support. Shock. She would field the calls downstairs, and protect him, and give him a hot breakfast. With lots of coffee.

## 09.35.

Pillay left the Captain's office a bit startled. The lines had been humming all night and they had worked through the whole thing, he told her, and those he reported to had in essence agreed with him. Nyawula's superiors usually ended up agreeing with him. Except for Major Swanepoel. But in this case even he had supported the request. So the Captain wanted her to know how hard he had worked at this deal, to get her on board. Because he had faith in her abilities, he told her. He hoped she knew that.

She had nodded and made to speak, but he had interrupted her.

'There are some rules being broken here, Navi. So please don't take this as a formal arrangement just yet. It'll take time to go through all the hoops, to satisfy the necessary protocols, and to sign off on everything, so we'll only be able to make a formal announcement in due course.'

'I understand, Captain.'

'But for now just consider yourself as Jeremy's new partner.'

'Yessir.'

'I'll brief him first, so try if you can not to be in contact with him until you have the go-ahead. Hopefully within a couple of hours, if Jeremy comes in today. I'll completely understand if he doesn't.'

'Me too, Captain'

'You'll receive the formal papers in a few days. Probably before the funeral, whenever that might be. I've thought long and hard about this, Navi, and I know it's a really sensitive issue, but I also thought there might be some therapeutic value in announcing only at Ed's funeral that you'll be the one taking over from him. I know that you and Ed and Ryder and KoeksnDips and the others have enjoyed a pretty good relationship in the unit. It's a difficult one, I know, but I've decided on balance to go for that option.'

'Makes sense, sir.'

'Above all, no-one must talk about a new partnership between you and Ryder beforehand. Especially at the function tomorrow night. That's not the occasion to talk about things like this. Let's try and keep it under wraps until the announcement at the funeral.'

'Will do. You can count on me, Captain.'

'Anyway, Navi. I'm sorry to have been so pernickety about this. In essence, despite all I've said, please consider the promotion a done deal. I want personally to let Jeremy know, so don't be in contact with him until that happens. In the meantime you can get back on the job. And given the circumstances, by all means work alone for the rest of the day. But be careful, until you have a partner to watch your back.'

Pillay had been unusually at a loss for words throughout most of this exchange. She walked in a daze to her car, her mind now racing as she considered the ramifications.

Nyawula stood at the window and watched her cross the car park. One of the few, he thought. Now partners. Pillay and Ryder. And soon, officially, Detective Pillay. No longer Sergeant Pillay. He wished he could have a few more like them and like KoeksnDips. Trewhella had also been damned good, despite his methods. Poor bastard. He and Ryder had been among the best he had seen. Perfect balance: good cop, bad cop was the impression everyone had of them, but in fact both of them were good cops. The best, and refreshingly clean, both of them, with no hint of corruption. To have a team like that broken up caused a real problem for Nyawula. Maybe Ryder and Pillay together could plug the gap.

Which one would be the bad cop, and which one the good, he wondered? They were both extraordinarily tough.

He had been pleasantly surprised that the Major had simply gone along with his proposal. It was unlike Swanepoel to let Nyawula just go ahead against strict HR policy and protocols. He usually put every obstacle he could in the way of Nyawula's attempts to turn this into an efficient operation. Racist bastard. It often seemed to Nyawula that the Major couldn't stomach a black officer making good. Always interfering. Usually wanted everything on paper, all the time. Dates, times, intentions: every damned thing that kept the team from getting out into the streets and doing the job they were paid for.

But at least for now he had patched up a big problem. Pillay would do well. He was sure of that. And Ryder would come around to accepting her as a replacement for his buddy

**10.40.**

Tony stood in front of Vic in his customary position. Vic's voice was even raspier than yesterday, Tony thought. It seemed more breathless than he had ever heard it. It seemed to emanate from a deep well, the air being forced up through a mountain of flesh as if through a cancerous larynx before emerging in a hoarse vocalised whisper.

'All hell's gonna break over this, Tony.'

'Sure expect it to, Vic. But, like I said, I really had to do it. The guy was getting too close. Like I told you yesterday, he had found the loose floor-board and the box and was about to go through the documents. What could I do? I've got the box in the car and I'll put it into the wall in Overport. I'll go over there right now.'

'OK. That's probably the best place for now. But I'm going to have to keep my ears close to the ground on this one, to see what action the cops are going to take. I suspect it's going to be like starting a whole new war. What about Ryder? He's a scary guy. Tough as nails, I hear, and apparently meticulous. Never lets go of a case. Follows it for years. I don't like that.'

'I'll watch my back. In the meantime, we really should bring in a couple of guys to help us, now that Dirk and Jannie are out of it. Do you have anyone in mind? From Cape Town or Pretoria, maybe? What about that guy in Maputo who's checking things out for you? What about Big Red? I've known him a long time, and you seemed to hit it off with him when you met, remember?'

'Let me think through that. I've also thought of Red. After that little runt Jannie I think we need more muscle like you, and brains. Like you. I like Red's muscle, but I don't know his brains well enough yet. I'll think about it.'

'OK. I'll wait for you, then. I know I can work with Red. He and I pulled some good stuff together in the old days. But I'll wait for you to tell me.'

'Will do. First I need to check that our lines are still safe. I'll let you know. In the meantime you get into the Overport place and store the box, sort out today's dispatch, and also clear out any traces that Dirk might've left. The cops might work on him inside, and get him to talk.'

'Will do, Vic. Is there any way we can find out where they took Dirk? If we could find out then maybe we could get someone on the inside to ensure that he remains cool. He knows a lot about us. If he talks...'

'I'm working on just exactly that. Leave it to me. I'll find out where he is in the system. Could be anywhere between hospital and a cell. I'll find him, through my connections.'

'Sure thing. I'll get on to Overport, then.'

Vic nodded and Tony turned to the door.

'Watch your back, Tony. I'm hearing things about Ryder that worry me. The *charra* woman, too. I hear they're gonna put them together, now.'

'That so? That small chick ? With Ryder? After Trewhella? Sounds like a panic decision. I thought she was still a junior. Anyway, I'll be careful. I can look after myself.'

'You do that, Tony. The estate agent's people are right now preparing Argyle Road. I want to check on their progress, then we'll be good to go later today, I hope.'

As he left, and closed the door behind him, Vic sat for a moment, then reached for his iPhone. He punched in a number and waited for three rings before the call was picked up.

'It's Vic, Red. I need to come and check the boat. It would be good to talk. Are we good for any time tomorrow morning?'


**11.00.**

As Tony walked through the casino, Thabethe slipped off the stool in front of the slot machine and followed him. Yesterday he had followed the gangster to his car, but having no transport he had been unable to follow any further. He simply noted the details, and watched Tony purr away from the casino.

Today Thabethe had arrived in his own car. Hired from Spikes Mkhize at Nomivi's for a cool four hundred rands cash for two days, *special price for Skhura alone.* A battered old red Mini, now barely roadworthy. Spikes had tried to interest him in the silver Honda Ballade, stolen in 2007, souped up and re-painted with new chassis numbers, and completely re-honed for speed and power, for only three hundred a day. Thabethe declined. He had to get used to driving. Better a bucket of bolts than a souped-up car that might attract attention, for now anyway.

He took some time to familiarise himself with the Mini, after his months in prison. But he soon got on top of it and had then driven slowly around the parking area until he found Tony's car. Black Mercedes-Benz 2.1 Sport. Not parked in the same area as yesterday, but instantly identifiable. So he had parked a couple of bays away from it. Now, as Tony got into the

Mercedes, Thabethe peeled off and walked over to the Mini.

He stayed a good hundred metres behind the Mercedes as he followed it onto Sandile Thusi Road and through to where it became the M17, then crossed over Lillian Ngoyi and Florida, followed by a couple of dog-legs and then on to Moses Kotane. As Tony slowed down, he fell further back. He then watched as his quarry pulled in and parked at the edge of the road.

Tony got out of the Mercedes, opened the trunk, and took out a long red box, half the width but twice the length of a shoebox. Then he walked across the road, away from the building next to which he had parked. He had clearly decided not to park adjacent to where he was actually going. Instead, he walked about thirty paces straight down the road and turned right into a place with a small forecourt, with space for five or six cars, fully visible to Thabethe still sitting in his car back on the road. Tony walked across the parking area, unlocked the front door of what seemed like a three-storey warehouse, looked around over his shoulder before entering, and closed the door behind him. Thabethe was intrigued, but decided to sit and wait rather than follow. He could take a closer look later, when everyone had left.

It proved to be the right decision. Within twenty minutes a white panel van arrived, and parked in the parking space, and Tony emerged to greet the new arrival. They both entered the building. Twenty minutes later they both re-emerged, struggling with what looked like a very heavy wooden crate. They took some time to manoeuvre it into the van. Then the door was locked, they shook hands, and the driver left carrying some papers. Tony in turn received a large envelope from the driver and stood there watching him drive off. Then he re-entered the building.

Thabethe stayed where he was.

## 12.20.

Pillay drove away from yet another search at the Montpelier Road house. Another largely fruitless search. Largely. Except for one flimsy possibility. A fourteen-month old receipt, scrunched back by the desk drawer into a scrap of bundled paper that no-one else had paid any attention to because it had become wedged in the corner of the drawer-space. She had unravelled it to read 'DA 68: Application for delivery of goods ex state warehouse... Section 17.' And an address in Overport scribbled in pencil, along with the words 'easy access to Sparks Road / Springfield, Mayville...'

Her mind raced through the possibilities as she drove toward the Berea.

She was dying to call Ryder, but she couldn't say anything, yet, about Nyawula's arrangement for them. Perhaps she should just get on with it, scout this place, see what comes up. If anything. The form DA 68 was more than a year old. Could mean nothing. Damn. She would love it if Ryder could join her.

Her dilemma was answered for her. Ryder on the iPhone.

'Jeremy? You OK?'

'I'm OK, Navi. Where are you?'

Within seconds Ryder had arranged to meet up with her at the Overport address. And within fifteen minutes the two of them had arrived in their separate cars, found parking in the forecourt, and then paused for discussion next to Ryder's Camry.

'Nyawula called me twenty minutes ago.'

'He told me, too, Jeremy, early this morning. How do you feel about it?'

'I'm OK, Navi. Don't think that...'

'I'm really sorry, Jeremy. I know I can't really – I know it will take some time – Ed was...'

'I'm good, Navi. No need to say anything else. OK? Nyawula asked me to let you know that he's talked to me, but to keep it between us until he's ready to make an announcement.'

'Thanks. I'll do what I can...'

'Let's check out this place of yours.'

They moved to the front door and Pillay knocked, loudly. After fruitlessly trying that for a few seconds, she tried the handle, with no great optimism. To her surprise, it opened. She called into the interior.

'Anyone home? Hullo! Anyone there?'

Nothing. They moved in, apprehensively. They were on a ground-floor passage leading to a flight of stairs. They could see a landing on the first floor, then beyond that another flight of stairs leading to a second floor. On a table in the passage just next to the front door, on their right, was a small collection of documents. They looked at first glance like no more than post, adverts for pizza delivery, business envelopes, junk. As Ryder picked up the pile to flip through them Pillay leaned in through the open door on their left. Nothing. There was a second door, also to their left, further down the passage, but Pillay was more interested in looking up through the stairwell to see how far the place stretched.

'I'll have a quick check upstairs, Jeremy. You check down here. OK?'

Ryder nodded, still looking through the post, and she moved to the stairs as he skimmed through the documents in his hand. She called up the stairs as she went.

'Hullo? Anyone home? Police.'

Her boots clumped upward on the stairs, deliberately loudly to add to the alert, for the benefit of anyone who might not hear her because of the noise of photocopying or some other possible reason.

'Looks like no-one's around, Jeremy. I'll start at the top.'

She moved up the flight of stairs toward the second floor rooms, as Ryder put the papers back down on the table. Nothing more there of any significance. Just letters to 'The Occupier,' advertisers, marketing junk, and charity appeals. He moved down the passage to the second room on his left, knocked, opened the door, and went in.

Tony stepped in behind Ryder as he entered, and brought the club down with such force onto the back of his head that it snapped the wood in two. Ryder dropped instantly, by no means unconscious but sufficiently stunned to preclude resistance and allow Tony to move his bulk rapidly toward him. Within seconds he had secured the detective's wrists behind his back, tied with nylon rope to the thick main plumbing line that ran an inch from the wall and three inches above the floor, just to the left of the doorway.

Tony immediately stuffed Ryder's mouth with a discarded oil rag and then stood back. Ryder, his senses still dulled by the blow, tasted paraffin as he tried to manipulate the rag with his tongue to stop himself choking. He could utter nothing more than a dull compressed grunt as his captor hissed at him.

'You're going to give me some information, detective. But you can give it to me after I've wasted your partner. She's useless to me. Just a hindrance. I'm going to take her out. Just like I did with your previous partner.'

Ryder struggled in vain. Tony moved to check through the window. All clear outside. Then he peered through the crack at the hinges of the door, up the passage. Nothing. He moved back to a spot six feet from the door, facing it, and facing Ryder sprawled on the ground, and waited.

It didn't take long. In the silence both of them heard a door open upstairs, on the first floor, followed by footsteps and then another door opening. Then another. Then more footsteps, this time descending on the staircase, rapidly. Heavy boots. Pillay. Ryder's brain was racing as he tried to clear the fog and focus. With his mouth full of oil-rag, there was no way for him to warn Pillay, who was already at the foot of the stairs and now moving quickly down the passage toward the door, calling out.

'Jeremy! Clear upstairs. What you got?'

Tony took a step forward toward the door, the Desert Eagle clasped in his right hand. Pillay wouldn't have a chance. He needed no information from her, so he'd just blow her away as she walked through the door. The downed cop was the guy who probably had the information he needed: how close the cops were to Thabethe, what they knew about the casinos, the plans for Saturday, and who their contacts were. She was nothing more than a hindrance.

He raised the weapon to shoot her point-blank as she entered the room. But Ryder's head was clearing rapidly. He saw the intent in the gunman, and from the sound of Pillay's voice and her heavy boots on the wooden floor he computed the exact moment of her arrival. Stretching every sinew in his body he chose his moment, thrust his body toward Tony, to the limit allowed him by the rope holding him to the plumbing, and as Tony raised the Desert Eagle he smashed his right boot into his adversary's left shin, just above the ankle.

Tony's shot angled to his right, as a result of Ryder's kick, and grazed Pillay's upper left arm, taking a fair piece of her flesh with it and initiating massive bruising of the muscle. A fraction to his left and the bullet would have shattered bone and knocked her off her feet. As stunned as she was, and immediately finding her left arm bloodied and useless, she had enough instinct to dive forward and head-butt Tony in the midriff with her full body weight behind the movement. The gun went sprawling one way, the gunman the other, and both he and Pillay struggled to get to their feet, but she had fallen awkwardly onto her right elbow, which instantly sent heat and a shock wave to her right hand, rendering it useless for drawing her own weapon in time. As she clambered up, she turned and saw that Tony was already on his feet, the dagger in his right hand. Seven-inches, inclusive of a three-inch blade. Double edged and very sharp. With a black Micarta handle, highly polished.

The pain from her left arm was unbearable. Tony was moving far too fast for her to draw her weapon with the numbed and almost equally useless right hand. He moved rapidly toward her with the dagger.


**12.40.**

'Any chance of a coffee in here, Piet?'

'Coming right up, Captain!' Cronje called from the next room.

Nyawula was troubled. Something was nagging at him. What was it? He certainly had enough on his plate to deal with. Four of his unit's Vektor Z88s had gone missing with Thabethe. Now within twenty-four hours two of them turn up in the Wilson's Wharf incident and another one turns up on the beach at the Suncoast Casino bushes. One of the weapons still remained out there, somewhere. No doubt connected with Thabethe. All of this looked bad for the unit and for him as the Captain tasked with bringing down the tally of lost weapons, not just for his specific team but for the whole unit.

But there was something else, too. He couldn't put his finger on what it was that was troubling him.

He doodled on the pad before him. His notes weren't hanging together. The man on the beach was a British tourist, so the office of the British High Commission was now involved. It had become a more important case than it might otherwise have been. The initial reports seemed to indicate that it was a straightforward – if ever these things could be considered straightforward – homicide, with robbery as the motive. As tough as it was on the victim and his family and the tourist industry, Nyawula was more interested in the weapon than the victim. Forensic Services were following up on the prints, and ballistics were doing their thing. The Z88 must surely lead them somewhere? He needed a break.

And then there was Trewhella. The team had been devastated at the news. And those in the wider unit. And those further afield in other stations, too. They had popped in and out of the office all morning as if on automatic. Faces grim, bodies bearing the weight of the endless fight. Some of them doubtless thinking of throwing in the towel. The annual party tomorrow at Mabhida Stadium would involve the usual speeches. Fight the good fight. Against what? For what return? Certainly not measurable by salary. He couldn't blame the men and women under his care for starting to question their careers in the face of rampant crime and corruption. He would have to try and muster some spirit in the team. Get them back to working closely together. Trewhella had been widely admired, despite his unorthodox habits. He had instilled fun into the team. He had been central to it. He had to try and rebuild some purpose and camaraderie.

Cronje walked in with the coffee and put it on the desk in front of him.

'Thanks, Piet. I appreciate it.'

'Pleasure, boss.'

Cronje turned to go, but Nyawula stopped him.

'Piet.'

'Yessir?'

'How long have you been with SAPS?'

'*Ag, jeez*, Captain, must be more than twenty years now.'

'Seen a few changes?'

'Sure thing.'

'Especially with detective stuff. Lots of changes since 1994 and all that.'

'Definitely, Captain.'

'How has it changed for you, Piet? What do you think the big changes were?'

'Seriously?'

'Seriously. You know you can speak freely.'

'*Yissus*, Captain. What can I say? I suppose the big thing for my dad was that under apartheid there was a bit of confusion between security police stuff and CID stuff.'

'Your dad?'

'*Ja*. He was a cop in the sixties, you know. Bloody good. Durban Criminal Investigation Department. His office was there by Smith Street – you know, when it was still called that. Anyway, I remember, *way back when*, hey, when my mom took me once to see him in his office. When I was still a *laaitie*. Must have been eight years old or something. My dad was a Detective Sergeant. Very popular *oke*. With the CID *manne*, that is.'

'Not with the criminals?'

'*Jislaaik* no, Captain. No way. He wasn't popular with those guys 'cos he was so damn good. But, hell, they respected him, you know? My dad had no time for politics, you know, and he didn't care if they were black or white or coloured or whatever. If they were robbing, murdering or breaking the law he would nail them. Never had a problem with a guy because he was, you know, black or something. Hated the government, you know? But, hell, man, he liked his work, hey? And I reckon even the crooks, like, respected him for that, you know? But he saw some things, I tell you, Captain.'

'Yes?'

'*Ja*. He saw some of the *kêrels* taking a few short cuts, you know? He was always the hell in with the security police *okes*. He wanted to just focus on crime, you know, but they kept on bringing the politics in. Some of them were bad, man.'

'But still good detectives, don't you think? Some of those old security police guys became even better sleuths when things changed.'

'*Ja. Struesbob*, hey, boss? Those *okes* were good at what they did. Their undercover stuff was brilliant, man. After his retirement my old man used to say that when they didn't have to deal with State Security stuff but could get on with the crime matters, they became bloody good detectives.'

The two of them could hear Dippenaar and Koekemoer arriving in the next room, so Nyawula called out to them.

'In here, KoeksnDips. Come in.'

'Hi Captain,' said Dippenaar, as they both came in, 'sorry to interrupt but Koeks and I were just passing through so we thought we'd drop off a bit of info we picked up.'

'What's that, men?'

'They've done all the autopsies on the three guys involved in the action at The Grove and Wilson's Wharf, and the reports show that all the bodies had exactly the same evidence of drug use just before they died. The summary says that the usual kinds of ingredients found in *nyaope* were present in all of the guys. The conclusion was that these guys were all higher than kites when they attacked the old couple.'

'They also show that the guys had been pumping the stuff into their systems for a few hours before they ran into Ryder and Trewhella,' added Koekemoer. 'They must have been like animals when they attacked the *ou toppies* in The Grove.'

'Sir, sorry, but I should just add something. When I was with Jeremy at the old lady's flat on Tuesday, when Ed was down at the Addington – er – interviewing the fourth guy – um...'

'Yes, Piet? What?'

'Um – well Ed phoned Jeremy while we were at the old lady's flat, Captain, when we were finding the money under her carpet, you know. It was after he had seen the fourth guy at the hospital. He said in the phone call that the guy confessed to him that the four of them had bought some *whoonga* earlier that night. They had bought it off some boat there by the wharf, Captain.'

'OK, Piet. Thanks. Right there, at the wharf? That's interesting,' said Nyawula.

'I'll check on the autopsy report for the fourth guy, Captain,' added

Koekemoer. 'It'll obviously be mainly about the strangling, but it'll probably also show that the guy was on *nyaope* too.'

'We'll also take another good look around the wharf if you like, Captain,' said Dippenaar.

'Thanks, Dipps. Thanks, Koeks. I appreciate the effort you're putting into this.'

They all paused. Nyawula was struck by the fact that the death of Trewhella had thrown a dark and heavy blanket over the normal energy and buoyancy of the team. These interventions of theirs had been unusually downbeat, given the importance of what they were reporting. Nyawula resolved to loosen them up a bit.

'See what I mean, Sergeant Cronje? This is good sleuthing. Always ahead of the game. Was your dad as good as these two guys?'

Dippenaar and Koekemoer looked perplexed.

'Sorry, men. Piet and I were just talking about the 'good' old days when his dad was a top Detective Sergeant in the CID. Sergeant Cronje is very knowledgeable about the old days. He has a whole theory about it. How did you put it, Piet? Something like *when investigative policing moved from spying on political activities to surveillance of criminal activities...*'

'*Daarsy!*, Captain, that's just what I meant just now when we spoke. I couldn't express it like that, myself, you know. But *ja*, just like you said right there.'

Koekemoer and Dippenaar teased Cronje, throwing in phrases like *Herr Doktor Professor Piet Cronje* and *investigative surveillance, oo la la! Not detective work but investigative surveillance, ou Piet!* To which he responded:

'*Yissus!* but you guys just don't stop, hey?'

'Piet and I were talking about the old security branch detectives. How so many of them were brilliant criminal detectives once they no longer had to do the political stuff.'

'*Ja*, Captain, you're right, there, hey,' said Dippenaar. 'Koeks and me, we knew some of those old security branch guys, and they were damn good, you know. Mandela must have *poeped* himself when those guys were looking for him in the old days.'

'*Dis reg*, Dipps,' Koekemoer contributed. Remember those reunion parties at Wentworth when those guys would talk about what they had been doing in those days? I was much younger then and I thought those guys were scary, *jong*.'

'Captain was just saying, guys, before you came in, how when things changed and the politics was different most of those guys then became as good as the old CID guys like my dad, who only used to do the crime cases and didn't have to bother with the politics.'

'*Ja*, Piet, that's right. Many of them did. But not all, hey?'

'Yes, Koeks. Not all. And, as Piet and I know you're thinking, not the Major, hey?' Nyawula said.

'My lips are sealed, Captain.'

'Mine too, Detective Koekemoer.'

They all chuckled.

'But you must have heard the April Fool's story back in 2010, Captain?'

'No, Dipps. What was that?'

'Well you remember the start of the new police ranking? It began on April Fool's Day in 2010?'

'Oh. Yes. That's right. That's the day it all took effect.'

'*Ja*. Well, the joke among the *okes* was about what a coincidence it was. That was the same day that Swanepoel became a Major.'

'Hmm! Yes, I suppose that would cause some mirth. But, men, I shouldn't be talking to you about these things, you know.'

'What did you think of the whole new ranking system, Captain?'

'Oh, well, Koeks, since you ask, I remember thinking at the time that it was all a bit too much like the army.'

'*Ja*, Captain, I agree,' said Dippenaar. 'The *okes* thought that it was like the Major saw himself as if he was on the battlefield with the rest of his men as the cannon fodder. Only he was on the phone all the time, not the battlefield.'

Nyawula was thinking that someone up there had made a really idiotic decision in thinking that Swanepoel needed to be known henceforth as Major, when it was fairly widely considered among all who worked with him even back then that he was an incompetent and rather obese racist relic.

'But serious, *ouens*, apart from the ranking, I think things got better very fast from 1994.'

'In what ways, Piet? I'm interested in how you see it. You've been a policeman much longer than the three of us.'

'Well, Captain, long story short, hey? I think there were some problems in the days when both the uniform *okes* and the criminal investigation *okes* had their own commanders at station level as well as district level. They had like – how do you say it – like separate controls. That was a good thing in some ways, but there was a problem with it, too, in my opinion.'

'What was that?' Nyawula prodded.

'I think it meant that there was no more discussion or working together. You know, like the *okes* in uniforms and in plain clothes did their own thing and sometimes they were working around the corner from each other in the same neighbourhood and they didn't know it. Uniforms bumping into detectives and saying *what the hell you doing here, boykie?*'

Dippenaar and Koekemoer were energetically in agreement, each throwing in from their own experiences various examples of clashes and contradictions and missed opportunities. The three of them became quite animated. Nyawula enjoyed the passion with which they argued the case, and the friendly cursing and swearing at each other.

'I tell you, *manne,*' Dippenaar said, 'it was much better when they changed the whole system and everyone came under joint command, with commissioners in charge.'

'I agree with a lot of what you say, Dipps. But I'm not sure it was all so rosy. Community forums working with station commissioners sounds good in theory, but there were a couple of problems.'

'What were those, Captain?' Koekemoer asked.

'All that consolidation stuff happened quite quickly. I wasn't in the game then, but I remember reading that when it all changed there were lots of new senior posts going. But very few of the senior detective guys could compete successfully for all of those senior management posts that suddenly appeared. It was those uniform guys that were well positioned. They were used to working in hierarchies. But detectives are like cats, men, if you don't mind me saying so. Hey, Piet? I'm sure you agree. They work alone or in pairs and they're so bloody individualistic.'

As the two detectives made to interject, Nyawula quickly continued.

'Don't get me wrong, I admire you guys. They're very talented sleuths, aren't they, Piet? But, hell, they haven't got a helluva lot of experience in managing personnel. You know yourself, Piet, that the great detectives we have in this unit not only can't be bothered with filling in forms. *They don't know how to even do it.*'

Cronje spoke the exact same last eight words in unplanned unison speaking with Nyawula, and all four of them laughed together about it. Then Cronje continued.

'You're telling me, Captain. Especially these two *ouens*, and Ryder and – God rest him – Trewhella. I'm like their bloody mother. Got to do everything for them.'

'That's why we appreciate you so much, Sergeant. So, anyway, at the time of the change all those talented guys were no match for the career professionals who knew office politics like the backs of their hands. The old uniforms, the station commanders, moved easily into so many of the new commissioner posts, and their underlings then rose through the ranks, too. So that's how we got people like Swanepoel climbing upward, higher and higher, like, well, like stuff rising to the top of the barrel.'

'*Yissus*. You can say that again, Captain,' said Cronje.

'*Ja*, I agree,' said Dippenaar. 'Once it became like the army you couldn't, like, speak to some of the top brass without them making you feel like you had no right to bother them, you know?'

'Yes, Dipps, I know what you mean. It's the way one interacts with the guys just above you and just below you that determines how happy you are in your work.'

Nyawula couldn't vocalise the rest of his intended sentence: *and therefore how easily one can be tantalised with bribes, and therefore how easily one can be corrupted.* Instead, he paused, and felt for a moment that he had been preaching at them.

'Sorry, men. I didn't mean to go on at you like that. But it helps me think through things to chat to you.'

They all protested together, Cronje's voice rising out of the joint babble more prominently than the others.

'*Jeez*. No, Captain. Not at all, I'm telling you' said Cronje. 'I told my wife the other night that I feel quite privileged, you know, after more than twenty years in the police, to have a boss who actually talks to us like this. So it's my pleasure, really.'

The other two heartily agreed.

'That's good to know. Thanks, men, and thanks for the chat. And for the info on the autopsies.'

They all took the signal and started to leave.

'Oh, one thing more, Captain.'

'What's that, Piet?'

'I'll need to bring you all the forms to sign off for the function tomorrow night. And there are some things to go through and decide so that I can clear it with my opposite numbers in the cluster. I'll be back with it all at about 4.30, if that's OK.'

'That's fine. We have to do it sometime.'

The three of them went out, closing the door behind them. Nyawula stared out of the window.

He was pleased with the people who worked for him. But he also realised that he was beginning to tire of the administrative burden that kept him away from the real task of leading a sharp team of investigators and sustaining their morale and energy and commitment.

He had been promoted to his own current position at an important time, coinciding with the football World Cup when the crime agenda was crucial to the country's image abroad. He remembered an international press report at the time, typically adapting and rendering sensational the much more accurate and detailed police report that it was based upon. About how just less than three thousand police weapons had been lost or stolen in a period of nine months, and about how four thousand replacement 9mm handguns from Beretta had been ordered, and how the recovery rate for stolen weapons was devastatingly low compared to the recovery of lost civilian weapons. He recalled insinuations in the media that the South African police were considered to be a major supplier of weapons to the criminal underworld. He remembered his dismay at the statement about how the murder rate in the country was one of the highest in the world for a country not at war. He also remembered how he promised himself that he would regard his promotion as giving him a mandate to turn these figures around.

All of which fuelled his incandescent reaction to the loss of four weapons from his own unit at the time Thabethe disappeared. Now he wanted to put that right.

But what was he doing instead? Wasting time putting together his part in tomorrow's police function in the stadium. Annual celebration. To celebrate what? To let some officers parade in uniform and others parade in their finest civilian clothes, with girlfriends kept in the background and wives putting on a show. People buying new suits and dresses for the special occasion. Hours wasted. Boring speeches. Awards to businessmen with dubious connections. Everything and anything to take him off the real work. He'd try and shift some of the load onto Cronje.

Worst of all, he thought, was the news that Major Swanepoel had indicated his acceptance of a formal invitation to the event.

## 12.50.

Tony made the same crucial mistake that others had made. He assumed that although Pillay was probably stronger than most women – she was, after all, a trained cop – she was still, in any case, a woman, and small. With one arm disabled by the bullet. No match for him.

Ryder was powerless. He could only watch as Tony advanced on her, the dagger expertly clasped in his right hand. He had clearly used it many times before. Pillay, her left arm hanging useless at her side and her right arm only marginally better, stepped slowly to her right and Tony matched her, moving to his right, circling, ready for the thrust that he would deliver and which would down her before he then cut her to pieces. Then her partner, after he had extracted the information he needed, knuckle by knuckle. Then he'd get rid of both of them. These two cops had to be eliminated, and he would burn the place down around their ears if necessary to ensure that.

He lurched forward to test her reactions. She was watching every sinew in his upper torso to spot the signals. She could sense immediately that his lurch was simply a feint. She reacted less quickly than he had anticipated, deliberately slower than she would have done had she suspected the incoming thrust to be real.

He registered the slowness of her response and immediately thought he had her measure. He shifted his centre of gravity, positioning himself for another apparent swing from the right, but then immediately adjusted for an upward stab from below. Pillay saw it in preparation a fraction of a second after he had made the decision. She stepped quickly to her right then immediately forward: one step onto her left foot to anchor her weight and then the right foot swinging as hard as any centre-forward might strike a ball, the shattering impact from her heavy boot onto his testicles producing a contorted gasp of pain from him as he dropped the weapon and fell to his knees, then rolled over onto his back with his knees drawn up to his chest.

In his agony, and having lost the dagger, Tony still had the instinct to reach for the gun, now within stretching distance of his right hand. But Pillay was immediately back onto him. As he lurched and grabbed the gun and started swinging it up from the dirt to fire point-blank at her, her right boot, leading her full weight as she jumped on him, came down onto his Adam's apple, thrusting down with brutal force, pushing muscle, sinew and cartilage through the throat and onto the bones at the back of his neck.

The thyroid cartilage shields most of the internal mechanism of the larynx. Tony's was able to protect neither his cricoid cartilage, lying just beneath it, nor the cricothyroid joint. Pillay's weight turned the circular tube with its untidy pack of cords and joints and muscles and sinews into a tangled mess, instantly destroying any elasticity that might have returned it into position, and separating the cartilage from the trachea.

Tony's scream was cut off a split-second into this massive damage, the vocal chords now useless, and his huge chest heaved as it struggled to suck air through the now useless compressed windpipe. Pillay stepped back, joining Ryder in stunned immobility as they watched him panic and then slowly asphyxiate, his legs pumping like the dog she had seen as a child, having a fit that took it to extreme panic and then slowly recovering to relative calm.

No slow recovery for Tony, and no calm. Foam started bubbling at his lips and his eyes nearly burst from their sockets with the strain to find air, his back arching upward from the floor with the effort. After what seemed an interminable struggle the panic faded away and they watched his final twitches.

In the silence Ryder and Pillay looked at each other. She pulled the plug of rag from his mouth, grimacing with the effort to get her right hand working again. He spat out a couple of threads and the taste of paraffin, before speaking.

'I've changed my mind about Ed Trewhella,' he said.

'What?'

'Compared to you, I think Ed was actually quite a gentle soul.'

'You think?'

'Maybe Nyawula thought it was time I needed to be toughened up a bit. With a tougher partner.'

She was still breathing heavily, and her good arm was trembling as the feeling started returning to her hand and the heat in the elbow dissipated. She shook her right arm to encourage the process of recovery.

'Get me out of this,' he said. 'We need to get that arm of yours sorted.'

'What about you?' she said. 'You need that skull of yours looked at, too. Let's get the medics in.'

'OK. And the cleaners for this guy.'

She freed him with her good hand, using Tony's dagger to saw through the nylon rope. Then they supported each other as they stumbled into the passage that led toward the front door.

## 13.30.

Thabethe had begun to drift off in the sweltering heat. Nothing had happened since the two cars had arrived shortly after the departure of the panel-van. Big white guy and small *charra* chick. More friends of the casino guy? No. Difficult to see at the distance, but he thought that the big guy was familiar. He had seen him somewhere, some time back. But he couldn't quite place the guy. From his observation point it wasn't clear to him but it looked as if they knocked at the door and waited, but no-one came. What's the guy inside doing? They knocked again. Paused. Then they just went in.

Thabethe waited. And waited. Nothing.

The sun was baking down on the Mini. Thabethe started drifting, when suddenly he heard a cacophony of sirens and hoots and squealing tyres. He went ice-cold as police cars lurched around the corner from both directions. How had they traced him? His instinct was to rip open the door and run, get into the side-roads, leap over walls, escape from cops on wheels. His hand was on the door-handle as the first car swooped past him and screeched to a halt at the entrance to the forecourt, backed up a fraction, and lurched forward again into the parking area. Two cars from the opposite direction followed the first one in. As uniforms bundled out of the cars two figures appeared at the door where he had last seen the casino man. People were shouting. Orders were being given. Two cops ran inside. Another one got onto his cell-phone, and was soon shouting into it.

Thabethe waited.

Onlookers started arriving. Crowds formed behind police tape. Double cordon. Where was the casino guy? Thabethe decided to get out of the car and join the crowd. Other cars arrived. He had seen this before. Forensics guys. He began to piece it together. No help from the crowd. They all had their own little rumours. None of them lined up with what he had seen over the last three hours. He decided to melt away. Come back after dark. Let the action settle.

As he walked back to the Mini, he remembered. The Mercedes. No-one seemed to be interested in the Mercedes in the road, up the hill. The crowd was far more interested in the action in the forecourt. It took him seconds to break in. It took him two minutes to do a thorough search. He found a cell-phone in the cubby-hole. Nothing else, other than papers for the car, service records, manual and standard warranty forms. He pocketed the phone, then stepped out of the car, squatted down, and started peeling back the carpet from under the driver's seat. He made a thin aspirated whistle of surprise as he revealed the prize beneath.

Six neat stacks of crisp brand-new two-hundred-rand notes, each pack neatly wrapped, as if just paid over by the bank, in its paper band. He dropped the carpet back into place and quickly clambered over to see if the passenger seat also yielded such delights. No luck. He knelt on the driver's seat and reached over to the back seat to check the carpets on both sides. Same thing. Nothing else. This was probably all of it.

He pulled back the driver's carpet again and stuffed the treasure into his pockets, into his underpants, and down his shirt, which he tucked more securely into his belt to hold the burden. Then he looked around, checking three hundred and sixty degrees before he slipped out of the car, and walked back to the Mini. He got in, with another casual look covering all directions, started the Mini, and pulled off slowly and unobtrusively.

He looked at the action down in the forecourt as he made a three-point turn, faced the car in the opposite direction from the police barricade, and drove away slowly back up the hill. Then, as he turned the corner and moved out of sight of the action his heart started pounding and his breathing escalated in growing excitement.

He went in search of somewhere to store his rich haul, and to find something to eat.

**16.30.**

Nyawula stood with Cronje leaning over the desk. They were looking at lists of names.

'I'll check with the other stations, and then when I get final agreement I'll get the seating plan down to the Stadium tomorrow morning. Then they'll ask you and me to do final checks and changes again tomorrow afternoon.'

'Thanks, Piet. I'm sure you don't need all this on top of the arrangements for the funeral. I appreciate it.'

'No problem. Ed's ex-wife – well, both his ex-wives – have agreed Monday for the funeral, so we've got some time there. I can wrap up those arrangements on Friday. Tomorrow is more difficult, with all the big guys coming.'

'Big in more ways than one.'

'*Ja!* You got that, Captain.'

'Speaking of him. I see he's coming alone. No partner.'

'Looks like it. Maybe we can put him together with Sergeant Pillay. They're the same size.'

Nyawula looked at him. Koekemoer and Dippenaar arrived as Cronje elaborated while gathering up the papers.

'Height, I mean. Not weight, of course. Pillay...'

'Let it go, Sergeant.'

'Sorry, sir.'

Cronje left, winking at the two new arrivals.

'Afternoon, men. Thanks for coming back. I just need you to do one more thing before you wrap up today.'

'Sure, Captain,' they chorused.

'I'd like you both to get to the warehouse at Overport. Forensics have finished and I'd like you both to go over the place to see what you can find. One thing that bugged them is that the corpse had car-keys but no ID and no wallet and no cell-phone, and no car in the parking lot or around the back of the building responded to them using the remote on the key ring. Not really their job, of course, but they had a quick look around for the car. I want you to get over there and see what you can find. Check with buildings in the area, find anyone who might have known what the dead guy got up to in there, and that kind of stuff.'

'OK, Captain,' said Koekemoer. 'Dipps and I have already had a word with Navi and with Jeremy down at the hospital. We went there as soon as we heard about the action. Piet told us they had been taken there to get patched up. They gave us a quick run-down. We told them we would be checking in with you before we went down to the place to have a look. We were going to get out there anyway, to see what we can find.'

'Thanks, men. One step ahead of me as usual. I appreciate that. Pillay and Ryder OK?'

'They're doing great,' said Dippenaar, 'Navi's raring to go but the doctor won't let her. She lost a bit of blood. Jeremy's fine. Got a plaster on his head and a bit of a bump, but he's OK. He boasts a lot about the thickness of his skull. Claims to be the head-butting champion in Durbs.'

'Thanks, guys. Let me know what you find in Overport. I'll be here late if you want to pop in before you wrap tonight. Otherwise just call me. I'll be here until I hear from ballistics: their top guys have promised me Speedy Gonzales work on testing the Desert Eagle they picked up from the scene today. We think it might match the weapon that put Trewhella down. They need a few hours on the case, so they're doing me a big favour with their top woman working into the night. If things pan out, then it looks as if Pillay might have put down Trewhella's killer today. Small compensation for Ryder, but it would be something, at least.'

Koekemoer and Dippenaar nodded their agreement, and exchanged a look. Koekemoer spoke for them both.

'If that's the case, Captain, then it'll make Ed's funeral just a little bit easier. We hear it's on Monday?'

'That's right. Not sure of the exact time yet, but Monday afternoon. Thanks, both.'

The two detectives nodded and left the room.

## 17.15.

Thirty-six thousand rands. Each pack had contained thirty notes. Six thousand rands. Six packs. Thabethe had stowed the money, apart from two packs, which he pocketed. Twenty-four thousand rands in a tin, buried in a spot unknown to any but himself. Impossible to find. His little emergency fund. For the future.

He sat in the corner of the restaurant, finishing his meal. He hadn't eaten real steak for more than a year, and he had never previously paid nearly two hundred rands for a steak. Ever. He had peeled off two bills to pay for the meal and the drink, and had pocketed the change. All of it. No tips for the bitch that had served him. She had given him that look that said *you're not my class, so don't try it on with me.* He sat, thinking through what had happened since he had met the young Afrikaner yesterday morning.

The Afrikaner had been right about these guys. *I'm working with these guys. I meet them each time at Suncoast Casino. They pulling big money... hunnerts of thousands...* Big money. Not just thirty-six thousand. There was more out there. Much more. Thabethe needed to find out how to get to it. *You remember Dirk? You met him once, right here. The fat guy. My friend...*

He worked through the possibilities, sipping the remainder of the wine. Then, as if only now remembered, he reached into his pocket for the cell-phone from the Mercedes. He switched it on. No password. Straight to the menu. He opened the contact list. No names. Message list. No messages. Then he clicked recent calls received, so that he could scroll through. No calls. Probably all deleted. Same with calls made.

He decided to call voicemail. One message. He listened. Then listened again. Then again.

'Tony. Vic. I found Dirk. He's in Addington. Call me. Now.'

Thabethe pondered for a moment. Then he tried speed dialling. He pressed each number in turn and got nothing until he pressed number seven and held it. The screen lit up as the call started connecting, showing three letters.

'VIC.'

And a cell-phone number.

He hung up before the call was picked up. There'd be time for that, later. He sat, deep in thought.

## 17.20.

Koekemoer and Dippenaar found the Mercedes immediately. They approached the Overport address the same way Tony had, and having the particular vehicle in mind was a great help. As they crested the hill there it was, alone, the only stationary vehicle at the kerbside. All other kerbside vehicles had moved for a good reason: the signs indicated no parking at this time. It stood isolated and begging for a traffic cop's ticket, but there were no traffic cops in sight. Just traffic. The passing drivers cursed the vehicle as they went by because with two lanes tightly squeezed together for peak hours there was the unavoidable funnel as they saw the Mercedes and had to swing out.

Koekemoer and Dippenaar attracted their fair share of hoots and bellows and curses, too, as they stopped behind the Mercedes and added to the congestion. There was no doubt in their minds that this was the vehicle that forensics had wanted to match to the keys they had taken off the corpse. They could also see, at a glance, that the passenger door had not been returned to a fully closed position. They quickly put out the red triangles and went to work on the car. Within minutes they had stripped back luxury carpets and stylish panels and high-quality rubbers and door sill panels with stainless steel inlays and... and that's where they found something.

Tight little rolls of two-hundred-rand notes. Hundreds of them: a quick and casual estimate, at a glance, of over one hundred thousand rands in cash. New notes, crisp, rolled in tight packs.

'*Daarsy! Bliksem,*' said Dippenaar, as he reached forward to pull out some of the rolls. Before he could say anything else, his phone rang. It was Nyawula.

'Yes, Captain. We've found it. In the road a little way up from the warehouse. And guess what? Lots of cash hidden away in the sill panels. Yes. Yes. No. Definitely. Good idea. *Ja!* We understand. OK, we'll do that. OK.'

He hung up and turned to Koekemoer.

'Nyawula says take photos of the hidey-hole and the money, showing exactly how much money, so there's no come-back on us later.'

'OK,' replied Koekemoer. 'Let's do that.' They got down to work.

'Not like the old days, hey, Koeks? Nyawula is cleaner than anything that was above us in the old days. No messing with him, that's for sure.'

As Dippenaar spoke he was preparing his iPhone and then snapped as many photos as he needed to cover the whole area stuffed with cash. Then they pulled out the cash, laid it alongside the empty panels, and took more photos. While snapping, they continued talking.

'Remember the old guys we reported to?' continued Dippenaar. 'Nyawula couldn't have been dirtier than any of them if he tried.'

'That's the thing with reporting upward, Dipps. What do you see above you when you report upward?'

'Arseholes.'

'You got it. This guy's different. He puts us all above him, where he can see us, and where he can check what we're doing. He's the one watching the arseholes, and making suggestions, asking questions. To make sure they don't screw up. Good guy. Hope he goes far.'

'His problem is that he still has to report to one of the old arseholes.'

'Old *Swannie? Ja!* And a fat one, at that.'

'*Ja.* Very fat.'

They finished the photos, then set about counting then stuffing the money into a bag that Koekemoer fetched from their own vehicle.

They called in for a tow-truck, and waited for it before moving down to the warehouse. They sat in their own vehicle, Dippenaar behind the wheel and Koekemoer with the bag of cash on his lap.

They traversed a bit of history while they waited. It was one of those conversations that, by the nature of their relationship, involved no disagreements or contrary views or contradictions or modifications. They found social intercourse easiest when it was peppered with *Ja! Exactly!* and *you got it just right, oke!* and *Ja, for sure!* and *Ja'k stem saam!* and *Strue, my china!*

They concurred. Trewhella and Ryder. A great team. Bloody good, in spite of the fact that they were *Engels* and couldn't speak Afrikaans to save their mothers. Trewhella genuine English because he had been born there and had only spent a few years here. Ryder just half-and-half, because he had been born in *Seffrika* and was here to stay, but he had spent a lot of time in England and spoke like them. A genuine *soutpiel*. In spite of all that, they were still both good guys. And *blerrie* good detectives. Got on well with the *manne*. Didn't get involved with the politics. Even when they came into contact with some of the old guys from Wentworth and Brighton Beach that time, and the Kings Rest crowd – those guys were tough Afrikaners and also good detectives but they were *gatvol* at the changes that had side-lined them and some of them had supplemented their pension pots with some shady deals with gangsters and *tsotsis*. When Trewhella and Ryder met those guys they made it clear that they themselves were not on the take. You could trust them. They were good at their jobs, but the old Wentworth guys preferred to steer clear of them. Didn't invite them to any of the old regular reunion *braais*.

Sad that Trewhella's gone. *He was a really funny oke.* Tough on Ryder. He lost Frikkie van der Westhuizen that time. And he also lost that Detective Ntshaveni *oke*. Now Trewhella. But he's damn good. Wonder who they'll put him with? Maybe get in a new guy from Durban North or somewhere. Another English guy, maybe. Or maybe someone like Frikkie. He'll have to be good, to team up with Ryder.

'I hear Ryder's doing the main speech on Monday,' said Dippenaar.

'At the funeral?'

'*Ja.*'

'Rather him than me.'

'Poor bastard.'

They went on for another half hour, chatting animatedly and reminiscing about the good guys and the bad guys, the good old days and the bad old days, pensions and politics. How the old station commanders had run their operations. The relations between uniforms and detectives. What Nyawula had said that morning. Then on to the corruption scandal with the head of the provincial Organised Crime Unit supposedly accepting bribes from those illegal casino operators. The years of lawsuits and countersuits over that. Clever lawyers and corrupt lawyers. Then the overturning of the charges. The allegations about corruption and gambling and kick-backs. The big stuff with the supposed hit-squad. The public starting to scorn the police.

Then the changes that had come in. The clean-up operations. The scramble for jobs and promotions. The old fat farts like *Swannie* getting promoted so that they could move him out and away. The arrival of new guys from other provinces. The arrival of Nyawula. The change in attitude. The growing efficiency. The arrival of Ryder and later on Trewhella, both from Johannesburg after serving time in England.

Eventually the tow-truck arrived. They helped them hook up the Mercedes, then watched the truck turn across the road and disappear back up the hill, almost colliding with a little red Mini coming in the opposite direction. Then they retrieved their triangles and drove down to the forecourt of the warehouse.

Koekemoer and Dippenaar spent half an hour going through the warehouse. Forensics had done what they could. They moved through the place carefully. Found nothing. Looked with particular interest at the marks and tapes in the downstairs room where the action had been. Then left the building, got into their car, and went back to the station with the money, before heading home to their families for dinner.

## 19.10.

Thabethe sat in the Mini, about three hundred metres beyond the forecourt, as the night crept in around him. Traffic had almost completely disappeared. A dog scavenged in the gutter in front of him. Newspaper, plastic bags, and dust drifted past as a gust of wind came in.

He thought back through the last hour and more. He had crested the hill coming down to the warehouse and had nearly smashed into the tow-truck doing a U-turn and towing the Mercedes. He had slammed on brakes with his heart in his mouth, instantly recognising the towed vehicle as the one he had broken into earlier. The driver of the tow-truck had glared at him as he drove past, as did the two guys standing at the edge of the road watching the truck leave.

He had driven on, watching the two guys in the rear-view mirror, but they lost interest in him the moment he passed, and had got into their car. He slowed down as he passed the forecourt, looking both in at the warehouse and back in the rear-view mirror. He watched as the two men followed in his direction down the hill, and then he saw them turn into the forecourt. He continued a little up the hill, and then pulled over. He got out of the Mini and walked over to the other side of the road, from where he had a view of the door to the warehouse. He watched the two men go up to the door, lift the police tape, fiddle at the door for a few seconds, and then enter the building. He stood, watching.

Half an hour later he watched the men leave. He then left his car where it was and walked back down the hill. As he came up to the entrance he saw that the police had put a heavy bolt and padlock on the door, probably in the afternoon after all the action, and had removed the Yale lock. He lifted the tape, picked the lock very easily, and entered the building. Ten or fifteen minutes later he returned. Nothing. Whatever had been in the building had been removed. Either by the police team that had arrived at midday, or sometime in the afternoon, or by the two guys he had just been watching. The place offered no clues. Except for the chalk-marks and tape on the floor of the second room downstairs. From his former experience as a constable, he knew that there had been some action in that room, leading to a death.

Thabethe turned on the ignition. Revved. He was about to pull away when something struck him. He paused. Sat for a moment, hands on the steering wheel, thinking. Then he switched off the ignition, pulled out the cell-phone, and thought for a moment. Then he pressed the seven for speed dial. Three rings, then:

'Where the hell have you been, Tony? We can move into the Argyle Road house. Entrance in Tenth Avenue. But I need you to set it up. First thing tomorrow. And bring back the box from Overport.'

Silence from Thabethe.

'Tony, What the...'

Silence. Then the line went dead.

Thabethe looked at the screen for a moment, then clicked off. He sat, contemplating. Then he switched on the ignition, turned on the lights, and pulled slowly away from the kerb, going up the hill.

*The Argyle Road house. Entrance in Tenth Avenue. I need you to set it up.* Thabethe tried to connect the clues. *Tony,* the voice had said. The dead guy, maybe. Argyle Road. These white bastards. They refuse to use the new names. They probably don't even know what Sandile Thusi did.

Thabethe suddenly swung the wheel, tyres screeching as he did a U-turn. He would go there now. Have a look at it. Sandile Thusi. Entrance on Tenth Avenue. Not far. Maybe he could learn something by just checking where the place is. Maybe this Vic is the big guy. The casino money guy, maybe. If he talks to Tony like that, then Tony is – or was – a smaller guy. A smaller guy with thirty-six thousand rands. Maybe this Vic guy is worth more than thirty-six thousand rands.

## 19.15.

Vic pulled the iPhone away from his ear, rapidly. He clicked the off button. His pulse thudded through his temples. He stopped breathing. Stared at the phone in his hand. He was ice cold with fury. Then he flung the phone against the wall. It shattered into countless pieces, but that provided no reason to stop him from smashing the heel of his shoe down onto the wreckage, again and again, screaming in fury as he did so.

He paused, breathing heavily now, sweat gathering in the lines of his forehead. He stumbled out of the room, slamming the door behind him, and found his way down the passage then down in the elevator. Then down and out across the hall then through the mass of gamblers, young and old, crowding around slot machines and tables. He walked in a daze, his huge bulk bumping into strangers, ignoring a member of staff who offered him a drink, pushing through the crowds, finally making his way out of the casino into the centre itself, and then down the passage until he reached fresh air.

He gulped the fresh air as if he had emerged from water. He filled up his lungs and stumbled out into the car-park. His mind was racing. Who? How? Where was Tony? What next? He had to get on top of this disaster, and he had to do it quick.

## 19.45.

Thabethe had driven round the block a few times, parked the Mini and walked in both directions, checking the house from every possible angle. He had also chosen his moment to clamber over the wall. He firstly threw a heavy rubberised mat from the back of the car over the barbed wire attached to the top of the wall. Then he clambered up and sat for a moment before dropping into the garden on the other side. He paused in the garden and then, peering through the windows, he was persuaded that it wouldn't be the right time to break in. It looked as if the house was empty, with minimal furniture, and waiting for someone to move in. No point in breaking locks or windows before they moved in. Wait for them to stash whatever goods they were dealing with and come back another night. Even though one of the window-catches appeared to be loose and almost inviting to any burglar. He peered through that window, the moonlight helping, and saw that the room was completely empty.

He took the opportunity to study every possible angle on the place. Back door into the kitchen and out to the back area and to the garage. Windows, garden terrain, types of burglar bars, window catches, door-lock mechanisms. Even the tree in the garden. The strength of the branches in case he ever needed to be up there. The depth of foliage for hiding in the branches. The massive hydrangea bush against the wall, large enough to conceal a couple of guys if necessary. The branch of the tree allowing access to the roof. Could be useful.

But as he was preparing to leave he had another look at the loose window catch. He slid the blade of his knife upward, jiggled a little, and saw the latch flip over. Opened and ready. For another night. When there were goods inside worth looking at.

He left as quietly as he had arrived, and walked back up the road to the Mini. As he got in, he thought it was time to change cars. Time to see Spikes again. Nomivi's would just about be starting to get hot. A good time to find Spikes.

*

One month full hire. Or, if he liked the car after one month, he could treat it as being a one-third deposit on the full price. Spikes Mkhize clutched ten thousand rands in crisp new two-hundred-rand notes, as he stood next to the red Mini, watching Thabethe roar off in the middle of the night in the silver Ballade. Thabethe was rising in the world, he thought.

Spikes had agreed, as part of the deal, and in preparation for a possible outright purchase after one month, to sort out the papers and licence and everything else, but in another name that Thabethe could use, rather than his own, along with the necessary new ID. Crisp new money could lubricate a lot of middlemen and forgers. He would have it all done within a couple of days. Skhura could collect the papers from Nomivi's on Saturday, latest. When Thabethe had peeled off the crisp banknotes from what looked like a wad of twice the amount he actually handed over, Mkhize couldn't resist putting himself out for further sales.

'*Eish!* Skhura. *Wena!* You *hit a big luck?* Spikes can help you move that money, *sharp-sharp*. You want police uniforms? I got. Bullets? I got. No guns – *hayibo!* – too much trouble for Spikes. But bullets I got. Plenty. You know Spikes. I can get for you.'

Thabethe had grunted something that meant *no, thanks*.

Spikes waited until the Ballade had disappeared into the night. He thought it was time to wrap up business for the night and get back to some serious drinking. *Tjaila*. Time to go. He got into the Mini and moved it around to the back of the building.

Thabethe felt the roar of the engine and felt vibrations in his hands as he spun the wheel. Things were going his way at last. Money made him powerful. The thought of more money, much more, made him feel invincible.

### 21.45.

Ryder reached the phone before Fiona did. They each had less than half a glass of Ondine Sauvignon Blanc, 2013, in their hands.

'Jeremy?'

'Captain?'

'Sorry it's so late. How's the head?'

Fiona nestled in to him and he tilted the receiver so that she could share the earpiece.

'It's fine, thanks. Fiona did her work on it. Re-did the dressing and put on a new plaster. Told me the nurses didn't know what they were doing, of course.'

She punched him on the arm, took a swig of wine, and went back to eavesdropping.

'I think I'd trust Fiona rather than Addington nurses, myself. Look, I thought you would like to hear this. Sorry, no, that's the wrong way of saying it. It's not at all something you would *like* to hear. But I hope you can take something positive from it.'

'What is it, Captain?'

'I had ballistics pull out all stops on both the bullet they took out of Ed and the Desert Eagle you and Pillay had to deal with today.'

He paused.

'They match?'

'As perfect a match as ballistics say they've seen. We're almost positive that the guy that Pillay took down today was the guy who put down Ed Trewhella.'

'Almost?'

'I've asked forensics to now cross-check with the Montpelier Road evidence to match up any possible traces of this guy at Overport, to place him at the scene of Ed's murder. I have no doubt we'll get the cross-check evidence we need, now that we know who we're looking for.'

Fiona pulled back to look at Jeremy. His eyes were dry. The anger was still burning away in him.

'Thanks, Captain. It *is* good to hear.'

'Take it easy, Jeremy.'

Nyawula paused.

'You, too, Fiona.'

She gasped, and pulled back from the receiver making all sorts of unintelligible motions with her hands, which Jeremy read perfectly as saying *Tell him he's mistaken! I'm taking a shower!*

'Thanks, Captain. Fiona is saying thanks, too.'

'See you tomorrow.'

'Bye.'

Fiona was aghast.

'You bastard. Why didn't you tell him I was…'

He kissed her passionately, spilling wine from both their glasses. When they came up for air, she said:

'He's a clever bugger, that captain of yours. Now I'm all embarrassed. How can I look him in the face at the function tomorrow night?'

'He sure is a clever bugger. No pulling the wool over his eyes.'

'You OK?'

'I'm fine. Ed would be pleased.'

'He would. More wine, or bed?'

'Bed.'

She pecked him on the lips, took his empty glass, and working together in a pattern they knew so well, they started switching off the lights.

# 4 THURSDAY

Ryder let the water burn into the wound on his scalp. He didn't feel like singing, for once. He stood, watching the water spool into the plug-hole. As it cascaded onto him he thought through the events of the last couple of days. Losing a partner was the very worst thing that had happened to him in his career. Three times, now. He wasn't sure he could cope with another experience like those three. Yet he had come close to the fourth, yesterday. Pillay had been his partner for no more than an hour – unofficially – before he had nearly lost her too.

No-one could replace Ed. But he had to admit that Navi was good. Damn good. It would be a special pleasure telling her what the Captain had told him, last thing last night, about the ballistics report. Much as he would have preferred to be the one to take out Ed's murderer, there was some kind of poetic justice in the fact that it was his new partner who had done it, and in a Trewhella manner, too. Crushed the bastard's windpipe and watched him die slowly. Ed would have approved.

The news of the ballistics report provided some comfort. He had been obsessed with chasing down Frikkie's assailant, all those years ago. He had lived that case night and day until he had run down the murderer. Same as when he had lost his good friend Ntshaveni to those other thugs. In this case it appeared already wrapped up, thanks to Pillay. Ed's side of things, anyway. There was still the stuff linked to the Overport address that would have to be investigated. But at least it wouldn't be complicated by having to find Ed's killer. If the forensics report backed up the ballistics information.

He felt comfortable working with Navi. Had always liked her. Spunky. Humorous. As foul-mouthed as Ed. And tough. Bet her arm was hurting right now. She'll have to take it easy for a couple of days. Partners. Both bruised, but both ready to go on.

There was something else in the back of his mind. But he couldn't put his finger on what it was that was eluding him. Maybe a cup of Fiona's coffee would get his brain-cells going.

He turned off the water and the day started.


## 08.00.

Vic eased the car from the left hand lane of the angry traffic in Margaret Mncadi Avenue and turned across the railway tracks into the entrance to Wilson's Wharf. He pulled into the parking in front of the Royal Natal Yacht Club. He was greeted by a red-headed, sun-tanned, burly man in his mid-thirties.

He was way more than a foot taller than Vic, and his biceps were as large as Vic's own. Except that this guy's biceps were hard muscle, not fat, Vic thought. He wore a plain white t-shirt primarily because he liked the ostentatious display of his body-builder's impressive six-pack and the muscular arms that sported two intertwined snakes on each of the right forearm and the left upper arm. His faded powder blue jeans stretched across thigh muscles suggested that his body-building was by no means restricted to the upper body.

They shook hands. His was a knuckle-cruncher.

'Good to see you again, Vic.'

'Thanks, Red. Thought I'd see whether we're still on schedule, and have another look around.'

'My pleasure. You're paying big bucks. You can hassle me any time.'

Red spoke knowledgeably as they walked along the pier, pausing a few times at some of the moored yachts as he pointed to the vessels and explained something of their features. In one case he paused and described the vessel at some length, and with great affection, almost as if he was a child describing the features of a personal favourite toy. Vic could see he was an experienced sailor. They moved on down the quay.

'I appreciate you doing this, Red. It's a longer voyage than I've done before, so you can understand that I'm a bit concerned.'

'No problem at all, *amigo*. It's a big trip, and it's perfectly natural for you to be apprehensive about it. As I said when we first met, feel free to come in as many times as you like. We could even take you through the old Maritime Museum stuff, if you want. Or we can sit you down for another detailed talk about boats and yachts, regulations and the law, coastal versus deep-sea sailing, and all that stuff.'

'Nah. I've had my fill of all of that. I'm ready. In fact, I can't wait.'

'As I thought. You don't really need to know any of that shit, anyway. The important thing, Vic, is that any client hiring any of the boats you see moored along here can have a crew of experienced yachtsmen who will do everything required. The crew I've got for you comprises some of the best people I know. They all love sailing. You're paying top bucks, *amigo*, so I've ensured the best for you. You just have to sit back and enjoy.'

'Any of them asking any questions?'

'None at all. Rest assured none of them knows anything about our deal. As far as they're concerned you're just a client who wants a break from business and wants to get away for a long holiday. None of these guys knows my business, let alone yours. Here we go, Vic. After you.'

Vic's voice sounded laryngeal as he replied while panting his way up the new aluminium Marine Wharf Gangway Ladder, arriving breathless at the top.

'I appreciate it, Red, believe me. I've invested a lot of time and money in this and I'm now needing the big change I've been planning on for a *helluva* long time.'

'OK, Vic. Sure thing. *No problemo*. Right. We'll take you around now to show you the extra fittings we did yesterday. There's still some stuff being fitted in the main berth, so we can't really go in there at the moment. But you can come along on Saturday morning if you like and have a final check on that and on the food and booze supplies. We're stocking up later today. Feel free to pop in anytime Saturday morning. We want to make sure we have everything you need.'

\*

After inspecting the vessel Vic puffed his way down the ladder and walked back over to where the cars were parked. Red stood on the deck, watching him go. He wondered exactly how much the fat man was worth. Maybe he should have driven an even harder bargain. Maybe some future deals will be in the offing. He contemplated the possibilities as Vic walked away from him and back toward his car.

Vic would normally have wanted to go straight into the Clubhouse for breakfast, but he had to pick up his new cell-phone. He was entirely satisfied with the boat, and starting to feel upbeat about that side of things. Red had proved to be solid and reliable. Maybe even more reliable than Tony. Maybe he would be up for a discussion about his future, once they were safely out at sea.

But he was deeply disturbed by the realisation that someone else had used Tony's phone last night. He had to get his new instrument. He'd feel safer with a new number. He had to make a lot of calls. Most of them were urgent final confirmations of deliveries and dispatches, none of which he could afford to postpone.

Where the hell was Tony? *And how do we get to Dirk?*

## 08.35.

Thabethe sat in the Ballade in Prince Street outside the Addington Hospital, waiting for Spikes Mkhize. He played Vic's message to Tony yet again: *Tony. Vic. I found Dirk. He's in Addington. Call me. Now.*

It was about the tenth time he had played it this morning. The first time had been at about 5.00 am, when his sleepless night had finally led to the realisation of the piece of the puzzle that had been eluding him. The fat guy. The friend of the Afrikaner boy. In the photo. The link to Overport, the other guy called Tony, and the big money. The idea had prompted him to get up, walk around in the pre-dawn cold, and force himself awake. By 6.30 am he was down at the Addington. He knew the hospital procedures well. It had taken him a couple of minutes to steal the clothes, find a trolley and look like a worker. After all, he had done exactly this for months way back when, and he knew the ropes. Few paid any attention to him in the bustle of morning preparations and breakfasts and bedpans and complaints and beepers and buzzers, and enquiries. It didn't take him long to track down the patient.

The problem was the police constable sitting in a chair outside Dirk's room. Thabethe had retreated, cursing. But within seconds he had worked out the way to solve this little problem. It would take a bit of time, but perhaps it would be better, anyway, to make his move only in an hour or two. In the down time, after the morning rush in the passageways of the hospital. To try now would be to run into people bringing breakfast and fetching dishes and delivering medications and checking patients. Better in an hour or two. He retreated to plot the next move.

Uniformed constable. He remembered Spikes' words of the previous night: *You want police uniforms? I got.*

It had been a problem getting Spikes first to answer his phone and then to speak coherently at 7.00 in the morning, but once the fog of the previous night's booze had cleared and he remembered the huge wad of cash that Skhura had been flashing around, he sobered up very quickly. *One constable uniform to fit Skhura Thabethe. And rope? Eish! Now? What's time? Now? Is 7.00 o'clock. Eish! I got a hectic babelas, Skhura, 7.00 is not so easy. I can come 12.00 o'clock.*

Thabethe told him that the price would go up from five hundred rands to one thousand rands if he could get there in an hour.

'*Eish*, old Skhura. For you, I can make the plan. I can be there 8.30 *sharp-sharp.*'

Thabethe now saw Spikes arrive, in the familiar red Mini, just a few minutes later than promised. He parked four bays away from the Ballade, and walked over with the package, something wrapped in brown paper, protruding from a very large black plastic bin-liner. Thabethe leaned over and opened the passenger door for him. Spikes sat with the parcel on his lap, tearing open the brown paper, and speaking animatedly about this line of his flourishing business.

'You hear, Skhura, about that case in Gauteng that time? Those guys in Tembisa Magistrate's Court. You see that guy in the newspaper, that *Tembisa Cluster Commander*, Major-General *fok*-face Leshabane. His guys caught my friends, that one. They were doing good business there for me, man. My guys had the constable uniforms like this one, with handcuffs, boots, and fake guns. Fake but look good, you know? They go up to people and say *Wena! We police! Give us your money...*'

Spikes roared with laughter, removing the items from the brown paper and passing them one by one over to Thabethe, who then looked closely at them, examined them, and was satisfied that the items were all completely authentic. He was well positioned to know. After all, he had done time in these exact uniforms. Spikes continued.

'That General Phiyega got that bastard Lieutenant-General guy and they messed up my business there, man. We had police uniforms, and police cars and blue lights, and all that stuff. When my guys stopped the people they thought *yissus! the cops!* Man, we laughed when we heard each time. My guys told them they were from the police K9 unit. Hell, Skhura, we laughed. But when they grabbed those guys, that station commander at Tembisa, Brigadier Jacobs, he started looking for more of my guys, so I closed down in Gauteng. Now I do only KwaZulu-Natal.'

Thabethe was satisfied with the goods, paid Spikes the thousand in cash, and Spikes left a happy man. As always, he gave Thabethe the assurance that no-one would ever know. Spikes knew better than most that to cross Skhura Thabethe in any way was to write one's own ticket to a very painful final result. They said that when Skhura Thabethe wanted to make you cry, he made you cry like a *vuvuzela*. Don't cross that one! *Hayi!*

Thabethe watched the red Mini drive away and then, with the bin-liner stuffed full, he went to find a toilet in the hospital.

Within minutes he had emerged from the toilet, feeling entirely comfortable in the uniform of a constable, exactly like the one that he had worn, two years previously, every day of his working week. Today he would be *Constable Dlamini*. He walked casually back over to the Ballade and emptied the bin-liner, now containing his own clothes, behind the driver's seat. Then he stuffed the bin-liner into his trouser pocket and crossed back over to the entrance that would take him back to Dirk's ward.

A quick friendly exchange and he had informed the constable on duty that his unit had decided to release him early from guard duty, at 9.00 am. He could now make his way back to the station if he wanted, or grab some breakfast before doing so, because his relief, Constable Dlamini, was happy to take over immediately instead of waiting for 9.00 am. The man needed no further prompting, and after telling Constable Dlamini in answer to a question that the nurses had already been and done their morning stuff with the patient, he was gone. Thabethe entered the ward.

Dirk, still on massive drugs to deal with the excruciating pain from his damaged knee joint, now supported in a hinged knee-brace resting on two pillows, was completely taken in by Constable Dlamini. The Constable told him to get into his dressing-gown because he was being taken back to the station for questioning. He then pulled out the bin-liner, stuffed the patient's clothes into it, and swept the boxes of painkillers and anti-inflammatories – neatly prepared by the nurses in a way that suggested to Thabethe that this patient was in any case scheduled for discharge this very morning – off the top of the counter into the bag. Then he wheeled the patient out to the street. And all of this with not a single person stopping them or even offering a second glance.

Dirk did not even flinch when Constable Dlamini handcuffed him, hands in front, and put him in the back of the Silver Honda Ballade, behind the front passenger seat, his braced leg stretched out and supported on top of the clothes stuffed behind the driver's seat. And he did not even register the fact that when Constable Dlamini drove off, they left the hospital wheelchair in the middle of the parking bay adjacent to the one they vacated.

Dirk dozed in the back of the car, the drugs having their effect on both his pain and his consciousness. Thabethe drove through the traffic, then north on the M4, past Umhlanga Lagoon Nature Reserve, turned right onto the M27 toward Umdloti, turned right again toward Selection Beach, down South Beach Road as far as he could before turning right and then left and finally nestling the car right up against the path into the bush that he knew so well from previous visits. This was one of his favourite spots.

The first hint to the half-asleep Dirk that something was not right was when the Constable pulled open the back door and thrust an oil rag into his mouth before Dirk could scream, and then tied on a gag. Thabethe checked all around for any witnesses. The coast was clear. With the coil of rope from Spikes Mkhize in one hand he used the other to drag Dirk by the collar of his pyjama shirt, forcing him to hop and whimper in agony as he tried to take pressure off the damaged knee. Dirk could not avoid putting some of the pressure onto the bad leg, even as he tried to put as much of his weight as he could onto the good leg. Within seconds they were in deep bush, and Thabethe allowed his victim to slow down, but he maintained a grasp on Dirk's collar and they moved into the thick foliage. Eventually Thabethe stopped, and allowed Dirk to collapse, whimpering, on the ground.

Thabethe uncoiled the rope and started tying the handcuffed prisoner, seated, to the base of a tree. Dirk was moaning in agony and fear. Thabethe finished and stood up over the wounded man. It was only then that Dirk was able to get a good look at his captor's eyes. Those eyes. He froze in horror as he recalled meeting the same man, along with Jannie, that time in the shebeen.

'You remember Skhura, white man? You and me. Today we talk.'

But before doing anything else, Thabethe turned and walked back the way they had come, to the car. He was back within minutes, with the bin-liner containing Dirk's things and having also stuffed his own clothes into it. He had also moved the car to an unobtrusive parking away from the pathway into the bush where it might otherwise have prompted curious passers-by to go searching. He pulled off his prisoner's gag, sat down opposite Dirk, and made himself comfortable.

'You and me, fat man, we spend some time together.'

Dirk was terrified and in agony. It was going to be a long day.


### 10.30

Sergeant Cronje was cursing with more than usual profanity as he put down the phone, just as Koekemoer and Dippenaar came through the doorway.

'What's the problem, Piet? Still working out the seating plan for tonight?'

'*Ag* no, Koeks, man. That's bad enough, but no, not this time. That was my favourite, how you say it – *gentleman caller* – as Ed would say.'

'Uh-oh! Major Swannie, again, Piet?' Dippenaar chirped in. 'What's he want? Wants you to seat him next to some hot chick tonight, I bet. How about Pillay? They're the same height. Should be fun.'

'No, man. He's just interfering again. Wants to know what's happening with the guy from Montpelier Road, is he still in hospital, and stuff, and when's he being taken back into custody, and stuff.'

'Oh boy! You're going to like this one, then, Piet,' said Koekemoer.

'*Ja*? What'

'Tell him, Dipps.'

'Tell me what?'

'You can call the Major right back if you want, Piet. You can tell him that our one-legged star escaped from Addington just over an hour ago,' said Dippenaar.

'Shit.'

'No shit, Piet.'

'*Yissus*. Does the Captain know?'

'Not to our knowledge. That's exactly why we popped in. We just heard ourselves and we dropped in to let the Captain know that we're on the case – we're going down to the hospital now to check it out. But you better let the Major know, I suppose, seeing he asked.'

'I'll call him right back.'

Cronje touched redial and within seconds was talking to the Major.

'Major Swanepoel? Sorry, sir, it's me again, sir. No, sir, Captain's still out, sir. He'll be some time, I think, sir. No, he's checking out details on a death – well, not really, but a death, you know, yesterday – in an encounter between our guys and a guy pulling a gun on them, clear self-defence case for us, but I – yes, sir, I just wanted – no, sir, but I just wanted to tell you – yes, sir...'

Koekemoer and Dippenaar looked at each other, a despairing shake of the head from the former and a long elongated sigh from the latter. They moved in on Cronje, tickling him under the armpits as Cronje tried desperately to ward them off and maintain some semblance of seriousness as he continued.

''No Major, I just wanted to come back to you, sir, after your phone-call just now, and tell you – no, sir. Well we've just got news, sir, but we still don't have the details. But the fact is, sir, that the Montpelier Road man escaped from the hospital ward, sir. Hullo? Major? Are you there, sir?'

Koekemoer and Dippenaar stopped their business as Cronje slapped Koekemoer hard on the wrist with a resounding clap that sounded like a gun-shot.

'Yes sir. No, sir. I thought the line had gone dead, sir. Yes. No, it wasn't one of our guys guarding him. I think the Captain made an arrangement with – yes, sir. OK, sir, when I find out more I'll let you know. Thanks, sir. No problem, Major.'

He hung up. Dippenaar and Koekemoer looked at him, waiting for comment.

'*Ja*. Well. No. Fine. He seemed OK with the news. Not such a big problem. I thought he would go ballistic. What a change. Maybe he's thinking about the party tonight. And – you heard – he wasn't even interested in me trying to tell him about Pillay and the guy she put down in Overport. *Yissus!* But you two guys give me a hard time, man.'

'Sorry, Piet,' said Koekemoer, 'we'll make it up to you tonight, and buy you a drink. If the Captain's looking for us, tell him we've gone to get ball gowns for tonight, OK?'

'So long, Piet. Call us if you need anything. We'll try and find out more about Addington and what happened, and we'll let you know what we find.'

'So long, *manne*. Check you tonight if I don't see you before.'

The two detectives left and Cronje turned to the seating plan in front of him.

He was irritated. Bloody Major. Always looking for someone to blame. Bloody top brass. Bureaucrats. Get a bee in their bonnets and just keep going at one thing. Irritate the hell out of us who do the real work.

## 10.35

Nyawula strode back to his office. He had been quick with the IPID people, and had given them the details on Ryder and Pillay at the Overport killing. That had gone well enough, for the moment anyway. Then back to base and immediately over to the HR people. They had been quite supportive for once. With the support of the top brass, things were going to be easier than normal, they said. There was also a lot of sympathy for him in the aftermath of the Trewhella shooting. He had to bite his tongue while enduring the tick-box exercise, as they commented on Pillay. *Found competent in training provided for the period 1 April to 31 March. No precautionary suspensions. Performance rewards. Progression to another salary notch. Employment Equity.*

'No problem there, hey?' the clerk had chuckled. 'Employment Equity. Two for one.'

Nyawula didn't react. The less he said, the better. He wanted this processed quickly so that he could get the hell out of there and so that both he and Pillay could just get on with the work. He had already endured the clerk reading out aloud – very slowly, with adenoids and a mouth that was too wet – the guideline that *Positions are funded over a multi-year period according to predetermined targets of the total establishment, taking into account personnel losses. Vacant positions at a certain level or in terms of a specific business unit are therefore planned and regarded as funded only upon the date of advertisement...* and then noting the agreement to waive advertisement in this case, and the extra note attached to the file and signed by various senior officers.

Nyawula had finally escaped, having secured the agreement that the papers would all be ready for final signature on Monday morning, so that the formal announcement could be made at the funeral of Detective Trewhella.

As he walked his mind traversed a range of things. Tonight's function was a chore but he would grit his teeth and do the right thing. The stolen Vektors were becoming a bit of an obsession, he thought, but he needed to get on top of them. Three recovered. One still out there, probably still with Thabethe, the elusive bastard. Dealing with IPID, who had wanted more information not only on Trewhella and Ryder putting down the guys on Wilson's Wharf, but also on Pillay and Ryder's encounter with the victim in Overport. Getting Koekemoer and Dippenaar to support Ryder and follow up on the murders of the old couple at The Grove. Checking with Cronje on Swanepoel's latest hassling. Updating the British High Commission, and getting Ryder on to that case while Pillay had her arm sorted out. Then following up himself with forensics on the cross-checking in Montpelier Road and Overport.

The burden was enormous. But no, the system determined that a major activity for today was to attend to a seating plan for tonight's party.

As Nyawula approached his office, Koekemoer and Dippenaar appeared.

'Bad news, Captain,' said Koekemoer, 'the guy with the leg, from Montpelier Road, he escaped from Addington this morning. We've just told Cronje.'

Nyawula looked up at the heavens and leaned back against the wall. Dippenaar thought he was remarkably calm, given the importance of the Montpelier guy to the Trewhella case.

'We're going down right now, Captain, to check it out.'

'Find out for me, men, who the constable on duty was,' Nyawula sighed. 'I know he wasn't one of ours, that's for sure. But I'd like to know how the hell this could have happened.'

'Will do, Captain,' said Koekemoer. 'We'll get down there now.'

'Just one thing before you go, guys. Can you also find some time to follow up on Trewhella and Ryder's work at The Grove? I've got Ryder doing some stuff for me on the beach murder, to satisfy the British High Commission who are hassling Cluster Command, but I don't want The Grove to go cold. Check out with Ryder how far he is with that, and see what you can do to help and take it further.'

The two detectives gave their assurances and left.

Nyawula strode over to catch up on things with Cronje. Who would probably greet him with a dozen new messages unrelated to all of this. Then he would have to work out how he was going to manage all of it while handling the incoming news of a stabbing homicide, three rapes, a brutal armed robbery just around the corner, two disciplinary matters involving new constables, and rumours of corruption in Inanda, all within the last twenty-four hours.

Apart from what was already on his plate.


## 12.00.

Ryder was on the beach at the site of Sunday night's shooting. He had prevailed upon Pillay to obey the doctors and get all the necessary attention to her arm, and then to catch up on paperwork. He had left her pouting.

He had spent the morning checking the movements of the British tourist, from his hotel to inside the casino, courtesy of a helpful hotel management and the CCTV from the casino. The cameras had picked up even more than he had hoped for.

The tourist had overdone just about everything. He had stuffed himself with food and booze. He had played the tables and the slot machines. He had gone back and forth to the bar. When he was in luck at the slot machines, the waitresses plied him with more drinks. Same at the tables. He started buying drinks for others with his winnings. He started becoming attractive, as grossly obese as he was, to a few young women. At first he paid no particular attention to them but then, as the booze flowed, he started becoming more and more open to conversations with strangers. Then he had got the big win at Blackjack. Then the popularity of the man grew exponentially.

Ryder marvelled, in his study of the visuals, at how it was almost possible to imagine the audio. Ryder could almost hear the guy saying, right near the end, *yes, well OK, you are a persistent little lass, aren't you, but is it safe?* Ryder shook his head at the naivety of the man. The management's camera technician and security officer both sat with him and could read the same things.

'It's so obvious, you can almost hear what the guy is saying to her, can't you?' said the technician.

'Sure is obvious,' said Ryder.

'Happens all the time in here. We watch these guys get taken by the floozies all the time,' said the security man.

'Anything you can do about it?'

'Not really. By the time we get someone down on the floor they've usually gone, or they deny doing anything wrong, or they say they're good friends, and that kind of stuff. Then we watch them go off to their hotel or they leave to go down to the beach. From then on we have nothing to do with it.'

Ryder managed to obtain hard prints of the last young woman who was with the tourist as he had left the casino and as they had then left the complex to go into the night. The external cameras showed them moving across the road into the dark, heading toward the beach. Then there were no other visuals.

He wasn't confident of achieving much, himself, with the photo of the young woman, but he kept the hard copy and arranged for the technician to scan a copy over to Sergeant Cronje. Then he called Piet and got him to do the necessary to put it into the system and see what they could find in the ether. Then he had gone down to the beach.

He had arranged to meet Nadine Salm, the crime scene investigator who had been brought in on Monday morning to the beach scene, at the time he and Ed had been busy having their own fun at Wilson's Wharf. She agreed to walk him through the scene as she had seen it.

'Been doing this a long time, Nadine?'

'*Shoo, I suppoose soo,* Jeremy.'

Ryder couldn't help thinking that the way she formulated a few of her vowels reminded him of an undergraduate student he had once met, from the University of Cape Town, who had also pursed her lips in the same way, like a native French speaker mouthing the informal *tu*. Whoever had said that there was no equivalent sound in English for the French *u*, he thought, had never met this particular UCT arts undergraduate. The student in question had had a habit of pronouncing *know* as *noo* and *show* as *shoo* and *Cape* as *keep* and table as *teeble*. She had told him that she had *choosen to read philosophy and soocial anthropology, because it's like, about real grooth and finding oneself, you noo? And it's so cool studying in the shadow of Teeble Mountain, you noo?* Nadine was not dissimilar to that student, he thought, as she continued. But as she did so, he filtered out of his consciousness the idiosyncratic diphthongs so that he could concentrate on what she was saying instead of how she was saying it.

'I started on this stuff way back, after I graduated, you know, Jeremy? I started as a CSI here in Durbs – well, first as a technician and then only later as a full CSI – then I went to the DNA Project, then back to SAPS. I suppose it's my life, you know?'

'Do you focus on one aspect of it or do you do it all?'

'Me? Well, as you know, we've got to be careful and avoid having the same person doing both the lifting of the evidence and the testing of it. Got to ensure cross-checking rather than conscious reinforcement of each other's findings. Corroboration rather than reinforcement. That's the theory. But in practice, with staff shortages and the number of cases, well, don't tell anyone, but, you know, we slip a little now and then. Which suits me fine. I like nothing better than lifting and testing my own stuff. As long as I cover the bases if we have to go to court on it. Anyway, I started with a focus on firearm and tool mark examination and then got myself into all kinds of stuff involving the full range of collection, preservation, analysis and interpretation. I particularly like shooting scene reconstruction, and wound ballistic determination. I hate the expert witness testimony side of things, though. I just like to follow the trail and find the evidence and let others make up their minds about what actually happened, you know? Don't see myself getting into trouble like a couple of the experts did way back during the Pistorius trial.'

They moved slowly around the site and Nadine pointed out with incredible insight and precision the key features she had identified. She discussed the initial report on ballistics, and impressed Ryder with the wide range of knowledge and experience she brought to the task. He had always been impressed with people who had had experience at the DNA Project. World-class stuff, he thought.

After just under an hour Ryder said he would be happy to walk further afield, alone, and think through what he had learned from her.

'Thanks, Nadine. I appreciate you coming back just for me.'

'Pleasure, Jeremy. Call me if you want any more, OK? I'm just across the way there for the next hour. I'm meeting my gorgeous assistant for lunch up at John Dory.'

She left and Ryder soon found himself probing into the bush at the upper end of the beach. He spent some time at it. He thought through what he had heard from Nadine.

It had been clear to the original crime scene investigators, supported by her meticulous reconstruction, that a third party, most likely a male, had joined the two on the beach. It wasn't possible to tell whether it had been a set-up and whether the woman had brought the guy down to be ambushed by a man, or whether the man had surprised both of them. It seemed from the reconstruction that the woman had then fled the scene in something of a hurry, and that there had been a bit of scrabbling around in the sand. When the CSIs found the weapon and Nadine had been able to re-imagine the scene, it seemed that the weapon had been lost in the struggle – right at the end of it, because the dead guy already had bullets in him – and that the perpetrator had then tried to find it in the sand, and had eventually given up on it.

Ryder moved into a thicket of bush and paused. If he was someone sitting in a thicket of bush like this in the dark, what would he be looking at? Foliage? How do you spend time in the middle of the night sitting in a bush? What's there to look at? The sea, surely? He moved, trying a few positions, to see whether there were any comfortable areas where there was also a view of the sea. He found three or four and tried them. Nothing. No insights there. Then he tried again, and found a perfectly-located hole in the foliage, and sat down, with his back against a tree. Nice view. Possibly even a nice view at night. He had checked the reports and had ascertained that the moon was full on Sunday from midnight. Must have been a nice view. Maybe this was where the guy had sat.

He looked around. Nothing. Then a small piece of twisted plastic caught his attention. Beneath the bush over to his right. He reached for it. Then paused. Looked at it more closely without touching. The familiar twist. The stuff inside. The colour. Unmistakable. *Nyaope.* He looked further, and found a joint, smoked almost to the end, under the same bush.

Ryder pulled out his iPhone.

'Nadine? Jeremy. I need you to come back. Now. Yes. Sorry, but I've got something. Something with finger-marks, I'm sure. Maybe fingerprints to match those on the weapon. I'm in the bush. I'll come out so that you can see me. Thanks, Nadine.'

Ryder took a white tissue out of his pocket. Fiona always ensured that he carried tissues. She wouldn't have handkerchiefs in the house. Foul things, she said. He hung the tissue on a bush, where it was prominent against the thick foliage. Time to play Hansel and Gretel, he thought, although he had no doubt about his ability to find his way back, and went to find Nadine.

## 13.40.

Koekemoer and Dippenaar got the full story from the constable who had been on duty at Addington. This Dlamini guy who had relieved him had obviously been an impostor. They had checked the CCTV cameras and picked off a couple of freezes from which they had been given hard copy photos of the guy. He seemed to know what he was doing, and had kept his eyes down and the peaked cap low over the forehead. He appeared to have had some experience with security cameras. Or with the cameras in this particular hospital, anyway. The photos might or might not be useful.

Then they had contacted Ryder by phone, and got his agreement to help him with the follow-up action on The Grove murders. As a consequence of this the two detectives found themselves having lunch at John Dory's, Suncoast Casino. *Thursday special platter for one*, seventy-nine rands each.

As utterly delicious as the meal was, their visit was not all pleasure. They had walked around the casino, asked casual questions, probed, observed, and got to understand some of the dynamics in the place. But nothing earth-shattering. They agreed that the highlight of the day – if not the lowlight – had been the unexpected pleasure of seeing the notorious pest Major Swanepoel himself, wearing civvies, waddling by, probably on his way from the casino to the car park. They had both behaved like children, they agreed afterwards, in ducking out of sight behind their menus in case the Major saw them and came over for a chat.

'Maybe he came down here to find a date for the function tonight,' said Dippenaar. 'There's some *lekker* young things hanging around the machines in there, looking at the *ou toppies* hoping to get lucky. So that they can then get lucky, too.'

The two detectives finished their meal and decided to do one more round of the slot machines. After some twenty minutes they suddenly heard a loud screaming and huge applause and bells and whistles, followed by the public announcement of *another Suncoast winner*. They went over and joined the crowd in gawping, with a mixture of amazement and jealousy, at the huge win claimed by a woman who must have been eighty years old.

'Nice to add that to your pension pot, hey Dipps?'

'Shit. You telling me, Koeks.'

People were congratulating her, she was cackling loudly and speaking to the amused crowd around her.

'*Ag*, you know, it's *rreally* nice, but it's not *rreally* for me that I'm happy. It's my daughter, you know. I'm going to buy her a new car. To replace her *terrrible* Citi Golf that's just falling apart, you know. And it's yellow, too, you know. Yellow like sick, you know? *Terrrible* ugly car. She brings me here then goes off to do the shopping then fetches me, and I get too *embarrrassed*, you know, driving off in that *horrrible* ugly car.'

The crowd chuckled, empowering her to babble on even further.

'I'm also going to buy my son a lovely present, you know. *Ag*, shame, his wife left him so he needs a little present, you know. *Ja*, man, no, I'm telling you, I've been coming here for years but this is my first *rreally* big win and you know, *dearrie*, this here is *my* machine, you know, I always play it. I even wait for it to come vacant if someone else is playing here, you know. You ask this lady here, she knows me because she comes here lots, too, and she knows I stand there and I wait for my machine...'

And then Dippenaar noticed two young men standing together, talking quietly. They stood out from the rest of the observers because their demeanour was so different. He caught the eye of his partner and indicated with a nod of the head.

They watched the two men, unobtrusively, throughout the process of them in turn watching the management arriving, checking the machine, taking the lucky winner's name and details, and handing her an envelope as they congratulated her.

The watchers watched. In due course, the crowd of well-wishers having dissipated and the old woman having played down to nothing the remaining credits on her card, she made her way slowly to the cashier, where, when her turn came, she handed over her envelope and chatted away to one of the women behind the counter, received her winnings, and then made for the exit. The two young men followed. The two detectives followed them. By the time they all reached the taxi-rank it seemed to the detectives that there was a clear *modus operandi* in play. The old woman was in some danger.

But it was shattered with the noisy arrival, with hooter blaring, of what was obviously the winner's daughter, in a yellow Citi Golf on which every part seemed loose and about to fall off. Within seconds the old woman was in the car and they were tearing off noisily. The two young men cursed, made an attempt to hail a taxi, thought better of it, and retreated, highly irritated.

The two detectives could do nothing. No crime had been committed. They were both totally convinced that the two had had the intention of following the old woman, with what purpose in mind they had no doubt. But they had been foiled by the timing of the daughter's arrival. They could only watch as the two men walked back into the casino.

'*Yissus*! Dipps. You thinking what I'm thinking?'

'No question, Koeks. Those guys would have followed her and mugged her, no question.'

'You think maybe that's what happened to the old couple at The Grove?'

'Maybe. Maybe this kind of thing should be checked out. Should we see what Jeremy thinks?'

'*Ja*. Maybe. Maybe it'll be worth a stake-out here to follow up on this kind of thing. Hard to track and to catch anyone in the act. But maybe we can identify someone with connections to other stuff. Let's talk to the guys. And to the Captain, if Jeremy agrees.'

### 14.20.

Vic was livid. No Tony. No Dirk. Big deliveries scheduled for tomorrow. Followed by big dispatches on Saturday to more than a dozen customers. Massive money involved. He had run down the battery on his new iPhone in next to no time, because of the constant calls he had had to make, which Tony would normally have made. He had closed it down for a while for rapid charging, and then had to sit next to a power source making further calls while the phone continued re-charging. He was cursing all the time.

Checking codes, confirming times and place of delivery, double-checking identities, paying the middlemen, moving money from numbered accounts to other numbered accounts. Screaming into the mouthpiece with frustration. *I said cash. I mean cash. I want it in an envelope. Or a bag. Or a briefcase. Or a bloody picnic basket if you want. But if it's not cash you don't get the goods. We've been through this before, goddammit!*

Where was Dirk? Where had he got to? Was he trying to get in contact? Has Tony found him and are they both trying to get back in touch with me? Is Tony in trouble? Unlike him to disappear. He would never. He would never betray me. Accident, maybe? Where's his car?

He undid the top button and loosened his tie. He found it difficult to breathe. The world was closing in on him.

He had to find Tony and Dirk.

## 15.10.

Nyawula, Ryder, Pillay, Cronje, Koekemoer and Dippenaar were crowded into the Captain's office. Nyawula spoke as they all settled down.

'Thanks, everyone. KoeksnDips had a word with me and I asked them to check things out first with Ryder. Thanks for joining us, Jeremy. How's the head?'

'Fine, thanks, Captain. I have an appointment to have the dressing changed again just after this.'

'Good. Your arm OK, Sergeant Pillay?'

'No problem, Captain. Just a flesh wound.'

'Good. Look after it. I asked Navi to join us, everyone, because until we replace Ed I'm asking her to pick up a few things for me.'

Ryder and Pillay exchanged the briefest of glances, not picked up by anyone else, while the Captain continued.

'I understand you're all on the same page with this thing at the casino?'

They all mumbled affirmations, which gave him the indication to continue.

'It's a really difficult thing to set up a surveillance operation with something like this, as K and D suggest. We could spend days waiting for the right winner on the slot machines to be picked out by the right muggers looking out for them, and then to actually catch them in the act. To be frank, I don't think we can do it. We don't have the person-power.'

Resigned acknowledgements all round.

'The best we could manage – if we were to even try this – is to get to the guys at the top in Suncoast and ask them if we can look at their list of significant cash winners over the last couple of months, then try and match those with any people in the city area who might have reported a mugging or burglary, and if we get any matches there then we could go back to Suncoast and ask them if we can look at the CCTV footage of those particular winners. To see what we can identify in the crowd at the time. Jeremy had some luck earlier today with the CCTV cameras down there, in the case of the British tourist. But to use them to track cases where we suspect that people are watching players, and then try to use that as evidence to pin something specific on people who we suspect *might* be thinking of mugging someone, seems like a long shot to me, with not much chance of success. Even if we got through the first couple of steps, to then try and trace the guys in the crowd and then pin a mugging on them seems to me to be a bit of a pipe dream. Agreed?'

There was general assent, and despondency to go with it.

'I'm not even sure we would get the cooperation of the senior management, to tell you the truth. As helpful as they were to Jeremy, that was only because of the publicity surrounding the murder of a British tourist, and the possible impact on tourism. And how it might hit their own business. But in cases where we think there are possibly going to be a few suspicious characters planning a mugging, well, I don't think so. I can't see Suncoast management being very helpful to us.'

'We would have to call on our *own* top connections,' Koekemoer threw in.

'*Ja!*' sniggered Dippenaar, 'maybe the Major can connect us.'

The Captain looked at Dippenaar.

'Sorry, Captain. Just a bad joke.'

The others all looked at Dippenaar, confused. Such peer pressure, without which he might have simply held his tongue, forced an explanation from him.

'I mean, sorry, Captain, it's just that Koeks and I saw the Major down there at lunchtime, and so we just joked a bit about it.'

'The Major in the casino? In uniform?' asked Nyawula.

'No, Captain,' said Koekemoer. 'He was in civvies. Day off, I suppose.'

They all chuckled.

'So how did you… You know the Major, all of you?'

'Yes, Captain,' said Dippenaar. 'We knew him in the old days, before you came. Before he moved on to greater things. He also came into the office a month ago to see you. And Piet. That time about the Customs bust, and the trouble at the Deputy Port Captain's Office in Point Road. We were all here then.'

'Not me,' said Ryder. 'I've never met the Major.

'Nor me,' said Pillay.

Nyawula thought for a moment, nodded, and continued.

'I'm sure if Ryder and Pillay stick with the unit the two of them will have the pleasure one day.'

Smirks all around as Nyawula continued.

'Anyway, I think we have to accept facts that the idea of a stakeout at the casino is not going to happen. I know that the chances are that that's what happened to the old woman at The Grove. We know she had a couple of big wins on the slot machines before she was attacked. But it's a long stretch to prove this through a stakeout, and even harder to prove a connection between the guys that Ryder and Trewhella put down on the wharf and any handlers they might have had at the casino. The case of the British tourist seems different. He went straight from the casino to the beach, loaded with money and on the arm of a prostitute. Stupid move. So, all I can suggest, people, is that we keep our ears to the ground for any possible connections that might come up with the casino scene. If anything develops we can have another look. But for now, let's concentrate on the things we have in front of us. And Sergeant Cronje and I have tonight's function in front of us, so unless there's anything else, Piet and I will get on to that.'

There was a general babble of sound as they parted, some nudging of Dippenaar along with sniggers, and they all left the office for their next tasks.

Nyawula and Cronje pulled up chairs around the seating plan for the function. Now began the enormous task of ensuring that last-minute changes to who was sitting next to who did not end up in turf wars between Durban North and KwaMashu or Hillcrest and Isipingo.

'Have you arranged lots of coffee for us this afternoon, Piet?'

'You can bet on it, Captain.'

## 16.20.

Ryder felt the dressing they had replaced on his head wound. The nurse had not even bothered to clean it up, because Fiona's work had already done the job. So she just changed the Elastoplast and pronounced it fine.

He was still deeply troubled. Had been all day. He had been trying to work out what it was that had worked its way into the back of his brain shortly after yesterday's action, still somewhat cloudy from the moment that Tony creep had dropped him with the club. What was it that his brain couldn't process? Something important. It had been nagging him ever since.

But he hadn't been able to recall it.

A major incident involving yet another xenophobic attack on foreign hawkers, and bringing out the riot police, had forced him to take a wide detour of the central business district. Now, at a standstill, caught in an unrelated traffic jam, he looked at another group of hawkers from the Warwick Junction market packing up for the day. Most of them doubtless disappointed with the day's takings and many thinking that they should have packed up with the others some time ago instead of hanging on in hope for something that would boost the day's takings.

His car edged forward a few feet. Shouts mingled with angry hoots from vehicles all around.

He stared vacantly at the devastating poverty of children earning a few coins by washing windscreens without first enquiring and then begging for payment from drivers staring resolutely ahead and ignoring them, windows firmly closed. Pavements meant nothing. Nor did stop signs or traffic lights. The cars edged their way through the mass of people with a combination of hooter and footbrake and cursing.

He eventually emerged from the cacophony into the relative peace of the Greyville Park area where the rough sleepers were already converging. It was too soon for most of them. These were the early arrivals. Once the sun had set the park would be illuminated by the many fires of homeless people gathering for the night next to the racecourse, home to the annual fashion extravaganza. The early rough sleepers were choosing their patches for the night. Some with large packs on their shoulders. Others with nothing but what was in their pockets. Others, as they gathered together, already making use of the tubes of glue or plastic bottles of meths.

Something wasn't hanging together, thought Ryder. There was a gap. They had overlooked something. What was it? His mind raced back over the scene with Tony. The agony of the blow to his skull. His confusion. The taste and the smell of paraffin. Why was that constantly coming back to him? What was it? The paraffin...

Then he stopped, stunned by his sudden recognition of what it was that Tony had said. *You're going to give me some information, detective. But you can give it to me after I've wasted your partner. She's useless to me. Just a hindrance. I'm going to take her out. Just like I did with your previous partner.*

Ryder played the sentences over and over again in his foggy memory. He visualised Tony's leering face as he had hissed through clenched teeth.

*...you can give it to me after I've wasted your partner... I'm going to take her out. Just like I did with your previous partner...*

125

Ryder stopped breathing for a few seconds as it became clear to him. Then he reached for his iPhone.

'Navi. It's me. We have to talk. Now. No, I'll come to you. It has to be alone. Where are you?'

## 17.10.

With Dirk still tied to the tree, Thabethe had removed the handcuffs and the gag, to allow him more easily to manage his burger and chips. He had changed back into his own clothes, dumping the constable's uniform under the bush and covering it with sand, and had gone off more than an hour ago to get food for each of them, leaving his prisoner cuffed, tied and gagged. Dirk was now gratefully slurping the can of coke that came with the food. As he did so, he watched Thabethe slip the key to the cuffs onto the key ring that also held the key to the Ballade. They both ate in silence.

When they had finished, Thabethe drew the iPhone from his pocket and played to himself, yet again, the message that he had listened to so many times already. Then he paused as he remembered the other call. The one that hadn't been a recorded message: *And bring back the box from Overport.* He played it over again in his memory, then stared at Dirk.

'What is this box at Overport?'

'What?'

'What is meaning this box at Overport?'

'I don't know what you talking about.'

Thabethe leapt to his feet and put his foot on Dirk's damaged knee. Dirk screamed with the pain.

'What is the box in Overport?'

'Stop! For God's sake, stop! *Pleeease*! I'll tell you!'

Thabethe released his foot and gave him a moment to recover. Dirk whimpered in agony.

'It's just a box I seen them carry. It has papers and stuff. I never saw inside the box. They just take it around with them everywhere they go. It's not in Overport. They keep it somewhere else. I never seen it in the safe in Overport.'

'Safe? What is safe? I been there. There is no safe in house in Overport.'

Dirk was desperate. He wasn't thinking properly. *Tony's going to kill me.*

*Why did I talk about the safe. The pain. I can't …* Thabethe moved in again.

'No! Please, no! I'll tell you. They have a small safe. In the wall. On the ground floor. The second room. I've seen it open. I've never seen anything inside. When I saw it that time it was empty. Standing open. But empty. I swear.'

'Good. You show me. Tonight, you show me. We go there and you show me, fat man. Tonight.'

Thabethe bent down and put the cuffs back on Dirk's wrists. Then he removed the ropes, and kicked the bag containing Dirk's clothes over to him.

'Now you take off pyjamas. You get clothes on. Then we talk some more.'

He watched Dirk struggle, handcuffed, to remove his hospital clothes and get back into his own, including shoes and socks. It seemed interminable, and the cuffs had to come off then back on again for the shirt exchange with the pyjama top, but Dirk finally finished, sweating profusely and groaning in agony every time his knee went even slightly out of alignment. Seeing the packet of painkillers and anti-inflammatories in the bag as he pulled out his shoes, he begged to be allowed to have a few tablets, which Thabethe allowed him. He swallowed them with the last of the coke, and sat down again, back against the tree, panting and sweating as he waited for the drugs to take hold.

Thabethe put his prisoner back on the rope, looped it once around the tree and through his arms then around his torso before tying it behind. He then kicked the pyjamas and dressing gown under the bush, and scuffed soil over them. Then he threw the gag and tablets into the bag, sat back, opposite him, and played the iPhone message again. And again.

Dirk watched him, helpless.

## 17.20.

Ryder and Pillay sat opposite each other, each nursing a coffee. Her left arm was in a sling. She was stunned by what she had just heard.

'I could kick myself,' said Ryder. 'For months, now, Ed and I couldn't work out how it was that they always seemed to be one step ahead of us. Every time we made a move on them, they seemed to have cleared out just before we got there. We put it down to bad timing. We didn't even pause to think that there might be some inside information involved. But when that arsehole had me tied and gagged he told me – at lunchtime, goddammit –

that he knew you were my partner. That was less than one hour after I myself had been told you were my partner. And he knew about Ed being my partner, and about him being wasted. How did he know that? The very next day. It could only have come from inside.'

'You think maybe one of ours? One of our own guys?'

'I don't know, Navi. I just don't know.'

'Should we go to the Captain?'

'Do we know it's not him?'

'Shit.'

'Exactly.'

'Can't be, Jeremy. It just can't — not Nyawula.'

'I'm sure that's right, Navi, but until we know for sure, it's just the two of us…'

'Wait a minute!'

'What?'

'It *can't* be our guys, Jeremy, and it can't be Nyawula. It has to be higher up. Nyawula told me at 9.30 yesterday about you and me. Told me not to tell anyone until he had spoken to you. You say he then told you only at midday. So it was only you, me and Nyawula that knew by the time we hit the warehouse. And the guy we wasted. *Who was already at the warehouse.*'

'And he couldn't have received the news about us while he was in the warehouse. There was no land line, and he didn't have any cell-phone on him, according to forensics. It was one of the things that struck them in the clean-up afterwards. Guy in a warehouse, smartly dressed, no phone. Mercedes keys in his pocket, but no phone. They searched all around the place and drew a blank. It was only later on, when Koeks and Dipps were sent back to the scene, and combed through the place, late in the afternoon, that they finally found the car in the road, up the hill. It had been broken into. No phone there either.'

'So he either left his phone in the cubby and it was stolen, or he didn't carry a phone at all on the day, which is unlikely. But whatever the case, *he received no call while he was in the warehouse.* Whoever told him about you and me told him before he got to the warehouse.'

'And he must have been told *even before Nyawula confirmed things with me,*' said Ryder, 'which means he was told by someone other than Nyawula. Before Nyawula could confirm things with me. Which means that it was someone higher up the food chain. Someone who knew that Nyawula wanted us in a new partnership without going through the normal procedures.'

'Someone in authority over Nyawula. Someone in the Cluster. Or higher. Or someone in HR or in IPID.'

'Or a business associate. Ed was always on about the Chinese business connection. They're too cosy with some of the units, he always said. OK. Let's go and see Nyawula, Navi. This stuff is just starting to get bigger than any of us ever thought.'

'Too late for that today, Jeremy. Piet told me as I was coming here that Nyawula was in no mood for anything other than the shit he has to handle tonight. He's already left for the big party, apparently, because he has to change into civvies, then he has to – in person – fetch a couple of big-wigs, then have a pre-party drink with the top brass. Apparently he told everyone at the station that he wants to be on the front line somewhere in deep KwaMashu tonight rather than deal with the fat-cat guys at the top of policing in this province.'

'Damn. I forgot about tonight. Fiona and I are also going. I need it like a hole in the head. I better go home and change. You going too?'

'Yep. For my pains. I'm going. Someone told me I can't wear trousers. Is that right?'

'Can't imagine you in a dress, partner. It would be like imagining Ed in a skirt. But you'll do OK. Let's hold this stuff for Nyawula for tomorrow morning, then. Can't raise it with him tonight.'

'See you at the party. Tell Fiona if she doesn't like whatever I decide to wear tonight that I'll be coming to her for advice about my wardrobe one of these days.'

'See you there. It's going to be a long night. Let's pick up this stuff again tomorrow.'


**20.05.**

The traffic had virtually disappeared. Thabethe pulled the Honda Ballade into the empty forecourt parking area, as close to the front door of the warehouse as he could get. He would have preferred to park up or down the road as he had done previously in the Mini. But the risk of attracting attention with a crippled man at his side, hopping down the hill in obvious pain, had to be weighed against the possibility of the police checking the warehouse again at this time of night. He had heard something on the news about some big police function at the stadium, so maybe they were all occupied anyway. Nevertheless, they needed to get in and out as quickly as possible, so he left the car with the keys in the ignition and pushed Dirk toward the building.

He picked the lock again and they entered the warehouse.

'You show me, quickly. Which room?'

Dirk motioned with his head, his hands still cuffed in front of him. Second door on the left.

'There's nothing left upstairs. It's all been moved out. Nothing down here, either, except for the one little place we keep a few things when we need to.'

'You show. Now.'

They walked down the passage, Dirk hobbling in pain, and entered the room where Thabethe had stared at the chalk-marks and tape marks the previous evening. Dirk was very agitated when he saw these. What went down here? Who was put down by who? Did Tony kill a cop? How could he contact Tony? Would Tony ever find out if he gave the information on the hiding place to Thabethe? Maybe Tony would just think that the cops had found it when cleaning the place.

Dirk hesitated, then found Thabethe staring at him. *Those eyes.* He moved over, grimacing with pain, to the corner of the room behind the door.

'Down there, I can't kneel. See there, that screw. Just pull.'

Thabethe told him to move back to the centre of the room. He waited till Dirk did so, then he squatted next to the screw that Dirk had identified. He twisted it counter-clockwise, and pulled. A perfectly disguised cavity covered by a wall panel, hinged on one side, swung outward with the screw, revealing a long narrow space into which was nestled a long red box. Thabethe recognised it as the box that the driver of the Mercedes had removed from his car the day before. He reached in and removed the container. Could this be the key to the big money the Afrikaner boy had spoken about? He laid it on the floor and removed the lid. Papers, receipts, invoices, gold and platinum and black casino cards, cash, more papers, more cards, more papers. He lifted pages at one end, wanting to keep everything in the box but still see everything that was in it. He was transfixed. More cards. More cash.

Then he heard the room door slam.

Thabethe cursed, dropped everything, lurched for the door handle, yanked the door open, and ran into the passage. Dirk, hopping in agony and terror, had made it to the front door. He pulled it open, hands cuffed together, and got his bulky frame through as Thabethe was two-thirds of the way down the passage, then he slammed the door behind him and slid the police bolt and hammered the padlock home, locked. Thabethe screamed and hammered on the door from the inside. Dirk hopped like a madman toward the Ballade, screaming in agony with each jolt of his body transmitting agonising shocks to his left knee. He fumbled with the door, scrambled into the driver's seat, and with his hands cuffed together and with his left knee eliciting from him groans of agony he turned the ignition key once, then twice, then as it took he thrust down as gently as he could onto the clutch pedal. He tore off from the forecourt, the engine screaming in first gear until Dirk found the means to rip it into second and then into third.

The hinges on the knee-brace were by no means tightened to a straight-leg position, but they had certainly not been prepared for the purposes of driving a car, so with only minimal flex in the knee Dirk was forced into a position where his buttocks weren't settled into the seat but hovered a few inches above it, partly supported by extra strain on the thigh muscles of his right leg and partly by his fat girth which allowed him to put pressure on the backrest, leaving the left leg stretched out to the clutch pedal and only partially bent. In this contorted position Dirk tried his best to manage the vehicle. The car swivelled left and right and out into the road and he was gone.

Thabethe ran back into the room, grabbed the red box, smashed a window with it, swiped at the jagged bits of glass to clear them, then clambered out, swearing every step of the way. He ran out across the forecourt into the night, clutching his treasure but cursing his stupidity.

\*

Dirk managed to drive no more than a couple of hundred metres before it became impossible to use the clutch any longer, his knee joint unable to respond to anything his agonised mind willed it to do. He swung the wheel and the car lurched into the first side-road he could find, then bumped and bounced into the darkest recess available in the road.

He switched off, removed the bunch of keys attached to the ignition, struggled with the key ring and found the key to the handcuffs. He freed his hands, slid the seat back to give himself more space for the injured leg, and sat panting in the dark. There was no way he would be able to drive any further. He would have to take his chances sleeping in the car tonight.

Thabethe had thrown the bag with the painkillers onto the back seat. Dirk struggled, leaning over the back of the driver's seat, snatched at the packets inside the bag, and swallowed four of the tablets, one at a time, with nothing but saliva, unsure of the dose but desperate to eradicate the pain.

He reached for and found the lever, tilted the backrest as far back as it could go, carefully stretched out his bad leg as far as he could manage, and lay in the dark, feeling the throbbing in his leg for another ten minutes before the tablets started taking effect and the pain began to subside.


## 21.05.

The Moses Mabhida, built as a FIFA Stadium for the 2010 World Cup, was described in the invitation to the event as a 'sporting cathedral.' Its grand arch, three hundred and fifty metres long and more than a hundred high, was a key feature, and for this evening's entertainment before the speeches and dinner there were rides for guests to the top on the funicular for a three hundred and sixty degree viewing of the city at night, and a range of different tours of the building and facilities.

Tonight they were not offering the normal tourist opportunity to plunge off the arch from one hundred and six metres on the Big Swing. Ryder might have tried that, just to escape the rest of the evening. Fiona had disagreed with him about doing the pre-event tour. He had wanted nothing to do with it, but she hadn't been to the stadium so she was going to have it her way. He meekly accepted. He knew this was one he wasn't going to win.

Parking was relatively easy, controlled by efficient and very polite and helpful traffic marshals. They were then ushered into the correct channels and tickets were checked, then clusters of guests were formed and eventually the two of them drifted along with the rest of their special tour group. Thankfully, for Ryder, they knew no-one else in this particular group. An excessively exuberant young man with a misplaced confidence in the quality of his rehearsed one-liners, and with serious adenoid problems, spoke too loudly and with far too much jollity. Ryder was on the receiving end of quite a few pokes in the ribs from Fiona, designed to prevent him from commenting on most of the guide's failed punch-lines.

They half-listened to the memorised speech. *World Cup 2010 ... world class stadium... New York has the Statue of Liberty, Paris has... and we have the Moses Mabhida... symbolises hope and victory... the greatness of South African sport... the great arch representing the previously divided nation now working together ... those of you who support AmaZulu would have been particularly proud...* at which point Ryder's muttered indication that Kaizer Chiefs was his team drew critical stares and whispered criticisms and a sharp elbow in the ribs from Fiona, so he decided to play it quiet for the rest of the tour. The guide went on ... *Neil Diamond chose to play here in 2011 ...* They saw the gymnasium, heard how the team from *Top Gear* had used the stadium not once but twice, and there was lots of *ooh-ing* and *aaah-ing* when they saw the VIP presidential suites, the change rooms and the tunnel. Finally, they were released from the torture to go off to the main function for a different kind of torture. At least one with a drink, thought Ryder.

The guests paraded in, some in uniform but most in the type of civilian clothes that struck Ryder as little different from uniforms. Uncomfortable suits, ties, new shirts and shoes bought especially for the occasion had already caused many of the men deep anguish. Women's dresses, many of them looking out of place and downright inappropriate on some of the bodies, given the amount of flesh in relation to the square meterage of cloth, were the focus of much of the initial conversation. They drifted in with the human tide, nodding, smiling pasted-on camera-smiles, and whispering on occasion to each other *what the hell is her name, again?*

They moved from the reception table where they had their names ticked off and were told their table number, and Ryder saw Pillay in the distance looking supremely uncomfortable in an entirely inappropriate dress. In fact, it was the first time he had seen Pillay out of trousers. Her arm was still in a sling. She and Cronje, Dipps and Koeks were in sombre conversation, doubtless about Ed and the agonising funeral to come on Monday. They waved, clutching their comfort-blankets of a welcoming glass of bubbly, all of them feeling as uncomfortable and as out-of-place as Ryder was. Ryder waved back. Fiona guided him on into the hall.

She knew that this was tough for him in every way. She would do her best to help him out in those awkward moments at which she was so good. As someone walked up to him with a *Jeremy! So good to see you!* and with Jeremy's face clearly demonstrating that he had no idea who this was, she would quickly intervene with *Hullo, I'm Fiona Ryder!* From which Jeremy would usually pick up an appropriate reply with the person's name. In the case of some self-centred idiots, of course, they would simply reply *Hello, Fiona, it's so nice to meet you,* and offer no name. In which case Fiona would exasperatedly have to add *Oh I'm so sorry, I didn't catch your name,* before she could then leave it to Jeremy to continue.

*What is it with some of these creeps?* she would say, when they got home at the end of an evening.

Ryder felt extremely uncomfortable in the jacket and tie, as they entered the main reception area. Fiona had tried to persuade him to get dressed in the formal navy blue suit and the new maroon tie that she had bought for him a few weeks previously, but that was a bridge too far. If he was going to be forced into a tie at all, then the subdued charcoal and navy check jacket along with the plain navy blue tie that he had had for twenty years was the most he was prepared to suffer in the Durban humidity. The jacket was of a lighter and softer fabric than any lounge suit could boast. Her attempts to get some colour into his outfit had failed dismally.

She had enough formal wear to cover for both of them, anyway. He told her she looked utterly stunning, and she did, in the black Sugarhill Boutique draped maxi dress with shirred waist and red ribbon trim to the sleeves, worn with simple but stylish black strappy sandals set against the elegant Jasper Conran clutch bag. He noticed the heads turning as they walked into the hall, and they certainly weren't turning for him.

Nyawula differed from Ryder in his approach to formal dress occasions. Ryder had never seen the Captain in evening dress, and he had to admit the guy looked impressively smooth and elegant in a simple no-nonsense dark navy pin-stripe two-button suit and dark maroon tie. He caught Ryder's eye as they entered, just as Fiona was touched on the shoulder by Dippenaar's wife and whisked away to meet someone that she had just been *dying for ages* to introduce to Fiona.

Abandoned by his wife, Ryder walked across to Nyawula, who had beckoned him over. He was talking to a very, very fat and very, very short man, wearing a charcoal grey Brunello Cucinelli wool, cashmere and silk-blend tuxedo with black satin lapels and stripe trim trousers. He still had his back to Ryder as Nyawula said, formally:

'Detective Ryder, I don't think you've met Major Swanepoel.'

The Major swivelled one hundred and eighty degrees on his Italian Tod's Gommino Driving Shoes with their one hundred and thirty-three rubber pebbles embedded on each sole, and put out his hand to Ryder.

'Pleased to meet you, Major Swanepoel,' said the detective.

The reply seemed to Ryder to emanate deep down on a column of air thrust upwards by a diaphragm struggling against the huge mass of weight. It rasped over tortured vocal chords and emerged as a hoarse half-whisper.

'Let's not be formal this evening, Detective Ryder. When I'm off duty, all my friends call me Vic.'

# 5 FRIDAY

**05.20.**

Ryder sat with Fiona at the kitchen table, each with a mug of coffee before them. He was dressed in the familiar black denims and khaki shirt under the dark-brown leather jacket. She wrapped up what she had been saying about the night before, and the difficulty she had had dealing with both of Ed's ex-wives.

'Anyway, I hope the two of them can put aside their differences at the funeral. It would be just too much if there was that bit of tension added to the pot. It's going to be difficult enough for everyone.'

'Sure will be.'

'You feel OK about your speech?'

'I'll be OK. Still a couple of days. Whole weekend to think about it.'

They both stared, silently, for a moment, into their mugs. Then she placed a hand on his.

'You seemed really quiet last night.'

'Really? I was OK. How do you mean? I had a good discussion over drinks with K and D, and then with Navi, and Nyawula also told me…'

'I meant when we got home.'

'Really?'

'Yes. And in the car, too.'

'Oh. Sorry. Just tired, I suppose. Tough week. Losing Ed.'

'Jeremy.'

'What?'

'Talk to me.'

'What about?'

'Jeremy. Talk to me.'

He paused. Looked at her. Thought again how extraordinarily beautiful she was without any make-up, sitting in her ancient dressing-gown. One that she had been wearing ever since they had got married. And he thought how extraordinarily beautiful she had been last night, too, with just a touch of make-up and dressed in formal black.

'Yeah. Sorry. I was just thinking.'

'About what?'

'That Major guy, I suppose.'

'Swanepoel?'

'Yeah.'

'Creep.'

'Yep.'

'I thought there was some minimum height requirement to join the police.'

'Me too.'

'I've never seen an adult so short. One that wasn't an actual dwarf, that is. He'd be taller lying on his side. What a slimeball. Couldn't take his eyes off my boobs when I came over to you.'

'Well, can't blame him, I suppose. They were at his eye level.'

'He has little piggy eyes.'

'Yep.'

'And probably a little piggy brain. What exactly were you thinking about him?'

'What?'

'You said you were distracted a moment ago because you were thinking about him.'

'Oh. Yes. I don't know. Just something about him. I don't know.'

She thought for a moment, cradled her coffee in her hands, and nodded.

'Yes. I must admit I was surprised at him talking so freely about you and Navi.'

'What?'

'You told me on Wednesday night that the formal announcement – about you and Navi teaming up – would only be made by Nyawula on Monday, at Ed's funeral. But Swanepoel was gushing to me about how they were sure that Pillay and you would make a good team. He certainly babbles on about things, doesn't he?'

She got up, reached across for his cup and took the breakfast dishes across to the sink. Ryder stared at her. As she turned on the hot water, she looked back at him. Then she stopped as she registered his stare.

'What's wrong? Jeremy?'

His eyes remained fixed on her.

'Jeremy?'

He got up, went across to her, and pecked her on the cheek.

'Sorry. Just thinking of something I have to pick up with Navi today. Gotta go. Love you.'

'Take care. Love you.'

And Ryder was gone.


## 06.15.

Dirk was shocked into consciousness by the iPhone blaring out somewhere in the car. Where was he? As he lurched upward, pain shot through his leg. He struggled to sit upright, suddenly remembering where he was. The windscreen was misted over, as were the side windows, condensation running off all of them. Where was the phone? Whose phone was it? He stretched and squirmed right and left. The sound was coming from below. Under the driver's seat. He reached down, felt, and retrieved it. As he looked at the screen he realised that the phone must have slid from Thabethe's pocket the night before, when they had got out of the car in the forecourt.

The screen was illuminated with the caller ID: *Unknown*. He pressed the *accept* icon and answered:

'Hullo?'

He paused and repeated:

'Hullo? Hullo?'

'Dirk?' came the shocked reply. The rasping throaty voice was unmistakable.

'Jesus. Vic? Is that you, Vic?'

'Where the hell is Tony, Dirk?'

'Vic? Jesus, Vic, Tony? I dunno. I'm in trouble, Vic. The cops got me and I escaped, but I'm in trouble Vic, man...'

'Shut up, Dirk and let me talk. I heard you escaped from the hospital.'

'*Ja*, Vic but it wasn't as simple as that...'

'Shuddup, Dirk! Listen to me. You don't know where Tony is?'

'No, Vic. I been looking for him. I need him bad, Vic. I got trouble.'

'Listen to me, Dirk. Listen, dammit. Where are you now?'

'I'm in a car, Vic, round the corner from Overport. I got into trouble last night and I slept in the car. I'm in the car now. I didn't know there was this phone in the car. I don't know whose phone it is...'

'It's Tony's phone, Dirk.'

'Tony's?'

'It's Tony's phone. I just called Tony's number on my new phone. How did you get hold of Tony's phone? Did you call me on Wednesday night? Who had this phone on Wednesday night?'

'Shit, Vic. This black guy. He must have had it. He kidnapped me from hospital early yesterday. He held me in the bush all day yesterday and then he took me to Overport last night, then I escaped from him. Took his car, but didn't know about the phone until now when you called.'

'What the hell did you take him to Overport for?'

'No Vic, not me. I didn't take him, Vic. He took me. I didn't take him there, Vic, I promise. He knew the place. He had been there before. He took me there, Vic. I swear, Vic. I would never...'

'Who is he? Do you know him?'

'Yes, Vic. I met him once before. With Jannie. He has these eyes...'

'The guy who sold guns to Jannie! What's his name? I forget his...'

'That's the one, Vic. A bad guy, Vic. He's a really bad guy, Vic. I think he killed Jannie...'

'Listen to me, Dirk. I need a man, now, to help me with some things.'

'Vic, I got to tell you, I'm sorry, Vic, I got my knee messed up. I can hardly walk, Vic. Can only just about drive.'

'Listen to me, Dirk, goddammit. I need you. Now. I need you to get over to... remember the Argyle Road house you checked out for me in the beginning? We went for that house and we finally got it. We've started operating there. But we don't have the stuff yet. I can't find Tony so I need you, Dirk. I need you to get over there.'

'Vic, I can get over there. But I don't know what I can do to help. I'm like a cripple, Vic. I can't walk. I got to get some help.'

'I only need you to be there, Dirk. There will be no action. I need someone there this morning at exactly 11.00 am, Dirk. Then again in the afternoon, a couple more times. Big trucks arriving. I need someone to be there for the deliveries, and to hand over some papers, and to sign for the stuff. It can't be me that signs, Dirk. I can't find Tony so it has got to be you. And you have to let them bring the stuff into the house. I'll leave a key to the gate and a key to the front door, both of them on top of the right rear wheel – listen to me Dirk – I'll put the keys on top of the right rear wheel of a White Ford Escort Mark 2 Van, that I'll leave outside the house, somewhere in Tenth Avenue. Depends where I find parking at that time of day. Look for the van. You got me, Dirk? 11.00 am!'

'I got you, Vic.'

'Tell me what you heard, Dirk. Repeat it to me.'

'11.00 am. Keys on top of the right back wheel. White Ford Escort van. I'll be there. You can count on me, Vic. I'll lie low for a couple of hours and then drive over.'

'You say you got the black guy's car? You better dump that once you get to the Argyle house. Some distance away from the house, Dirk. We don't want snooping around his car. The bunch of keys on top of the Escort's wheel will include the keys to the van itself, as well as the garage and side door leading to the back of the house. Once you have the keys, and after the delivery, you can use the van for yourself. There's no trace back to us.'

'OK, Vic. Thanks, Vic.'

'After the delivery stay low for a bit until I reach you on this number. You OK?'

'Yes, Vic. You can count on me.'

'I'll remember this, Dirk. We can look after you, you know?'

'Yes, Vic. I know that.'

'We can talk later, Dirk. Got a pen or pencil or something? I want you to write down a cell-phone number.'

Dirk searched through the cubbyhole and found nothing, cursed, looked in the storage space in the side of the driver's door, found nothing, cursed again, then in the equivalent space in the passenger's door he found the stub of a pencil.

'I got a pencil, Vic. Shoot.'

Vic called out the number and Dirk scribbled it down on the box of anti-inflammatories, the only place where he could find a white space big enough on which to write.

'Call me on this number when the delivery is in the house, Dirk.'

'Will do, Vic. I'll be there at 11.00 am.'

'Don't let me down, Dirk.'

And Vic was gone. Dirk breathed a little more easily. Maybe there was going to be a way out of this after all. Vic would look after him. *Where the hell is Tony?* He opened the driver's window and let in some fresh air. Turned on the wipers to clean the windscreen. Then reached into the bag for the rag that Thabethe had used to gag him. His mind raced as he wiped the rag back and forth over the moisture that had collected on the inside of the windscreen. *Why did he save this rag and the rope and just kick my pyjamas and dressing gown under the bush out there? The bastard was planning some more bad stuff for me!* He shook his head to clear the cobwebs.

He keyed into the phone the number he had written down, hit the button to dial then killed it immediately so that it wouldn't connect. Needing now only to press once for the redial next time, he put the phone in his pocket and then paused a moment while trying to work out the geography. Overport to Argyle. Argyle Road was no longer Argyle Road. He knew that. It was now Sandile Thusi, *whoever the hell that was.* Then he returned the driver's seat to its normal position, turned the key in the ignition, and let the engine run while he thought through what he was going to do until about 10.00 am, when he would have to start making his way over to the Argyle Road house. There was one major thing he had to do. He had to get the hinges on the knee brace re-set by someone who knew what he was doing. He couldn't survive the day in this condition without some support for his leg. And he knew the place in Westville that would help him. He could already picture the conversation. *Playing rugby again at your age, Dirk?* This is the second time in two years the guy at Propaedic would help him with a knee-brace. He would arrive, say it was an emergency, and pay cash. Like last time, when Tony had advised him. This time he was on his own.

*Where the hell is Tony?*

**06.55.**

Pillay and Ryder sat in his car outside the station. Ryder thumped the steering wheel with his right hand.

'I couldn't put my finger on what it was about the bastard that was bothering me. I thought it was just that I couldn't get Ed out of my head, and that I was just distracted all the time he was talking to me, but I should have listened more carefully to what he was saying. I suppose I also couldn't get my head away from how gross he looks. Fiona took an instant dislike to the creep. She picked up the contradiction immediately, last night, but only mentioned it to me this morning. If Nyawula was so determined to keep things quiet about you and me until he could make a formal announcement at Ed's funeral on Monday, she said, why was it that Swanepoel was shooting off his big mouth about it last night?'

'Was he talking openly? About you and me?'

'Yes, dammit. He told Fiona that he thought you and I would make a good team. Fiona only mentioned it this morning.'

'Was there anyone else within hearing?'

'Fiona wasn't sure, but she got the sense that he had no problem at all in just talking freely about it.'

'Do you think he's the one who...'

'He *must* be, Navi. He's the one who's been giving Nyawula problems, too, with all sorts of things over the last couple of months. Remember the constant complaints we picked up from those random comments made by Nyawula? And by Piet? Swanepoel's constant interference, always asking for reports, wanting information, getting his fingers into nitty gritty that shouldn't concern him. Drove Nyawula up the wall.'

'Time to see Nyawula?'

'Maybe. Maybe we need to tighten our facts a little before we go making accusations.'

'What do you suggest?'

'Let's try and find whether Swanepoel's hassling of Nyawula had any particular themes. Was he hassling on petty administrative details because he just wanted to be on the black Captain's back? Or does he have some other agenda? Let's go and see Piet. No-one knows the Captain's thinking as well as Piet.'

'OK. Good idea.'

'Piet's inside right now. Poor bastard. He was saying last night that he'll be up to his ears in it from first thing this morning, because he has to account for a lot of the follow-up from the function. Let's go.'

They left the Camry and strode over to the front door of the station. Before they could mount the stairs, Cronje opened the door, mug of coffee in one hand and a cigarette between his lips.

'Talk of the devil,' said Ryder.

'What's that, Jeremy?'

'Nothing Piet, we were coming in to talk to you. Got a minute?'

'*Ja!* Definitely! Anything to take me away from the stuff I got to do for the Captain. Follow-up from last night...'

'We need to ask you a couple of things that might sound strange. Hope you don't mind.'

'No problem, Jeremy. Shit, you guys look worried.' They walked back into the parking area and stood next to the Camry.

'Piet, can we ask you a bit about the Captain's problems with the Major?' said Pillay.

'Major Swannie? That *oke*? *Ja*, no problem, Navi. He calls me nearly every day, sometimes a couple of times a day, always asking for the Captain. Drives the Captain crazy. And me, too, I'm telling you. The Captain is always getting me to tell him that he's out and that he'll call back later, even when, you know, he's in the office. He just can't spend all the time ...'

'Does the Major ever tell you what he's looking for?'

'*Ja*, definitely, Jeremy, he's always asking me details about investigations, what reports are coming in, when so-and-so is expected to report on such-and-such, and have we collected the evidence, and when's this going to court, and stuff like that, you know? Captain goes ballistic.'

'Sorry to ask you this stuff, Piet, but it's important. We'll be speaking to the Captain, but we want to make sure we're on the right track with him. Are there any things that the Major seems more interested in than others? Like, does he have a particular interest in homicide, or car theft, or...'

'Gambling, no question.'

'What?'

'Gambling, Jeremy. Casino stuff. No question. Captain and I once joked about it. Captain said maybe the Major's looking for tips on what to put down on red next time he goes down to the Wild Coast.'

'How long has he been interested in gambling cases?'

'*Ag*, Navi, even long before your time here, you know. Even before he moved up with his promotion, you know, we used to joke about it. Way back in 2008 I remember one day here in the station when he was really *gatvol* with the government bringing in the Gambling Amendment Act that year. He was complaining about how the government was trying to control everyone's lives, and now this new Act, and stuff like that. The *okes* began to joke that he must be running a string of casinos and was scared he might have to pay taxes. *Ja*, even now, I tell you, the Major is always asking what's happening in the gambling world and who are we tracking and are we busting anyone, and that kind of stuff. Funny thing is...'

'What?' Pillay was on the verge of snapping her fingers in front of Cronje's face as he seemed to drift off.

'Funny thing is, you know, that we should be speaking about this just when I was wondering, before you two arrived just now, I was wondering...'

'What, Piet?' Jeremy demanded.

'You know when we were writing up the stuff on both those two young guys on Tuesday, the one who died near Nomivi's Tavern and the fat one in Montpelier Road who Navi put in hospital?'

'Yes, what about them?' asked Pillay.

'It was you, Navi, who told us in your notes on those two guys about the knuckle-dusters and the daggers that each of them had on them.'

'Yes? So?'

'The notes on their files also mention that they each had a gold Suncoast casino card.'

## 08.30.

Thabethe sat with the contents of the red box spread out on the floor in front of him. It wasn't the cash that interested him: it amounted to no more than half the amount he had retrieved from the Mercedes. Small change, as far as he was concerned, compared to what he thought this would all lead to. Of more interest to him was the large pile of casino cards – black, gold and platinum – which he had stacked together and which he assumed might be worth trying out later in the casino to see what credits they might each hold.

But even the cards paled into insignificance once he had scrutinised the papers from the red box and had separated them into batches. One batch now held his attention. It comprised what he could identify as six delivery notes stapled to invoices and then scrawled upon, variously, in pen or pencil. The scrawls were of enticing significance. *165k. 420k. 185k. 210k. 145k. 375k.* If he was reading things correctly, the owner of the red box was either planning deliveries to, or had already made deliveries to, six different parties and had received or was going to receive payments amounting to one and a half million rands.

Thabethe sat back, thinking through the possibilities. Then he set to work looking more closely at the other papers. A document entitled *Customs External Policy State Warehouse - effective date 22 February* was of only marginal interest and he threw it aside – until he read a few other papers, each stamped *DA 68* in the top right hand corner. After perusing the contents of these forms he came back to the eleven pages of the policy document and skimmed through it with growing interest. He began to ponder the meaning of phrases like 'uncleared imported goods,' 'goods detained subject to compliance,' 'goods seized,' 'disposal of the goods condemned and forfeited to the State.' He rifled through the other forms again, looking at heavy exclamation marks in pencil against one definition: *Cargo manifest: A listing of goods comprising cargo... carried by a means of transport. The cargo manifest describes the particulars of the goods, e.g. transport document number, consignors, consignees, marks and numbers, number of packages, etc.*

Why would someone want to be on top of these boring definitions? Why mark something like that as worthy of attention?

Thabethe skimmed further and soon began to think that the little red box functioned also as a proud achievement record for its owner, because he then found some interesting slides torn from photocopies of *National Gambling Board* slideshow presentations, one of them under the heading *Confiscated Gambling Machines - F2006*, in which each of four quarters of Financial Year 2006 displayed comparative provincial statistics. It was clear from the bar chart that KwaZulu-Natal ranked second to North West, and a wise guy remark scribbled across the page at this point read '*second to N. West, guys!!!*' Another, headed *Case Convictions - F2006*, reflected an outright win for Limpopo province and a nil recording for KZN, which had prompted a comment in the same handwriting of '*well done, men!*' A slide entitled *Admission of Guilt - F2006* showed KZN top of the list with no competitors coming near. There was no comment scrawled on this slide.

Neither were there any handwritten comments on a slide headed *Destroyed Gambling Machines - F2006* that showed KZN way ahead of the competition. But there were three prominent thick exclamation marks drawn in black ink on this one. And there were no comments on a different kind of slide, a summary slide listing all provinces under the heading *Illegal*

*Gambling Statistics 1 April 2008 - 31 March 2009,* that showed KZN leading the pack on the line item *destroyed gambling machines* with a number pegged at two hundred and sixty-two, higher than any other province. At the end of this line was a large asterisk drawn in pencil.

Thabethe began to get the picture. This information covered more than a decade. The red box was the key he had been looking for.

But to use the key effectively he had to find the fat Afrikaner called Dirk, and the guy he reported to.

## 09.35.

Vic had breathed a sigh of relief when he put down the phone to Dirk. Tony's disappearing like that was a real problem. Left him with no-one reliable. He had to be careful of his own exposure here. He was too easily recognisable. Couldn't afford to be seen at the Argyle house. But unless Tony showed up in time, he would have to do it. He could drop the van and the keys there himself, then walk round to Butcher Boys or somewhere like that and get the hell out of the place with a taxi. No. Maybe better to call a taxi to pick him up near the house at a fixed time. He can't afford to be seen walking around the area.

Vic was furious. Tony had never let him down before. What was his game? Or had he genuinely lost his phone? Maybe he's had an accident? Maybe he's in hospital! He began to realise how much he had come to depend on Tony. Tony had been the one to find Big Red, and had commissioned the yacht, organised the crew, put together the papers and passports, got everything in shape for a dawn departure on Sunday. He had always handled all the paperwork, signed for things, dispatched and paid, nailed the guys who reneged, rewarded the guys who played along. Above all, he was the guy who received the cash. Without Tony, who was going to receive the cash? Can't be Dirk. Or can it? Maybe if I do it myself. But then I'm identified as the guy who handled cash. Never done it this way before. What am I going to do without Tony? How the hell am I going to find the red box? Should I have a discussion with Big Red? Tony had said they'd worked together in the past, and that he could be trusted. Do I bring on a new guy at this late stage? No. Maybe when we're out at sea. Find out more about Big Red. Maybe he could be the new guy. If Tony is out of it.

The tightening of the whole industry by the Gambling Board guys had been a signal that it was time to quit. After more than a decade it was time. One last batch, and he could be done with it. Melt away and cut all ties. A million and a half to add to his pension pot. The Argyle operation was the last one. At least for a while. Maybe for good.

If Tony was out for whatever reason, he would have to use Dirk.

He got back on the phone. Calls to confirm times for Saturday's collections. This is to confirm. The goods will be there. As planned, Saturday. Cash. I'll be there in person.

\*

After another interminable wait, Vic had finally given up on Tony. Later on he would look into whatever had happened to the guy, and do whatever he could to retrieve the red box, but for now he had to deliver the white van and the keys. He found parking at a spot about thirty metres from the corner, and walked up to the gate. Checking that he wasn't being observed, he opened the gate and moved into the property. He locked the gate behind him and moved to the front door, unlocked it and went inside.

He was out again within a few minutes. Everything was as he had been promised it would be. Lots of space. Ready for the next round of deliveries. And for Saturday's dispatches. He locked the front door, locked the garden gate behind him, and waddled back to the white Ford Escort van. He placed all the keys on the top of the rear right wheel, ensuring that they were balanced safely and out of sight. Then he walked down Tenth Avenue to the corner of Clarence to meet his taxi.

## 10.45.

Ryder, Pillay and Nyawula sat together in the Captain's office. Nyawula was incandescent, but controlling it amazingly well, thought Ryder, as he and Pillay added further pieces of information.

'Navi and I have also checked out the gold cards. The Afrikaner kid and the Montpelier fat boy were probably given the cards from the same supply pack on the same day from the same counter.'

'You couldn't get a closer match if you tried,' added Pillay, and Ryder continued.

'We've got Koeks and Dipps under cover in Suncoast to see what they can find out, but they know to go very carefully in case someone has already been alerted down there. They're only there for an hour or so because they're then going to the hospital to follow up on a lead down there.'

'Thanks, Jeremy,' said Nyawula. 'Now wait for this, both of you. Which you will simply not believe. Bear with me while I take you through this.'

Ryder and Pillay exchanged surprised glances.

'I received a phone-call just before the two of you came in. Some truly fascinating information from ballistics. It was you who raised the question on Tuesday, Jeremy, in the discussion with me and Koekemoer and Dippenaar, about the homicide from last year. The one in the bush next to Suncoast, Navi. Last year's one. Jeremy thought that there might just possibly be a connection between that case and the third Z88 that you yourself identified on Monday when you were looking at Sunday night's homicide with the tourist. That weapon, too, was found, as you know, on the beach. Near some bush. Not just any bush. In the bush near Suncoast Casino.'

'Don't tell me...' said Ryder.

'No, Jeremy. Not what you're thinking. Last year's guy was killed with a 9mm fired from a Z88, that's for sure. Sunday night's guy died, we know, with a 9mm fired from the Z88 that Navi identified. But the clever woman in ballistics...'

'Nadine Salm?'

'The same, Jeremy. I'm beginning to think she's the best in the business. She assures me that the bullets in those two corpses don't match to the same Z88.'

'So, what are we...'

'Something even more interesting than what you were hoping for. Nadine tells me that she looked further into the other stuff we've been dealing with – I love these guys in ballistics who love their work – and she found that the guy who died in the bush last year was killed not by the same Z88 that finished off the tourist on Sunday night, but by one of the two Z88s that were used in The Grove killings on Monday morning.'

'Shit. Sorry, I mean, *omigod*,' said Pillay.

'How very interesting!' said Ryder.

'So what we have here, guys, is something that connects Thabethe via three of the four Vektor Z88s that disappeared from the station when he left, to a homicide last year outside Suncoast Casino, a homicide this Sunday night outside Suncoast Casino, and two homicides at The Grove involving money which we can trace back to Suncoast Casino. Put all of that together with what you two have just told me about gold casino cards found on the two creeps from Nomivi's Tavern and Montpelier Road, and we have the common factor here being *casino*.'

'Add to that, Captain, the money found by K and D in the Mercedes at Overport,' added Pillay.

'And the ballistics on the Desert Eagle linking the Overport guy back to Ed,' said Ryder.

All three of them paused, as if in deference to the memory of Trewhella, as these linkages fell into place. Then Nyawula picked up the momentum again.

'Now, back to what you were telling me when you came in about Major Swanepoel's interest in gambling. How about this? Swanepoel kept on hassling me about the Z88s all week, from Monday first thing. Not least of all at the function last night. Can you believe it? I had been wondering why. I should have stopped to think through why he was pushing me for details, but the prick has irritated me for so long that I lose perspective when dealing with the guy. Anyway, I'm starting to join a few other dots in my head – I have to be careful here because a lot of it is just circumstantial – but we have lots of dirt in the past on illegal gambling operations, as you know. This ranges from the Head of the Organised Crime Unit being acquitted after spending years in claims and counter-claims, to all those rumours – *none of them proved* – about the guys who had connections with the old cops at Wentworth and King's Rest, and also through one detective at Durban North with dubious friends. And we think there might be some other cops in Durban North, lower down in the system at constable level, with dubious connections, too. This thing, I'm saying, could be much bigger than any of us know. On the other hand we have to be very careful about one thing. We've done some work in the past on this and the big operators come up completely clean. There might be some individuals within their operations who are operating illegally, but the organisations themselves always come up clean. Suncoast Casino we know is fully compliant. It's the guys operating *outside* the Gambling Board guidelines that we need to find. And it looks increasingly as if Swanepoel is connected way outside those guidelines.'

Both Pillay and Ryder noted how the Captain's cool control at the start of this speech started eroding as he progressed and he grew more and more angry until he reached the final sentence. He then paused, and added:

'The fat prick. I've got his number now. Damn! I should have picked it up earlier. I should have stopped to think, the time I got into a really heated argument with him about the National Commissioner and the Scorpions and the Public Protector. In retrospect he was far more agitated that time than he should have been, about what was in essence merely a difference of emphasis between us.'

'What was the debate, Captain?' offered Ryder.

'I think I said something a bit crass and undergraduate about the anti-corruption agencies being threatened by the very institutions and people who are supposed to uphold the law and protect the Constitution. I found myself lecturing him on Chapter Nine institutions. Perhaps a bit naively academic on my part, I admit, but I remember being really surprised at his outburst. We had been talking about Phiyega's announcement – way back in July 2013, I think – at about the same time that the minister was talking about a new general public anti-corruption bureau. The National Commissioner announced, around about the same time, plans for the re-establishment of the old police Anti-Corruption unit that ran from 1996 to 2002.'

'Before being closed down by Selebi,' said Ryder.

'Before he got bust for his own special brand of corruption,' Pillay threw in.

'So I was arguing with Swanepoel about how we move from an Independent Complaints Directorate to an Independent Police Investigative Directorate, and I probably allowed myself to run away with it, which prompted his outburst.'

'It sounds, with wisdom after the event, as if he let down his guard with you,' said Ryder.

'I think back, now, on why that would have happened. I remember I got a bit carried away by saying that we had the best anti-corruption legislation in the world but simply lacked the calibre of people to enforce it. I was depressed, I think, because I had learned just a day or two before the exchange that once again Transparency International was ranking us way down the list on the corruption index, and I had despaired yet again about how that reflected on all of us. Maybe I hit the wrong chord with him because I mentioned, in the argument, that our own internal police audits told us that of about fifteen hundred serious offence convictions for police corruption far too many were in senior ranks. What did he reply? That given the size of the organisation that was only a small percentage of bad apples! He was right, of course, in a purely statistical sense, but it was what I said next that triggered his big reaction.'

'What was that, Captain?' asked Pillay.

'I told him that what the statistics missed – and I still believe this emphatically – what they missed was the fact that these convictions of corrupt police officers completely omitted all the countless undetected guys who were both cops and crooks, running their own corrupt businesses on the side while functioning as squeaky-clean cops but still using their police connections for manipulating their private business. The statistics would never tell us the full picture, I said to him.'

'That must have hit home quite sharply, given what we now know about him,' said Ryder.

'I wish I had had the conversation on video, because I think you're right. It was that single moment, in hindsight, that exposes him for what he really is, and I missed the significance of it. In retrospect, I should have left that meeting and gone straight out to do some research on our friend the Major. But all I did was wind down the discussion with some excuse and get the hell out of his obnoxious presence.'

Nyawula paused.

'OK colleagues. Now I have to be ultra-careful. Before we move on Swanepoel I need to get to the Cluster Commander. Who I happen to know can't stand our fat friend. He'll probably want to take me to a discussion with the Provincial Commissioner. There's no way something like this can be bust by us without someone up there knowing what's happening before we go in with all guns blazing. So let's just sketch through a couple of lines of action here. If it all comes together then we can move tomorrow. I can't see it happening today.'

He took them through what he had in mind. The two detectives added a few tentative observations of their own, drawing on some of the stuff they had discussed with Cronje in the car-park. Within minutes they had agreed some lines of action and enquiry. Ryder sketched out a quick plan of action for himself and Pillay for the next two hours. They would be going their separate ways and then coming back together to join things up. Nyawula agreed, but added another task.

'I hate to throw this at the two of you, but there's an additional chore that's needed from each of you.'

'What's that, Captain?' asked Pillay.

'Both of you were involved in *actions resulting in death* this week. There are IPID forms we have to complete. They're on their way over, and if you can complete them sometime this afternoon that would be good. Jeremy, you just need to report on your guy at Wilson's Wharf. I'll do Ed's two guys, and a separate report on the guy he wounded. Navi, you need to do the guy in Overport. Sorry, both. Has to be done.'

'No problem, Captain. Navi and I can get back here in an hour or two and do them then.'

They then took their leave of Nyawula. As they passed through the outer room and made for the door to the cars, Cronje whispered to them.

'Sounds like the Major is going to *kak off* now that the Captain...' He was interrupted by Nyawula's voice booming from the interior.

'Sergeant Cronje! A word, please.'

'Yes, sir. Coming, sir!'

The two detectives chuckled as Cronje brushed past them.

'Good luck, Piet,' whispered Pillay. 'The Captain's on a mission. I've never seen him so determined.'

'You can say that again, Pillay!' boomed the Captain's voice.

Pillay was startled, much to Ryder's enjoyment. As they descended the stairs into the car park she blurted out in astonishment:

'How the hell did he hear that? He's got ears like your dog, Jeremy. Unless the place has been miked up.'

'Don't whisper near the guy, Navi. He's very sharp. Fiona's learned that, too. Let's go.'

They made for the Camry.

## 11.10.

Dirk was in agony. The painkillers were supposed to be taken every four hours but he was in unbearable pain again every two hours. He sat on the low wall in the back garden area of the Argyle house, as Tony called it, catching his breath and watching as the workmen delivered the equipment.

There had been no problem getting the hinges on the knee brace adjusted. Exactly the same process as the previous time. And enduring the questions from the guy who talked the hind leg off of a donkey. *Stupid. Yes, I agree. No more rugby from now on.* Forced merriment. It was unbearable having to make conversation with the guy, but he did know his stuff, that's for sure, and Dirk finally left, having had clear though extremely lengthy instructions on how to manage the hinges in the brace for the purpose of driving, which he would definitely keep to an absolute minimum, he promised. *Why doesn't the guy just stop talking and let me get away?* Yes, he agreed that he should have gone back to the hospital for them to do it, and he would, but for now he just wanted some adjustment to ease the pressure. Yes, he would see a doctor again as soon as he could. Yes, it would be an *orthopod*, not just a GP. Definitely, he would not play rugby again any time soon.

He had arrived at the entrance to the Argyle house in Tenth Avenue in time but had been in far too much pain to heed Vic's words about parking far away from the house. There was no way he was going to hobble a block or two with this knee. It was bad enough parking thirty metres down the road.

He'd locked the Ballade and pocketed the keys, then limped down to the house, retrieved the bunch of keys from the wheel position on the white Escort van, clicked the remote for the garage door, and entered the property. The van needed to remain in the street, because he knew there would be lots of activity in the garage for the rest of the day.

He had waited no longer than ten minutes, apologised to the man in charge of delivering the hardware for making him wait outside for a few minutes while he opened the garage, opened the kitchen door and the security gate, and then sat on a low garden wall inside while the delivery truck moved in. Once in, he had clicked the remote to lower the garage door so that the offloading wasn't visible from the street.

He sat on the wall, checking off the items as the heavy crates were moved in one by one by four burly workers. He told the main guy to move them down the passage and stack them into the front room. He sat on the wall checking off the crates on a list, trying desperately to find a position to ease the pain in his leg, and wishing that they would move faster. He desperately needed to tell Tony that he couldn't manage with his leg. He would need a few weeks off. The cops would be looking for him. He needed to get away. Maybe Vic could use him for work in the Cape or Gauteng. Whatever Vic decided, he needed some time off. He couldn't go on like this, on painkillers.

After what seemed an eternity the truck was emptied, Dirk signed the papers, handed over an envelope, got the guy to sign a receipt, confirmed the arrangement for the second consignment which would be there at 15.00 promptly, opened the garage door with the remote, and watched them depart before lowering the door again. He moved in agony to the house, and lay down flat on his back in the passageway, trying to find a position that would allow at least some release from the throbbing pain.

## 12.20.

Big Red sat on the turquoise chaise lounge, an expensive but tastelessly upholstered semi-couch that had once been advertised in a luxury furniture store in The Pavilion in Westville as a *classic authentic French style* piece of home furniture. It had been produced in Hangzhou and sold, finally, at almost ten times its first price after it had worked its way through all the retail stages. All around him in the sumptuously furnished room were the accoutrements of ostentation and indulgence, exhibiting enormous cost but little taste.

'I suppose while I'm at sea you won't be moving away much from my Lazyboy, hey, Ben?' he said, as he shaped and stacked on his knee the pile of more than thirty A-5 pages, upon each of which he had been scribbling various notes and prices.

Opposite him sat a thin and dirty man aged about thirty years who looked like a refugee from the sixties, with greasy shoulder-length hair caught by a rubber band in a ponytail, and facial hair that belonged at the first Woodstock Festival. His rheumy eyes were those of a much older man, and reflected a brain that an observer might conclude had been burned dry by years of inhaling a range of different corrosive substances. He was reclining in a *Legendary La-z-Boy Gizmo Recliner.* The recliner had originally attracted Big Red partly because it came fitted as standard with a cool box under the left arm pad and a full ten-point built-in massage system. Ben reached down for a bottle of Castle Lager as he replied.

'*Yissus,* man, my favourite chair in the whole universe, Red. It was a *bakgat* purchase, my *china.*'

He added an unnecessary guffaw after his reply, showing grossly discoloured teeth. Before slurping from the bottle he removed from his left ear the earphone of the MP3 player that was plugged into the audio connections on the side of the recliner. He snuggled deeper into the Full Grade A Brown Mocca Leather as he brought the bottle to his lips and slurped loudly.

'OK, Ben. I've done all the pages. When I come back tomorrow night I want all of the stuff ready in one box, with one of these pages attached to each bundle.'

'Sure thing, Red, my old *tjommie.*'

'I'll be here after dinner, between eight and nine. We can talk through final arrangements and then I'll take the stuff to the yacht just before midnight.'

'I'll be ready, *bru.* You think the stuff will sell?'

'I reckon the guys in Maputo have their own version of *nyaope,* but from what I've heard this stuff is much stronger than anything else that goes down there.'

'No question. I thought I knew all the Durban *gif* before I found this stuff. This batch is amazing, Red. Really *kif.* But you gotta be careful, hey? After one minute you can be in a real *dwaal,* you know?'

'On the other hand, once the guys are hooked they'll pay anything, right?'

'*Struesbob* Red. I reckon you're gonna sell at double the price the *dronkgats* pay here.'

'Well, if it works, I'm going to open a whole new shipping lane between here and Mozambique.'

'Does your secret *pallie* know you won't be just playing sailor to him tomorrow? You think he'll *sug* if he finds out you're running your own business on the same trip? Does he know you'll be doing stuff of your own?'

'He doesn't know yet. But as soon as we're out of SA waters I'll tell him. From what I've heard he's loaded, and I think I can talk him into coming in with me. Buy a share, you know? Maybe with his bucks we can grow the business? The guy's well connected with the cops, and I hear he's got his own funny business on the side, so he's not so clean, hey, Ben? Funny, I got a feeling when I was talking to him yesterday that he might even be talking to me soon about a business proposal of his own. Maybe we can do both: me help him with whatever stuff he's selling, and him come in with me selling *nyaope*.'

'You *scheme*? Really? And what about me, Red?'

'Hey, *china*. You were the one who first told me about *nyaope*, remember? I'm not going to cut you loose.'

'*Ja, struesbob*, hey? I just wish you would try a hit with the stuff yourself, Red.'

'Not for me, Ben. I'm happy to let the guys smoke the stuff. I'll just trade it. It'll rot the brains, man. You should slow down, yourself. You're too deep into it, Ben.'

'*Ja*, I know, hey? You sound just like my *boet*, man. But it's so *lekker*, man, Red. Anyway, don't worry, *china*. While you're away I won't be getting into the stuff too much. I'll stick to the beer.'

'Don't get up to any stuff while I'm away, Ben. Don't pull that stuff you did on Sunday night, OK? Selling *nyaope* from *my* boat to those four *tsotsis*. From *my* bloody boat!'

'*Yissus, s*orry, hey, Red. I didn't know they would go and cause that *gemors* across the road. I crapped myself the next morning with all the cops around, hey?'

'That's why I say, Ben. That stuff is dangerous, man. You shouldn't have sold to those guys. There are *okes* out there who take the stuff just so they can go out and kill and rape. I heard some guy being interviewed, and he told the guy on the radio just that. *I take nyaope because it makes me feel strong so I can fight anyone. Jeez,* stay away from guys like that, man. What the hell are you selling to creeps like that for? And right under the nose of the guys in the yacht club!'

'I dunno, Red. Someone must have told them where they could get some *nyaope*. They woke me up and got me going before I even knew what I was doing. The *ous* actually told me, hey, that they had been looking all night for some and then someone told them we had some *kif* stuff on the boat. I didn't go looking for them. They just arrived, man. Woke me up and said they needed some of the stuff and they heard I had the best stuff and all. They were scary *okes* but they had the *geld*, hey, so I thought I'd just sell them some, quickly, and let them go. They even came back a short while later – I think to get some more – but I pretended there was no-one on board and they went away again. When I heard the next day what they did to those people in The Grove I *poeped* myself. I wouldn't have sold to those guys if I knew they were going to go and rob someone and kill them, promise, Red.'

'Well I hope it's a bloody lesson to you, Ben. That's the last time I let you alone to look after my boat. Next time I need you to do that, I'll make sure you have someone with you. *Yissus,* man! Selling to people you don't know! How damn stupid!'

'I'm sorry, hey. Promise I won't do something like that again, Red.'

'I'm taking no chances, Ben. This whole week, since that stuff on Monday morning, there've been cops snooping around Wilson's Wharf. That's why I moved the stuff here until tomorrow. These cops are taking *nyaope* more seriously than anything, and I'm watching my back all the time in case they bring their sniffer dogs. If those four guys heard about us selling the stuff from a boat, then there's a good chance that whoever told them will tell the cops too. From now on we load the stuff onto the yacht only a couple of hours before we sail. No more stocking it at the yacht club.'

'OK, Red. I got you. I'm with you, hey?'

'OK, Ben. I'm off. I'll see you tomorrow night. Tomorrow we start ratcheting up the business.'

## 14.20.

Ryder and Pillay were in Cronje's office struggling to complete their part of the forms required by the Independent Police Investigative Directorate after their *actions resulting in death* during the week.

'More forms. I can't stand it Jeremy. *Cause of death*: I stood on his throat, your honour, because I was sick of the crap he was talking.'

'Don't think it will fly, Navi.'

'Which one, then? I got these options: *suicide*, or *during apprehension*, or *in transit with SAPS vehicles*, or *self-defence*, or *during escape*, or *due to motor vehicle accident*, or *unknown* or *other*.'

'Why don't you tick *suicide*? The guy took you on in hand-to-hand combat. I suppose that could count as suicide.'

'Very funny. I'll just tick off *self-defence*. What are you going to put for your guy at Wilson's Wharf? You shot him in the throat, didn't you? Think they're going to start asking why we go for the throat, the two of us? *Because we don't like what people say to us, your honour. So what is it that you are trying to say to me right now, your honour?*'

'Here we go, Navi. Here's one for you. *Classify deceased*: was your deceased *suspect*, or *sentenced*, or *witness protection*, or a*waiting trial*, or *mental patient*?'

'Definitely mental. Anyone who takes me on must be mental.'

'Agreed. I can hear Piet coming. Smoker's cough, if ever I heard one. Let's get done with this, Navi. I want to take a look at the stuff that K and D are bringing in from the parking opposite Addington Hospital.'

'Oh? What have they got?'

'Sorry. Meant to tell you. Piet called me at lunch-time and said that Koeks told him they have CCTV showing our one-legged hospital patient being pushed in a wheelchair over to a Silver Honda Ballade in Prince Street. By a kindly SAPS constable in a nice uniform. Friendly constable apparently is a bit absent-minded, too, and left the wheelchair in the middle of the parking bay.'

Cronje arrived at the door, having finished his smoke and tea in the car park.

'Here, Piet. We've done as much as we can on the IPID forms. Can you let the Captain have them?'

'Sure, Jeremy. K and D have just arrived. They're parking. You can use the Captain's office. It's free for at least another hour or two.'

'Thanks, Piet.'

Koekemoer and Dippenaar arrived as Ryder and Pillay were moving into the inner office. There was a hubbub of greetings and exchanges and they settled down around Nyawula's desk to look at the photos the two new arrivals had brought with them.

'Good images,' said Pillay.

'Amazing, isn't it?' said Dippenaar, 'when you really want them to be good they're usually so grainy you can't see anything, but in this case, look – have you ever seen such a clear number plate?'

They pored through the photos, exchanged views, enjoyed some merriment at Pillay's expense about the injured man in the wheelchair, and all agreed without hesitation that the so-called Constable Dlamini was in fact one Skhura Thabethe.

'Have you got anyone looking at that number plate, Koeks?'

'Done, Jeremy. They're doing a trace. I already had a call saying there's something funny about the papers and the licensing, but they're onto it and I should get another call soon.'

'*Yissus*! Just look at that bastard. I could never stand the *oke*. Me and the Captain, we were in competition about who hated the guy most.'

'If you can bring him in, Dipps, you'll be Nyawula's buddy for life,' said Pillay. '*Jeez*, I've never seen the Captain so the *moer* in as when he talks about Thabethe.'

Koekemoer's iPhone rang, and he answered.

'*Ja!* That's right. No, no problem. OK. OK. OK. *Ja*, OK. No. I see. Can you check out further and see what you can get? *Ja*. OK. Thanks, I appreciate it.'

As he closed off the call, the others waited expectantly.

'Guys, a really *lekker* piece of information. They still haven't got the full picture, but maybe you'd like to know that the Honda Ballade we see in the photo there was registered until a few hours ago at an address you all know. The new address is fictitious, but the old owner is a guy called Mkhize. And his address is Nomivi's Tavern.'

'*Shit*.' said Pillay.

'*Fok*.' said Dippenaar.

'How very interesting.' said Ryder.

Koekemoer told them he had got assurance that the car would be put on a police alert and unless it had been burned or sent to a chop-shop or dumped somewhere they would track it down.

'OK, guys,' said Ryder, 'we need to get out there and follow up a few things. Koeks, are you able to follow up on CCTV footage further down the track and see which way the car was heading when it left the hospital?'

'Sure, Jeremy, leave it to me, I'll get on to that right away.'

'Dipps, could you de-brief Piet so that the Captain knows what we're up to, and then get on to that idiot constable who Thabethe clearly bamboozled, and see what else you can get out of him?'

'Sure, Jeremy, no problem.'

'Thanks, guys. Navi, what about if you and I get out to Nomivi's to follow up on this Mkhize guy and then take it from there?'

'Sounds good.'

'Let's go in separate cars in case we need to split after that. Koeks, if your guys call in with a location for the car...'

'You'll be the first to hear, Jeremy.'

'Thanks, Koeks. Let's hit it, Navi.'

The office was vacated amidst fist punches and high-fives, and Ryder and Pillay strode across the car-park to their cars.

**15.05.**

Dirk repeated the process with the second delivery. Slightly more crates, slightly longer to off-load. They moved them into the second room down the passage. But when they had finished the work he was in a better frame of mind than after the morning's delivery. The papers were signed and handed over as in the previous session, and the delivery guys left, having arranged that the third and fourth – and final – deliveries of the day would be at around 6.00 pm. Maybe earlier, if the traffic was OK. *Two trucks this time*, said the lead guy.

The painkillers were having the desired effect. Dirk could treat himself to something to eat and drink. Debonairs Pizza delivery, just around the corner in Florida Road. Perfect. While he waited he hobbled through the house to have a look at the equipment, now packed into two of the rooms.

**15.20.**

Pillay and Ryder spoke to Mkhize outside the tavern. Ryder leaned back against the Camry while she stood directly in front of Mkhize, who was animatedly denying just about everything that had been suggested to him by the two detectives.

'*Hayibo* detective, not me. *Aikona!* Not Spikes. Spikes is one-time clean. Me, I'm not a *mampara*. Not me, no *shibobo*. That Thabethe is a *skabenga*! I'm telling you. Spikes does no business with *skollies*. No more. My business is clean.'

'So if we find the car,' said Ryder, 'you say it has nothing to do with you because it was sold by you to a Mr Buthelezi for cash and you have no idea where Mr Buthelezi lives, and you had never met him before he bought the car off you?'

'Is right, detective. Is right! I'm not *moegoe*! I know there is big trouble with cars. This Buthelezi, he must be a *skelm*. He is supposed to make the changes for the registration, not me. He promised me. *Eish*, is bad.'

'So if we trace the owner and we bring him back to stand here and talk to you, face to face, you're happy with that, Mr Mkhize?' said Pillay.

'Is good, detective, is good. *Ek is skrik vir niks*. Spikes is good. *Struesbob!*'

'And you can't tell us any more about Thabethe?' Ryder interjected, as he could see Mkhize preparing to extend his assurances.

'That one? *Eish*. Skhura. He is *spookgerook!* People here, we are scared of that one. Spikes has nothing to do with that one. *Tsotsi! Hayi!*'

It was fruitless. There was no way they were going to get anything more from him. They let him go and he retreated with as many obsequious assurances and gestures and genuflections and touches of an imaginary forelock as they had ever seen. They had never seen such oleaginous grovelling.

'What an unctuous creep,' said Ryder.

'Greasy slime-ball. Maybe we need to stake out this place and see what he gets up to.'

'I think you're right, Navi. Let's get K or D to help out. This guy reeks of it and I reckon he could lead us to Thabethe.'

Ryder's iPhone sounded.

'Yep. Dipps? Yeah. Fine. OK. Yes. No, not at all. No problem. OK. Look, Dipps, Navi and I had just been wondering, when you called, whether you or K could help us out with something. You called, so you get first go at the lucky dip. This is the thing...'

When he had finished with the call he briefed Pillay on what Dippenaar had told him. Nothing had come from the interview with the Constable at Addington who had been bamboozled by Thabethe. He had confirmed the physical description of Thabethe that Dipps had provided – no problem, because the eyes were the first thing the guy had mentioned – but there had been nothing else of value. Dipps would be on his way right now to take over from them at Nomivi's. He'd watch the place and tail one Spikes Mkhize for as long as was necessary.

They agreed that Pillay would stay to brief him.

Just as Ryder set off in the Camry, with Pillay remaining behind for Dippenaar, another call came in on the iPhone. He stopped, spoke briefly, then dropped the window of the Camry to tell her.

'That was Koeks. They've found the Honda Ballade. Quite close to the Montpelier house. Couple of blocks down. I'll get out there and see what I can find. The uniforms will wait till I get there. See ya.'

'OK, Jeremy. I'll let you know when Dipps takes over here.'

'OK, Navi. See you later.'

*

He was there very quickly. The two uniforms were waiting for him. After glancing at Ryder's ID, It took only seconds for one of the constables to slide his adapted *slim jim* into the rubber seal of the driver's window and free the Ballade's mechanism. As he opened the door for the detective, he proudly explained how his thirteen-year old son was the one who had made the simple modification to the *slim jim* in order to foil the manufacturer's deterrent mechanism.

'*Eish!* My son, he's a *skelm* that one. He can get into any car.'

'Useful talent to have in the family,' Ryder replied.

A couple of minutes later he had checked the vehicle throughout, while the uniforms watched. Then he sat in his own car having found nothing useful other than the torn-off piece of cardboard from the pharmaceutical box that had housed Dirk's anti-inflammatories. He looked at the cell-phone number scribbled in pencil over the chemist's label, and called in to Cronje to arrange for him to track the number without actually calling it.

Ryder checked the area quickly, doing no more than walking briskly past and glancing at the four or five properties in the vicinity of the vehicle. He arranged for the constables to remain with the Ballade until the tow-truck arrived, and then he drove off. He didn't notice the man standing in the shadow of the palms on the far side of Sandile Thusi, who had been watching since the first arrival of the two constables.

Thabethe now moved his position from under the foliage to sit on the low wall next to the palms, and stayed there throughout the next hour, watching them as they joked and smoked then helped to hitch up the Ballade to the tow-truck when it arrived. He watched the exchange of papers and signatures, and finally watched the two constables leave.

He remained where he was, eyes staring across and up Tenth Avenue as the first hint of dusk began to descend, erasing the lengthening shadows.

He did not have long to wait. He saw a large truck arrive, laden with wooden crates. It hooted outside the wide double-garage door, and after a couple of minutes the door was opened by remote control and a man hobbled out onto the brick-paved concrete apron.

The fat Afrikaner.

Thabethe watched as the truck was ushered in and the garage door closed. He was about to leave his perch across the street when suddenly the door opened again and the fat man limped out, much more energetic than he had just been. He appeared frantic. He walked a few paces up the street, into the middle of the road, peering in both directions. He had suddenly realised what was missing in the street. The Honda was gone.

Thabethe, sitting back in the shadows, was not visible to Dirk. He watched the fat man smack his forehead with the palm of his right hand. If he had been a little more proficient in languages, he might have been able to lip-read the anguished man's self-inflicted curses.

'*Fok! Doos! Jou bliksem!*'

Dirk was utterly devastated, and retreated back into the garage, the door coming down again almost instantly.

Thabethe changed his mind. He would wait a little longer.

Fifteen minutes later another truck arrived, and hooted. The garage door opened, and both the first driver and the Afrikaner came out onto the apron. It soon became clear to Thabethe what was happening. The first truck had been almost cleared, and they'd bring it out of the garage and into the road. The new truck would then not enter the garage but move onto the apron so that the cargo could be moved into the garage and not into the house.

Over the next half hour there was a lot of shouting from the workmen, complaints about the weight of the crates, some calling into the interior of the garage, and finally papers were signed and the two trucks drove off, with shouts and laughter indicating that the day's work was done and it was time for beers all around.

Thabethe crossed the street to get a different angle on the open garage and could see even before he had fully crossed, and before the garage door came down, that the garage was crammed with crates that had been offloaded from the last truck.

It grew darker.

Then the side door to the left of the garage opened and he watched as Dirk came out, limped over to the White Escort Panel Van, and drove away.

Thabethe watched and waited a little longer. Then he chose the right moment and repeated his actions from two nights ago. The barbed wire presented no problem. This time a heavy blanket provided the service previously provided by the rubberised mat from the Mini. Within seconds he was in the garden, then at the window with the loosened catch. He clambered in, and stood in the room, listening.

His eyes grew quickly accustomed to the dark, and he found himself in front of a room crammed with slot machines, of every conceivable make and size and shape, interspersed among various wooden crates containing other hidden equipment. He used the penlight to scan quickly over the room. It was impossible to estimate how many of the machines there were. He guessed at least fifty in this room alone, assuming the unopened crates contained the same machines.

He moved into the passage and into the next room. The same. Crammed full of the stuff. Then the kitchen, at the end of the passage. Also almost full. Boxes, plastic-covered slot machines, huge crates. Impossible to even access the minimal household stuff there – the dishwasher and washing-machine, and even the wash-basin were all partially obstructed by the crates.

He moved out of the kitchen back door and across the short open area to the back of the garage, and could see at a glance the same picture in the garage. He then retreated the way he had come in, finally making his way back over the wall and across the street just as the White Escort van pulled up again a few paces away from the garage door.

He drew back into the palms and watched as the fat Afrikaner clambered out of the vehicle with some difficulty, looked around to see if he was being observed and then, seeing nothing to concern him, placed something on the top of the rear wheel before limping toward the side door next to the garage, carrying a brown paper bag and what looked like a litre bottle of coke. He fiddled with keys at the door, and entered the property.

Thabethe crossed the street to check the rear wheel of the vehicle. He felt and retrieved the single key, which he could see immediately was the ignition key for the Escort. He thought for a moment, placed it back on its perch, then walked slowly back to the cover of the palms across the street.

Not tonight, he thought. This fat boy is not the man with the money. Tomorrow. All this equipment. It's not going to stay here, in this house. Maybe tomorrow. Maybe then. The big money.

He stepped into the road and flagged down a taxi.

*

Dirk's quick trip to Masinga Road for a couple of burgers and chips and a litre of coke and extras on the side were to be his only comforts during another night of pain. The one bed in the house was as uncomfortable a bed as he had ever slept in. Solace would come through food. And painkillers. Vic had promised him a big reward. Tomorrow and Sunday the stuff would be moved out, and Vic would get his money. Dirk would receive a bonus like he had never imagined possible. It was worth it.

Where was Tony? Neither he nor Vic knew where the bugger was. What was he up to?

Dirk munched and drank and mused.

## 19.15.

Dippenaar was finally rewarded. The Friday traffic had been against him getting there, and it was long past 5.30 pm by the time Pillay had filled him in and then left him. He had settled comfortably and watched the dusk descend over the neighbourhood around Nomivi's.

He watched the first *whoonga* trades of the weekend go down, and marvelled at the experience of the traders. It was almost as if they didn't really care if they were being watched by anyone, because they had the moves down perfectly. Passing car slows down. Young ten-year-old kid goes across. After a quick exchange he tells the driver to move down to a designated spot. Packet passed from driver to second kid. Second kid whistles. Car drives on another thirty paces. Older guy emerges from nowhere, walks over to the driver, greets him, high-fives him, and leaves a small packet in the driver's hands as he walks on. Laughter and greetings. Driver moves on. The team ready for the next one.

Dippenaar was wondering how it would ever be possible to stop this stuff from happening.

He had been prepared to do this watch for a few hours before calling in for relief, but it turned out that his initial watch was less than two hours long, because he saw his suspect emerge from the tavern. Unmistakable, from Pillay's description. Within minutes, while briefing Ryder on his iPhone, he was tailing Spikes Mkhize, who was less than a hundred metres ahead of him, driving a little red Mini.

## 19.45.

Fiona had been happy enough for him to go out again. She also had a lot to catch up on, anyway, and at least they had had a nice quick tuna salad together. He thought he'd be back before eleven, but as always they knew that it depended. She said she might be up. She might not. Hugs and kisses.

She watched him ease the Camry out into the road, heard the throbbing beat of Fleetwood's *Tusk*, probably louder than she had ever heard it, and shook her head in despair. She couldn't see any point in tackling him about it when he got home. She could already envisage him arguing *Oh, OK. I thought you said only in the morning. No-one hassles with the volume early evening. But if you insist...*

Dippenaar had tracked Mkhize to an interesting spot, he said to Ryder in his second call.

'Any guesses?'

'None at all,' Ryder had replied.

'A nice little place we all know well. Called Suncoast Casino.'

Ryder replied that he was five to six minutes away.

'Come to the bar in the main playing hall.'

Ryder had called Pillay once he hit the freeway, and she had already left home. He now followed up with a second call and she replied that she was seven or eight minutes away.

Spikes Mkhize nursed a tall lager at the bar.

*

Thabethe arrived and immediately saw Mkhize at the bar. He moved a few paces toward him and then paused as he thought for a moment. His eyes swept the area and he picked up the cop within seconds. Dippenaar hadn't registered the new arrival. He was too concerned with appearing inconspicuous to Mkhize, so his eyes were fixed on his drink as he faked a telephone conversation into his iPhone.

Thabethe silently cursed the moment he had responded positively to

Spike's suggestion. *Idiot!* He should have told him they'd meet in the bush, not the casino. Why the casino?

At that precise moment Spikes saw him, and was about to hail him when he realised that something was wrong. Skhura turned, deliberately, and was walking away from him, his right hand stretched out toward his right, the index finger and the little finger extended, and the other fingers and thumb folded in. Spikes followed the line of the gesture, and saw Dippenaar. He sat back into his bar-stool, clutched his beer, turned his back and fixed eyes on the television screen, paying more attention than he had ever done before to a replay performance of Orlando Pirates, who were leading Mamelodi Sundowns by one goal at half-time.

Spikes maintained the same position until Ryder slipped into the seat next to him on his right, and Pillay on his left. Dippenaar stood directly behind. Thabethe had vanished.

'Better beer here than at Nomivi's, wouldn't you say, Detective Pillay?'

'I don't know about that, Detective Ryder,' Pillay replied.

'*Eish!* Two detectives. Not one detective. Two detectives. *Hayi!* There is no more crime in KwaZulu. The police they have no work. They look only at poor Spikes.'

'Correction,' said Dippenaar from behind him, 'not two detectives, three detectives.'

'Allow me to introduce Detective Dippenaar, Mr Mkhize. He, like me and Detective Pillay here, are very keen to have another discussion with you.'

'*Hayibo!* Detective, my friends, if they see me talking to you, Spikes she is finished. *Mina, impimpi? Aikona!* Not Spikes.'

'So you have friends here in the casino, do you, Mr Mkhize?'

'*Hayi!* Mr Ryder. No friends here. Sometimes I see some people I know, but no friends here. I come here to try my luck, and sometimes for beer, you know?'

'So if we hang around here with you for a while – we can even buy you a beer, if you like – you won't have any friends joining you for a chat?'

'*Aikona!* Mr Jeremy. I come here for one-time one beer only. Quick one. Me, I want to do the machines, you know. Quick one, then I go home to my wife. No, not my wife. She is gone long time. To my woman.'

'We were thinking, Mr Mkhize, me and Detective Pillay and Detective Dippenaar, that maybe we can interest you in a job.'

'Is what job, Detective? Spikes she is not qualified too much.'

'It's very easy, my friend. We ask you a few questions and you give us some information. The salary could be quite good, depending on the quality of the information we get from you. Interested?'

Mkhize laughed loudly and with genuine mirth.

'*Eish!* Is good, is good, Mr Jeremy. You pay Spikes the money and Spikes she get his throat cut sideways one time. Is very funny!'

Dippenaar couldn't contain himself, and started laughing too.

'*Yissus, ou broer!* You a funny man, you know? The detective is offering you good money here for an easy job. You think we going to tell your friends that you now a policeman?'

Pillay added her piece, leaning in to him and speaking in a hushed voice, trying to get them all to attract less attention than they were.

'All you have to do is tell us a few things and then we can decide whether we're going to do anything with the information. We're not going to take out an advert in the Sunday Times and say *We are pleased to announce our thanks to Mr Spikes Mkhize for his support!*'

Mkhize laughed again.

'Is right, Detective. Is right! You will not do that, I know. But I'm not *moegoe!* You think the people they are stupid? You think they see me talk with you and Inspector Dippenaar and Inspector Ryder and they say Spikes he is just talking business there by the police. He is talking politics. He is talking soccer. They are all supporting Amazulu and they are laughing together when Pirates miss the penalty. *Eish!*'

Ryder was about to call an end to it when Mkhize added a suggestion.

'But I tell you what, Mr Jeremy.'

'What?'

'Me, I'm happy to talk to you one time, no witness, you only, not Detective Dippenaar and this lady detective – she is a nice lady, I can see, but no, I talk to no witnesses, I talk to you only. Outside. By the cars, maybe. Not here inside.'

'OK. You and me, then. Let's go. Navi, Dipps, hang here and I'll be back.'

The two detectives nodded in agreement and Ryder and Mkhize left. As they did so, the television blared out *ladoooma!* and cheers and groans emanated from the individuals and groups watching the game. Mkhize's eyes flickered up to see that Pirates were ahead by 3 goals to nil.

'Is a replay, Mr Jeremy. I seen this game. Sundowns they are finished. Final score. *Moegoes!'*

They threaded their way through the crowds making for the exit.

As they did so, Thabethe emerged from one of the aisles crowded with Friday night slot-machine hopefuls. He followed them at a distance of some thirty paces, out of the gambling hall and into the car park. He watched them throughout their twenty-minute conversation, until Ryder reached into his jacket, pulled his wallet, and handed something over. Mkhize touched his imaginary forelock more than a dozen times, walking backward as he did so, until Ryder turned and went back into the building.

Thabethe watched Mkhize walk across to the red Mini, get in, and pull away.

Tomorrow. Tomorrow he would drop into Nomivi's. He would hold back, at first, and see whether Mkhize volunteered any information. If his story was that the cops had hassled him a bit and then eventually left him in the casino, Spikes would get the spoke. If his story was that the cops took him into the car park and bribed him and that he took the money and spun them a tale, well then maybe he could be trusted.

Tomorrow for Spikes. One way or the other.

**20.35.**

Ryder, Pillay and Dippenaar were wrapping up the evening at the bar.

'Can't tell whether what he told me was anything more than soft stuff designed to just get the money and give me enough to go on with, but he wasted no words in telling me what he thought of Thabethe. Slimeball, evil, malicious, a violent murderer that Nomivi's wanted nothing to do with, and stuff like that. If you didn't know the guy you would think that his worst enemy on the planet was Thabethe.'

'On the other hand,' said Pillay, 'all of that sounds like an accurate version of what anyone might say about Thabethe. So maybe it's just easy for him to spew out stuff like that. Did he give you anything about Thabethe's movements or whereabouts, Jeremy?'

'Nah. He says that no-one knows where Thabethe hangs. He just appears. Some say he lives in the bush. Others say he has a shack somewhere. Mkhize says he is very careful about arriving at Nomivi's, when he does. He scouts the terrain very carefully to ensure that he knows who's doing what and when, before he enters the place.'

'I don't know if either of you ever spoke to Thabethe face to face,' Dippenaar threw in, and in response to the two negatives from them he continued. 'Well, I did, a couple of years ago just after he joined us and before his problems with the disciplinary stuff. I tell you, I never seen a guy so evil as that. Everyone talked about how they were scared of being alone in a room with him. Maybe old Spikes is just plain scared and will tell us anything we want to hear just to keep us off his back.'

'While taking the informant money, of course,' added Pillay.

'Either way, guys,' Ryder intervened, 'we'll test Mkhize on one thing he did offer me, in return for cash. This was his idea, not mine. I think he did it because he thought I wasn't going to put him on the informant roll unless he gave me something tangible.'

'What did he give you, Jeremy?' asked Pillay.

'He said that Thabethe had lost his cell-phone and was sure that he would need one very soon. He's sure that he'll be in contact soon, maybe even tomorrow, and when he is, Mkhize will offer him a cell-phone. If we prepare the phone for a trace, Mkhize will ensure that Thabethe gets it. Then, says Mkhize, it will be over to us and he wants nothing further to do with it.'

'Fair enough,' said Dippenaar, 'and tell you what, Jeremy, I've got a meeting early tomorrow with van Rensburg in the comms section. He's the Industrial Technician and he's setting me up with my new iPhone. I'll take the opportunity to fix up a phone for Mkhize, shall I?'

'That would be really great, thanks, Dipps. Could you also get it out to him at Nomivi's?'

'No problem. I can get it out there by ten, latest.'

'Brilliant. That's it, then, guys. Don't know about you, but Fiona expects me home, so if you're intending gambling your life away here, Navi, I'll leave you to it.'

'You have to be joking. I already look like a one-arm bandit as it is. I'm also going home.'

'Me too,' said Dippenaar, and the three of them made their way through the sea of gamblers, most of them with grim and depressed faces, back to the car park.

Thabethe watched them leave the bar. He followed them to the car park. He watched each of them as they drove away.

He put his hand into his trouser pocket and felt for the joint. Tonight he needed some *nyaope*. Where that might lead him tonight he didn't know.

Then tomorrow he would question Spikes.

# 6 SATURDAY

**06.59.**

Fiona hit the buzzer before it went off, just as Ryder was also surfacing.

'See! I'm becoming like you,' she said, yawning. 'Look at that. One minute to go and I beat the buzzer. Maybe I'm becoming as paranoid as you.'

'What do you mean?' He yawned and stretched and felt clicks all through his spine.

'As paranoid as you are about being woken up by alarms.'

'Oh. Hmmm. Weird, isn't it? It's not just body clock stuff, 'cos it's Saturday, so it has to do with some deep-seated desire not to be shocked by the sound. Got to beat the alarm.'

'How do you mean, *because it's Saturday*?' she asked.

'Two hours later.'

'Oh. Yes. I see. Hmmmm. Or do I?'

'Do you what?'

'Do I see what you mean. I don't know.' She yawned again, loudly. 'I still think we would get up if we had no alarm at all.'

'Coffee?' he enquired.

'Hmmm.'

'Nice industrial strength hot coffee?'

'Hmmmmmmmmmmmm.'

'With frothy hot milk?''

'Hmmmmmmmmmmmmmmmmmmm.'

'Sound good?'

'Hmmmmmmmmmmmmmmmmmmmmmmmmmmmm.'

'Good. Bring us a whole pot.'

'Whaaat?' she exclaimed. 'Oh no. You were the one who offered.'

'I wasn't offering. I was asking.'

'Screw you.' She stretched and yawned.

'OK. Now?'

He suddenly leaped on her, taking advantage of her full-stretch above the shoulders, and tickled her under the arms as she arched her back, cat-like, for the yawn. She screamed in mid-yawn.

'No! Please! You bastard!'

She fought back, digging her fingers into his ribs and eliciting a matching scream from him. They cavorted and rolled. And giggled like children. Then their lips made contact and their hands began to wander, and their rumble in the duvet was just turning from childish to more mature stuff when it was shattered by the phone. He cursed and grabbed it.

'Hullo? Oh, yes, hi Captain.' She sighed and they both raised eyes to the ceiling as he continued. 'Yes, I got the message. We're meeting at 9.00 am. In your office. What? OK. Oh, all right. That's good, thanks, that'll make a nice change, but you don't have to… well, great, OK, that's very generous of you. Yep. Same time. See you.'

'What's that about?'

'A turn-up for the books. He's taking me to breakfast at Mugg & Bean.'

'Musgrave Centre?'

'No, Suncoast.'

'Lucky you. Can I come?'

'No.'

'Oh.' She pouted.

'He didn't invite you. Wants to have an informal chat. Says you're far too formal for him.'

'Well, your loss, both of you. Anyway, OK then, because you're getting breakfast from your bossy Captain, you can get coffee for me, now.'

'OK. Fair enough.'

'And if you do, you might get a reward.'

'Hmmm. Serious?'

'Hmmmm.'

'Before coffee, or after?'

'After,' she said. He pouted. 'Go,' she instructed.

He went.

She completed her yawn and stretched, luxuriously.


## 08.50.

The Major waddled across the tarmac toward the Royal Natal Yacht Club, entirely satisfied with the yacht. Red walked alongside him. It was the third time Vic had checked it during the week, and now he was ready, and hugely excited. It was fully stocked and perfectly clean, and expertly fitted. Wired for efficient communications, and ready for an inconspicuous departure with a fully competent crew in a little over eighteen hours.

'I'll be bringing my own luggage on board only late tonight, Vic. I'll arrive at about midnight. I'm seeing a friend in Westville just before that. He's looking after my house while I'm away. The rest of the crew will already be on board when I get here. They know they have to be in place from 10.00 pm, all of them. I've told them you'll arrive a couple of hours before sailing.'

'Thanks, Red. I'll get here about one or two o'clock, latest.'

'That'll be perfect. Couple of hours to settle in before we go.'

'*Lissen*, Red. Once we're out there you and I can have a chat, if you're up for it. About some ideas I have for the future. I think you know from what Tony said, and from the little bit I told you, that I've got a few businesses going. I'm going to need some more help as we go forward.'

'I'm all ears.'

'Great. Not now. Let's get out to sea first. I think you'll be interested in what I say. But we'll talk.'

'Good. No problem. I'm looking around at the moment for a few new things, so it would be good to see what we can work out.'

'OK, Red. OK. So we'll talk. Thanks again, then, and see you tonight. Or should I say tomorrow early.'

'After midnight, Vic. See you.'

They shook hands, and Red turned to go back to the yacht.

Vic had long been a fan of the RNYC breakfast on the lower deck of the clubhouse. 2 fried eggs, bacon, sausage, mushrooms, grilled tomato, 2 slices of toast, filter coffee. All clean and dry and hot, minimum grease or fat. The waitress always greeted him with *The usual, Major?* and he always grunted in the affirmative.

It had been here, in his favourite haunt, that the idea of a final departure by sea had first hit him a year ago. He had spent months with Tony, the two of them asking around, getting tours aboard different vessels, being taken out into the bay and beyond to get a feel of the experience, and understanding how club membership worked, the relative merits of buying and renting, and, finally, the widely varying costs of commissioning a yacht and crew to take one to Mauritius or to Mozambique or to Zanzibar or to destinations even further afield. Learning about the immigration regulations, and the ways of circumventing those. Meeting the best forgers in the business, and buying their services.

In addition, through Tony, finding the right guy to captain the vessel. As expensive as Big Red had proved to be, he seemed like the right kind of guy. Maybe even, if Tony drops out for whatever reason, he thought, a future replacement for Tony.

As he stepped into the bright sunlight he paused a moment to look up at The Grove across the Esplanade. That's where that idiot Jannie had screwed up. The murder of that old woman and the old guy. Jannie's sights should have been set on skilled burglars, not hit men. As a result Trewhella and Ryder had got in on the scene, and from there the whole thing had started falling apart. It was beginning to leak like a sieve, he thought, and it was time to sew up the whole operation and get out. Today's business had been long in the planning. Today was harvest day after months of planting the seeds and tending the crops.

He walked across the parking area, stuffed himself into his car, and then drove slowly out, over the rail-tracks and across Margaret Mncadi to turn right. Last day at Sunsquare Suncoast Hotel. Things to wrap up there.

## 09.15.

Ryder and Nyawula sat in the Mugg & Bean. The Captain was having the *Tropical Breakfast*: fruit salad, muesli and honey, with mango juice. What Ed might have called fairy food, thought Ryder. *Wouldn't touch it with a barge-pole*, he could imagine Ed saying. He himself was having a *Mighty Morning*: scrambled egg, back bacon and tomato, not for any particular reason of taste preference or desire for a cholesterol fix, but simply because he had read the menu too quickly and had mistakenly thought that he would have to order one of those in order to qualify for the bottomless mug of coffee. Mistakenly because the bottomless would have come anyway.

They covered a bit of ground on the funeral preparations for Monday afternoon. Who would speak, what order, how long, and which journos might be present. Then they moved on to a bit of shallow gossip about what had happened at the function on Thursday night, and eventually they turned to the matter in hand.

'The Major-General is having a second meeting with the Brigadier at 10.00 am. A justice of the peace is involved. The three of us had a useful discussion last night. I could have phoned you late last night but the three of us had our phones humming past midnight as we put things together, and it was only this morning – even after I spoke to you – that the last piece of the puzzle came in.'

'I'm all ears.'

'What I can tell you is that this goes way up the line and a key person in Pretoria is now aware of what we're doing. All of those who know can be trusted. Nothing will break until I press the button. A useful piece of information for you right now is that the Major's reputation stinks all the way up the line. He's considered to be the worst kind of relic from the past and there's a widespread view that he's been planning his exit for some time.'

'A guy of that calibre must be aiming for a career in politics.'

'No, the guys higher up the chain think he's long been stashing things away in a Swiss bank or a bank in the Caymans, or somewhere else. They've never been able to pin anything on him. Everyone thought he'd die of a big fat cholesterol attack before he put a foot wrong. Or before it became necessary for someone to bust him. Anyway, I expect a call from the Brigadier in just over an hour. I suspect it will be to tell me that all the warrants are in place and that we can go ahead and arrest pig number one. But until that happens I want to fill you in on some interesting stuff that came out in our discussions last night. Short of giving you a brief history of illegal gambling in this province, I need to highlight a few things.'

'I suppose the fact that we're eating in a casino is not unrelated to this?'

'Definitely related. In fact, our friend Swanepoel has a room a few floors above us which he has been renting for the last three weeks.'

Ryder paused, looking quizzically at him.

'And I can see you're not joking.'

'Not one bit. He's turned a normal guest room into something of an office, with printers and that kind of stuff. Irritated the hell out of the management, apparently, when they found out, but there was nothing they could do about it. For whatever reason. Probably some money changed hands somewhere. They say that today's his last day of a three-week long reservation so they probably decided to grin and bear it. So if today's Swanepoel's last day then we have our timing down perfectly. But, Jeremy, I'm going to hold back on an interesting piece of news that was phoned through to me at the crack of dawn this morning. You'll find that snippet really interesting in the context of a few of the things I want to tell you about now, so I'll hold back on it for a few minutes.'

'Intriguing. You've got my attention, Captain.'

'Sibo.'

'OK. Sibo.'

'Look, Jeremy, since Tuesday evening I've wanted us to get together informally to discuss Ed and Navi and some ideas for the future, but the phone-call I got this morning made me think through a bit of history, and made me decide to focus our discussion a bit differently from the way I had intended. In fact, I could kick myself for not having put this stuff together earlier. In brief, following our initial discussion yesterday, I've got more to tell you about illegal gambling in this province. I hadn't even realised that this thing has been bubbling away in my subconscious. As I told you and Pillay yesterday, I certainly don't think the casino operation here is dirty. We've had a really good look at this place over the years, and they always come up clean. No, I just think it happens to be a magnet for a lot of crooked chancers and parasites who ride on the backs of the genuine players, but I don't think there's any problem at all with the management of the place.'

'OK. I've also heard that. For some time.'

'What I've been thinking through, since the phone call I received this morning, is this. More than a decade ago a whole swathe of illegal casinos in Durban operated with the knowledge of both the police and certain provincial officers of the Department of Justice. Shady places manned by bouncers, none of which had licenses to operate, were making big money. How were these guys doing it?'

'You've got me there.'

'Can you believe it? There was actually a formal agreement in place between the police, the Department of Justice, and some of the worst criminal types you could imagine who were running illegal operations. The agreement allowed those operations to continue to run under the police radar.'

'You've got to be joking. A formal agreement?'

'And guess what? Our colleagues in Pine Parkade at the time decided to raid one operation. If I'm not mistaken they also had the army supporting them in that particular action. They removed illegal equipment and bust the big guy concerned. Guess what next? He promptly produces the formal agreement signed by both Justice and Police showing that he's allowed to operate. The police are humiliated, have to acknowledge that the agreement is genuine, and then have to return all the equipment. That's how it came to light that there was this undercover agreement. Some clever lawyer for the illegal operators then had the police over a barrel for wrongful arrest and wrongful impounding of equipment. Wrongful in the sense that they had a written agreement with the police to operate their business, so how could it be wrongful? Never mind that it hadn't been authorised through the correct channels. So what does he do, this clever lawyer? The police are scared of massive damages in the courts, so they sign a *further* undercover agreement with him that these particular operations are to be allowed to continue in return for dropping charges for the wrongful raids.'

'*Jeez*, Captain.'

'Sibo.'

'Sibo. So this agreement remained private?'

'Well. Depends on what you consider to be private. It actually included a clause not to make the agreement public!'

Ryder, still astonished, probed for more detail, which Nyawula happily provided, taking the detective through the intricacies of the legal arguments at the time, the outcomes of some of the cases, and the PR disasters. He concluded by describing how the whole illegal gambling scene after that little episode started to be cleaned up with the new legislation and the tightening of gambling regulations. Then he paused, while the waitress cleared dishes, before continuing.

'The new regulations didn't change things overnight, although there were some high-profile busts, both before and after the new policy. I remember reading that back in about 2004 there was one instance where slot machines worth about six hundred thousand rands were found by the KZN Gambling Unit in a police raid in Matatiele and they were busting quite a few illegal casino operations at that time, but what bothers me is the follow-up. Who controlled the confiscation of those machines? Where did they end up? And who got paid what?'

The waitress returned to refill Ryder's coffee and there was another pause while she did so. Then the Captain continued.

'OK. Now to my phone-call this morning. It was from a guy I trust who works in Gauteng. He's been tracking through a whole lot of history for me, and he's finally come up with an identity for the guy who Pillay took out in Overport. The guy who killed Ed.'

'Who is he?'

'His name is Antonio Vietri. Tony Vietri.'

Nyawula took from his briefcase a large envelope and spread four or five photos on the table.

'He has an interesting history. You remember that a few years ago – it was before your time here but when you started in Durban I remember you telling me about the stuff you had read in preparation for moving in – there was a lot of stuff happening which included allegations against the head in this province of the Organised Crime Unit?'

'Allegations of police taking bribes in return for not shutting down illegal gambling operations.'

'That's it. Well, one Tony Vietri was a section 204 witness in one of the trials.'

'Exemption from prosecution in return for giving evidence?'

'Yes. This guy was one of the big players and I remember friends groaning when they heard he was to be let off the hook.'

'I can imagine.'

'Well, he did the dirt on his accomplices and then disappeared. Surfaced in the Cape a few months later, then in Gauteng and then finally made his way back down here. But probably played a back-seat role in whatever he was involved with. My contact is networked into the Forensic Technology guys in Silverton and in the last twenty-four hours he has run a whole lot of things through IBIS which show our Mr Vietri popping up all over the place during the last ten years in a whole string of – until now – unsolved shootings. Once they got the stuff on his weapon from the Overport scene, and the GSR and the other evidence putting him at Montpelier Road, and ran all of this through the systems, all the dots started to get connected. Then he did some research for me and took it even further than I had asked. I owe this contact of mine big time, because what he took me through this morning gives me a lot more than I thought we had.'

'So we've got the confirmation evidence from Montpelier Road?'

'Yes. It's all come together. He's without doubt the guy who did Ed. And in addition to that, hold on to your hat for this.'

'What?'

'Vietri's prints are all over the guy who was strangled in Addington Hospital on Monday.'

Ryder stared at the Captain, thinking through the implications.

'We can come back to that. But first, back to the illegal gambling scene. One of the things that had been pinned on Vietri at the time he was bust was his involvement in a very interesting little business which involved the interception of illegal gambling equipment – slot machines as well as wheels and tables and all sorts of other things – merchandise that had been confiscated by the police and then, while in police possession, mysteriously disappeared. This included machines that had been supposedly destroyed. Also newer stuff that had been imported from abroad – mainly China – and discovered in police operations. These machines were then sent to warehouses to await destruction or some other fate, and time after time the warehouses were opened and the goods had disappeared. There was huge suspicion about police involvement, but they could never nail the guys. Then it went quiet when the new legislation came in and the whole gambling thing tightened up under the National Gambling Board.'

'And you think that Vietri was part of a new operation trying to resurrect all of this?'

'Exactly. I think we might be on to quite a sophisticated operation, and we think Swanepoel is a key part of it. He's been on top of the information about police operations. He knows when there's going to be a raid. He knows when illegal machines have been confiscated. And he knows when they are taken to state warehouses to await proper claims. He has his grubby fat fingers in a whole lot of these pies. And now we're on to him.'

'Ed and I talked a *helluva* lot about how so many of the unit's carefully planned operations were blown at the last minute. We often thought that there might be some inside information getting out to people to warn them. But every time we came down to it, we thought it can't be. We scrutinised every one of our guys. Even you, Sibo, I have to admit.'

'Thanks.'

'Yeah. Well, the good news is you came up clean each time so we dropped it.'

'Pity you didn't look harder at the Major.'

'Yeah.'

'And me, too, dammit. I should have looked harder at him. In retrospect it seems so obvious. All his irritating questions about detail. When were we planning to bust, where, who was involved? All of that I put down to the guy just trying – tiresomely – to prove that he was the know-all and that he was gunning for me, trying to derail me, for no other reason than his racism. I never for a moment thought it could be anything else.'

They covered more ground, first looking back at some of the history, and then coming back to the anticipated events of the day. They played back and forth various likely and various possible actions once the warrants were in place and the arrests were made. They also mapped out a PR strategy for the coming week. A Major being bust for corruption. That was going to bring the journos in big time, so Nyawula wanted all bases covered.

Nyawula agreed that Pillay should be called in to accompany Ryder on the arrest of the Major. Her arm was still in a sling, Ryder told him, and she was feeling a bit frustrated being left on the side-lines. Ryder made the call and she responded instantly. She would come down to the casino immediately and join them for a briefing. By the time she got there the Captain expected to have the go-ahead and the papers signed off.

## 11.10.

Mkhize had sent a message back with one of the staff at Nomivi's. Tell the policeman asking for him at the front entrance that he would meet him in the road. Tell him to wait in his car. She had come to the back room in some agitation worrying about why the police were there. Maybe it was something to do with that murder around the corner on Tuesday. Whatever it was, it felt bad for business to have the police visiting all the time.

Mkhize had then gone out a few minutes later and had got into the detective's car so that he could take the cell-phone and charger from Dippenaar without being observed by anyone else. Dippenaar told him that he wouldn't have to do anything with the instrument. It was already primed and set up, and all he had to do was let them know once Thabethe had taken possession of the phone. He wouldn't be called upon to do anything else from that point on. They would handle everything.

The cop had driven off and it was just over half an hour later that Thabethe arrived and after scouting the place satisfied himself that it was only Spikes and the normal staff on the premises. The two of them sat in the same seats Thabethe and the young Afrikaner had occupied on

Tuesday. Spikes was cackling loudly.

'*Struesbob*, Skhura! The cop he gives me money. Me, Spikes, police informant! Paid with police money! Maybe they promote me to detective one day. Maybe I get a raise! *Hayi*! These guys. They know nothing. Nothing! They think I sell out my friends.'

'Is good you tell me, Spikes. Is good.'

He was relieved, after what he had observed the previous night. He needed Spikes. He would have had no hesitation in cutting the guy's throat or giving him the spoke, but at least he knew now that Spikes was on the level.

'This one is funny, Skhura. You like this one. They ask me, they ask *What you think of Skhura? What kind of man is Skhura Thabethe?*'

He guffawed, spluttering his coffee and then, after a fit of coughing and more laughter, he continued.

'I tell them *Skhura Thabethe, that one, that one he is a skelm number one. Tsotsi big time. Bad man. Spikes never like that one.* Is joke, you know, Skhura. Is big joke, 'cos you know me, *nè?*'

'I know you, Spikes. I know you.'

'But this inspector Ryder, I'm scared of that one, Skhura. I must play along with him, you know? I don't say *no way, I'm not wanting your money.* 'Cos then he makes things bad for Spikes, you know?'

'I know, Spikes. I know.'

'So I say things. Now he thinks I am against Skhura. You know?'

'I know.'

'So he asks me, that one, he asks me to say where you live. I say I don't know but if I find out I will tell them. He says they will give me money if I tell them. I say give money first and they say no, they want something from Spikes first then they give money. Then I have a big idea, Skhura. You like this one. I tell them something and then they give me money.'

He collapsed in another hysterical fit of laughing, wiping tears from his eyes.

'What you tell them, Spikes?'

'I tell them....' He lowered his voice to a whisper and leaned in to Thabethe as he continued conspiratorially. 'I tell them I got a big idea. I see it on television. I see the cops do it on television, so I get a great big idea.'

'What, Spikes? Tell me, *mfowethu*.'

'I tell them they must fix a police cell-phone for you with bugs and things like that and I give it to you then they can trace you where you are.'

'*Whaaat?*'

'Easy, *broer*. Easy *my bra*. Is a trick. Is a trick from Spikes. You take the phone, you see, you throw it on a train or hide it on a bus, or put it in some lorry going to Jo'burg in the middle of the night, and they follow you to kingdom come, you know? Is a good idea, *nè?* They think Skhura is there by Pretoria and Skhura is here all the time. *Fokken moegoe* police.'

Thabethe calmed down. He saw some merit in the idea.

'Is good, Spikes. Is clever. But then they come for you again.'

'Is no problem, Skhura. I tell them, then, I tell them *Hayi! That Skhura he is a clever! He maybe found out the bug! He is clever! He is a big skabenga!*

Another fit of laughter.

'Is good, Spikes. Is good. When they think you going to give me the phone?'

'I tell them when I tell them. I say Skhura he has now got that phone. Until then, nothing. They wait for Spikes to tell them.'

'Is nice. Give me the phone.'

Mkhize handed over the phone and the charger.

'Ready to go one time, my brother. Me, I know nothing how this bug thing works, you know. Inside there somewhere. That bug she has got ears. They can tell when you are talking, when you are moving, when you are shitting. *Hayi!* these police they want to know everything we do.'

'OK, Spikes. OK. Good thing. You wait for me and I tell you when to tell them. We send them far away just when they want to catch me. But you wait for me, *nè?* Only when I say *tell them now, Spikes.*'

'I wait for you, Skhura. Nothing from me to them until you tell me. You can trust good old Spikes, *nè?*

Thabethe nodded, and they punched fists.

'You say you lost the car, Skhura? You want 'nother one? I can get 'nother one Monday. No problem. I can get new papers. I get you Mazda. Or Toyota? I got a Ford 1974. You want?'

'Maybe, Spikes. Maybe. Maybe I come next week. For now, is safer with a taxi. I let you know.'

'Anytime, *my broer*! Anytime. Spikes works for Skhura. We are big friends. I know if I have trouble with guys who come to mess up my place I find Skhura and say these guys must go, and Skhura will sort it out, *nè?* With Skhura my friend *ek is skrik vir niks.*'

'Is right, Spikes. Is right. You call me and I fix you up. I know. I trust you.'

They punched fists again, finished their coffees and Thabethe left, after checking through the windows to see that the street was functioning exactly as it should on a Saturday morning.

### 13.25.

There had been frustrating delays as a call from the Colonel had caused a hold-up while they got more information to him. Then Ryder finally got the go-ahead, along with paper warrants hand-delivered by a trusted constable from the Cluster Commander's office. All of it was sweetened by an additional personal call from the Brigadier, confirming everything, and they set off. He and Pillay stepped out of the elevator and walked briskly down the passage to Swanepoel's room.

The Major hardly hesitated after checking the peephole, and opened the door, having doubtless decided that jollity was the best defence.

'Jeremy! What a nice surprise.'

'Only my friends call me Jeremy, Major. We have a warrant for your arrest.'

'You have the right...' Pillay started, but the Major, sensing immediately that they must have more information than he had assumed possible when looking through the peephole, changed tactics and interrupted her.

'I know my section 35 rights, detectives, so there's no need for that...'

'Not good enough, Major, we still...'

'*Lissen*, girlie, I was doing this long before you...'

Nothing could rile Pillay more. She was on to him immediately, her wounded left arm proving no deterrent to her ability with the handcuffs as she produced them from nowhere and pushed past Ryder, forcing the major back into the room, thrusting the cuffs into his chest with her right hand as she spoke.

'No-one calls me girlie, fatso. Now listen to your lesson on constitutional rights and be a good fat *boykie*. Your rights are as follows...'

Rather than her small physique having anything to do with him staggering backward, the Major deliberately over-reacted to her forward movement. Before either she or Ryder could work out how her action had managed to propel him backward against the desk, his enormous buttocks almost crushed the HP desktop as he tilted back, and his right hand stretched out behind him, apparently in an effort to prevent his bulk from crashing through the desk. But he suddenly steadied himself and brought his right hand high overhead. He had retrieved the desk clock mounted on its slab of inch-thick glass and brought it smashing down on Pillay's head. She went down instantly, crashing to the floor. The Major maintained the momentum forward and to his left, stumbling now toward Ryder, who had followed Pillay into the room.

Ryder could deliver a punch that would drop most two-metre, two-hundred-and-fifty-pound men instantly. He could wriggle his way out of almost any adversarial grip that a powerful wrestler might offer. He could kick his way out of most close-combat situations with any of the top kick-boxers around. But here was an adversary who broke all the rules. He had never encountered in hand-to-hand combat an opponent this shape, size and weight. Ryder wouldn't get two arms around the man's girth. Any blow he landed on the huge torso would be dissipated, its energy being swallowed up by layers of fat interwoven with flabby muscle.

The Major's strategy was to crowd into Ryder and keep him close. He sensed the power in the detective's fists and was determined to keep him too close to deliver any effective punch or kick. If he could collapse them both to the ground, with himself on top, he stood a chance. He rushed forward, arms initially wide, and then drawn down rapidly to smother the detective's incoming right uppercut. The weight and momentum of his three-hundred-and-fifty pounds sent them both crashing through the flimsy counter with its tea, coffee, kettle, jug of water and the rest of the crockery and condiments, and smashing into the Xerox Phaser 7100V Printer, destroying it beyond repair, then spinning around twice before falling onto the floor and skidding through the door into the bathroom, with the fat man on top.

Luck didn't favour Ryder in the fall. He ended up wedged under the twin basins. He took two seconds longer than the Major to extricate himself. Which gave the fat man the chance he needed. He hauled himself up and out of the bathroom, smashing his weight against the door and locking it, with Ryder inside. He knew that the door probably wasn't strong enough to keep the detective occupied for more than a minute, but that was all he needed to make his escape, slamming the main door behind him as he left the apartment.

**13.40.**

Dirk was agitated. The dispatches were due and Vic was nowhere to be seen. He had had another pizza and two-litre coke delivered to the side door and he had derived comfort from it. He had been through the lists that Vic had given him, and he had counted and re-counted, and checked and re-checked the stock.

He had broken up some of the wooden crates to confirm their contents, but had left alone the ones covered in thick plastic. They were identifiable. Those that were neither covered nor boxed were the ones that had not been imported but had been confiscated from illegal operations and stored for months in warehouses before being somehow, miraculously, claimed by Vic and shifted to alternative venues and then finally delivered here to the Argyle house. Vic was a genius, thought Dirk. The guy had so many contacts. He knew exactly who was who in the business. He knew how to do business, and he had promised Dirk an extra bonus tonight, for taking on Tony's work as well.

Who knew where Tony was? Who cared? It was almost over. Vic had said they should all lie low for six months to a year and he would then find them and start a new project. Maybe in Zimbabwe, Vic had said. Maybe in Mauritius. He wasn't sure. He had advised Dirk to head for Gauteng. Lie low. The cops were still looking for him. It wasn't safe in KwaZulu. Vic himself was thinking of dropping out for a while. But he would make sure that Dirk was looked after.

Where was Vic? The first dispatch guys were going to arrive.

*I can't do this without Vic.*

**13.45**

The Major drove like a maniac. He had reached the elevator just as it was – miraculously – about to close for its downward journey, with no-one inside. He had made his way through the lobby without steam-rolling into anyone. And he had got into the car, then lurched out of the parking and through the control point, without a single hitch or pause or queue. He tore around the corner onto Sandile Thusi, controlled the vehicle as it hit top speed, and had his foot flat as the road became the M17.

He had to get to the Argyle house. Ryder would be on his tail, probably no more than a minute or two behind him. The cops had no way of knowing anything about the Argyle house operation. Once he was there and away from CCTV cameras he and Dirk would be safe from prying eyes.

They would spend the rest of the day simply clearing the stock through the garage entrance point and receiving piles of cash in return. By tonight there would be no trace left of him or the operation. There would be nothing but cash. Dirk would be paid in cash, and he would go his own way.

Then he would make his own move after midnight. The cops would be watching everywhere. There would be road blocks. Ryder must already be free and he would have already put out the alert. Every cop in town would be looking for him. They all knew what he looked like. Unmistakable. There was no possible disguise for someone like him. He had to stay low. He had to get to the house.

The first dispatch was scheduled for less than an hour from now. At 2.30 pm. Then on from there, all through the afternoon and into the evening at meticulously scheduled times. If he could stay off the cop radar for eight hours he would make his way down to the harbour after midnight. With the cash. A million and a half in cash. No-one would expect him to make his escape by sea. He had planned this for a long time. Andre Stander had planned his own final escape from the country by yacht more than thirty years ago. It had been his own dream to do the same, but to succeed where Stander had failed. Before dawn he would be doing exactly what Stander had planned to do. Everyone was briefed. Everything was a go for an hour before dawn.

He screeched to a halt, abandoned the car in Clarence Road and waddled his way, breathlessly, down Tenth Avenue to the house, to join Dirk.

*

Ryder cursed as he dragged himself up off the bathroom floor. He knew, even before he could recover from the awkward position into which he had fallen, that the Major would be locking him in. The bastard had had a few seconds advantage, and had taken it. Ryder kicked at the door to no avail. It was solid. He searched wildly around the bathroom for something to smash against the window. The best he could find was the metal trashcan. Hopeless against the thick glass. Last option was to shoot out the lock of the door. He pumped a couple of bullets into the door catch before it weakened sufficiently for him to kick again and break his way through. His first thought was for Pillay, but a quick look showed that she was already recovering. She looked OK. It was a tough choice to leave her but he took it. He ran.

By the time he reached the closed elevator door he realised that the stairs would be quicker. He took the stairs four, five, six at a time. By the time he hit the car-park he knew he must be more than a minute behind the Major. Then an old woman going home after her Saturday fling on the tables created a jam at the exit point by boasting about her good fortune to a disinterested gate-keeper, and by the time he reached the road he knew he was fully three minutes behind his prey. And now he had no idea what direction the Major had taken.

Ryder pulled over and hit the iPhone. Within seconds he had given Cronje instructions. First, get the medics to the hotel to check on Pillay. Next, every available source was to be used to track the Major's direction. Traffic cameras, witnesses, GPS trackers, anything he could find, had to be called in. The Major was a priority suspect on the run. He was *the* priority suspect.

Ryder hung up. He had to get back to Pillay.

## 14.05.

The office was a hive of activity. There was a cacophony of shouts and calls and people entering and leaving the main office and the inner office. Cronje, Koekemoer and Dippenaar were frantic. Each of them was on a different phone. They were calling in extra hands from Durban North and Westville, supported by station commanders who had been instructed from higher up the chain. They had people checking CCTV cameras all the way from Suncoast through to Overport. Cronje had been called by Cluster Command and hassled by someone seeking updates on what he called 'the Ryder mission.' Everyone was trying to get hold of Captain Nyawula. Medics had responded instantly and Cronje had his intern Mavis Tshabalala reporting on progress in that quarter as well as screening reports coming in from comms.

The intern rushed up to Cronje and whispered in his ear. He in turn called out to the others.

'Navi's OK. The medics are with her. Bump on the head but OK and no concussion.'

There was relief all around. The unspoken thought had been the possibility of another Trewhella disaster. That would have killed off the spirit and the energy that had been building all day since the news had broken that a move had been made on the Major.

The relief was palpable. The office returned to a hum of quiet and efficient business as calls were put and received, and the telephones worked overtime.

## 14.10.

The medics had got there in record time. Pillay was already receiving treatment by the time Ryder got back to her. He could hear her swearing and cursing from the moment he stepped out of the elevator and as he stepped through the door he could see at a glance that she was OK, but that she would soon be sporting a bump on the head even worse than his own.

'Jeremy! Oh my god. Report me to the Captain. Go on. For me to get stymied by a big slob like that is just unforgivable. What an idiot. I didn't see it coming. The slimy bastard.'

'You OK?'

'Yes, dammit. I'm fine. Just wanted a bump on the head so that everyone could identify me as your partner. These guys tell me the glass didn't crack, but they're not so sure about my skull. I told them they must be mistaken. My skull is thicker than that slab of glass, any day. What an idiot!'

'She OK, guys?'

The medics grunted in the affirmative, confirming that they had checked her thoroughly. No concussion, no problems. Just a strip of Elastoplast necessary. They'd cleaned the wound. No problem at all. Except, one said, they had no cure for her foul language. They had never seen a case quite as bad as that, he said. He felt that the only treatment for the language problem was surgery. Which elicited another response from Pillay.

'And fuck you too, doctor. Fuck you very much. Did you get him, Jeremy? What happened? Where's he?'

'Nah. After you and he had your little disagreement I just decided to step out for a moment and leave the two of you to go at it together. I don't like violence, as you know. I just went downstairs for some ice-cream until the two of you had sorted out your differences.'

'Shit. I'm sorry, Jeremy.'

'Rubbish. I didn't see it coming, either. Fat bastard moves faster than I thought he was capable of doing. We'll get him. Cronje's all over the case. Alerts are out. We'll pick him up. Guy with a body like that can't really go into disguise, can he? Take it easy, Navi. Let's get you settled with a cup of something.'

The medics finished their business, muttered their goodbyes, and left the two detectives to it.

'Coffee?' said Ryder.

'Please. Yes. No. Wait. Some of that ice-cream you mentioned sounds better right now.'

'OK. Good idea. On me.'

**15.30.**

Thabethe thought he must have missed a couple of loads. He had arrived at his viewing spot next to the palms across the street from the house, just as a panel van emerged from the garage. It paused. Then it turned left toward Sandile Thusi, as the garage door descended behind it. The van paused at the end of Tenth Avenue, turned left again and disappeared into the traffic.

If it was emerging from the garage that meant the stuff in the garage had already been cleared. They had already been at it. For how long? How much had already been moved? If the van was parking inside then they might already be clearing the kitchen, or maybe they've done most of the stuff there, too, and are already at it in the front room? When did they start? How much had he missed?

Thabethe wasn't sure whether he should get over the wall in broad daylight, risk being seen, and have a look through the windows. Maybe up in the tree? In broad daylight? Maybe he should wait and see what happened. He waited an agonising fifteen or twenty minutes and was about to go for the wall option when he saw another panel van coming from the top all the way down Tenth Avenue toward him. He remained in the shadow of the palms and watched.

There were two people in the van, the driver and a passenger. It was a non-descript panel van, like the one that had just gone. Thabethe was quite good on the makes and models of cars, but neither the first nor this one could he identify. *Sommer 'n van, jy weet?* he could imagine Spikes saying. *Who cares, if it's got wheels!* The driver hooted. Thirty seconds passed, then the garage door opened. The van reversed in. Ten minutes passed. Twelve. Thirteen. Then the door opened and the van came out, turned left, turned left again and disappeared up Sandile Thusi. Thabethe waited.

**15.35.**

On arrival back at the station, after the initial expressions of concern and the round of well-wishing, Pillay and Ryder were teased mercilessly. Jokes about Moby Dick predominated.

'*Ja, okes,*' said Dippenaar. 'I told the guys that Navi was the perfect Captain Ahab. Now she's obsessed. Has to catch the big fat albino whale. Except she should have her leg in a sling, not her arm. Couldn't you have done better research before going whale hunting, Sergeant Pillay?'

'Who was that harpoon guy? Queer something? That's you, Jeremy, according to Dipps. Pillay's harpoon-man.'

'Thanks, Koeks. I think you mean Queequeg, as I recall.'

'*Daarsy.* That's him. Bloody tough guy, that one, old Dipps told us.'

'Thanks, Koeks. Very kind. I appreciate the compliment, Dipps.'

'We were all saying how you two make a good team, *okes.*'

'*Yissus*, Dipps. You Afrikaners are always so bloody tough on both us *charras* and *Engelsmanne*,' said Pillay. 'Don't you know, guys, that Jeremy and I are the ones who built this country. You guys were just farmers. We're the ones who invented business and entrepreneurship in this country. Me and my cousins from India on the sugar farms and Jeremy and his guys with the help of their empire. This country would be nothing without us. Nothing but boer wars and zulu wars.'

'I don't know what you guys are talking about,' said Cronje. 'I never read that whale book. My *boet* told me when I saw *Jaws* that that was it, and I didn't have to read the book.'

Cronje's intervention succeeded in creating a pause in the babble of conversation, so he continued.

'Jeremy, that phone number you gave me, written on the back of that chemist's cardboard box for those tablets...'

'Yes, Piet. What about it?'

'I got the guys to follow up as you asked, and they've now come back to me to say something like they got triangles or something from the cell-phone company...'

'Triangulation.'

'*Daarsy!* There's it, thanks Jeremy. That's exactly what the *oke* told me. So they followed these triangles and came up with a very interesting spot where they say the guy with the cell-phone was at today.'

'Where's that, Piet.'

'Well, they eventually lost the signal for some reason, but they were able to, before that happened, they were able to find out that it comes from the Royal Natal Yacht Club there by Wilson's Wharf.'

'How very interesting.'

'*Ja*. I thought so, Jeremy. So anyway the guys tell me they were able to have a really close look at the spot their machines and equipment and stuff took them to, and then they couldn't understand why it all ended up in the water there, then they had another look and they said it must have been on a boat, there in front of the Yacht Club.'

There was a babble of excitement, capped by Pillay.

'Looks like Captain Ahab is on the right track after all, Koeksister. Looks like we might be getting onto a whaling boat to go and find some fat whales.'

'*Yissus*, Navi. It looks like it. Want me to come along with my harpoon, too? It will be my pleasure to serve with you.'

It didn't take long for them to haul out a laptop and do a quick google-earth search and then for Ryder to announce a line of action.

'OK, guys. Here's the thing. I think Navi and I should go and take a look at the boats around there and see what we can come up with. Piet, are your guys still tracking the phone?'

'Yes, but they're saying it might be switched off or something, or their equipment is not handling it properly, but they haven't got any track on it right now. They say the fact that it stayed in one place down by the boats for more than an hour might be worth something for us to think about for now, but they'll keep on trying and will let me know if they pick it up again.'

'You're going to be hanging around here, Piet? What will your wife say?'

'*Ag*, Jeremy, you know her. She's like Fiona, man. She wouldn't mind. But I have to tell you anyway, it's her birthday today and I do have to get home for dinner with her and her mom and dad, you know. But I told the guys in comms that they could call me anytime on my cell-phone. So if they call I can escape the dinner and get back here, no problem.'

'Thanks, Piet, but no need to come in here. Just call me and let me know if they give you anything more. We can take it from there.'

'OK, then. Will do. But, guys, really, there's no problem if you need me, hey? Just give me a call and I'll be here.'

## 16.25.

A pattern began to emerge. The vans were arriving outside the garage in Tenth Avenue almost exactly every twenty minutes. Thabethe began to do sums in his head. He thought back on the red box. He tried to remember the exact figures scribbled on the paper but he couldn't. He started estimating how many slot machines a van could carry, and how much one might pay for each of the machines. Then he remembered how different some of them were. There were those with every ornament and colourful accessory imaginable. There were others that were plain boxes with a few lights and numbers. He remembered the machines he had experimented on in the casino. He remembered the faces of the old men and women all shoving hundred-rand and two-hundred-rand notes into the slots to reload their casino cards.

He remembered having seen the older versions – those with arms and levers rather than buttons – at cafes and tea-rooms up and down the coast in the old days. He remembered having read about laws and regulations preventing gambling, about arrests and seizures. And he remembered hearing people in prison talking about the money to be made.

He brooded, in the lengthening shadows under the palms. It was time for him to start making serious money.

## 18.15.

Pillay and Ryder had been watching the yacht for almost an hour. They had scouted every vessel in the enclave and had finally focused on only one of them. They had seen unusual activity there, compared to the other boats. The one they were interested in was a forty-one foot Hunter 410.

Under pretext of undertaking a casual survey of moored vessels in the area, they had then obtained the very willing permission of a crew member – who didn't seem to have any understanding at all of his rights – to have a look around. He gladly gave them a guided tour, explaining that the rest of the crew were at dinner somewhere in Mahatma Gandhi Road before coming back at about 10.00 pm, and that the Captain was having a quick dinner just up the road before going out to meet someone in Westville tonight. He would be back only at midnight. The guy babbled without hesitation, Ryder thought, and wondered whether the yacht's captain would approve of how much information his crew member so willingly gave.

Ryder and Pillay were treated to a quick tour and proud descriptions – almost as if the man was intent on selling the boat to prospective buyers – of the additional teak storage, the enormous centreline king berth, and the freshly waxed hull and decks. He particularly boasted about the in-mast furling main and one-hundred-and-ten percent roller furling jib. He pointed out the interior design that boasted almost seven feet of headroom, eight opening ports and ten overhead hatches along with ten fixed windows maintaining a bright and airy feel to the U-shape saloon, which seemed to be his pride and joy.

Pillay commented with particular interest on the sumptuous fabrics in the vast master stateroom aft hosting the centreline berth. The two detectives, neither of whom had ever stepped onto a vessel like this, took in almost casually the separate shower stall and Corian vanity top.

The real interest was not just the description of the lavish suite. What was of much more interest was their guide's mention of a special VIP guest expected to join them after midnight.

'I don't know much about it, except that the boss says he's a very large man, like, you know, fatter than he has seen, you know, and that partly because of that the king berth was the key thing that attracted him. He was looking for a yacht to take him out to sea, you know.'

Having ascertained that the departure time was as soon as possible after 4.00 am the next morning, and that the large visitor was expected to come on board an hour or two after midnight, the two detectives gave their profuse thanks and made to depart.

'Ah. Just as a matter of interest,' said Ryder, 'you said the captain was having dinner up the road. We're looking for a place to get a bite to eat, too. Any place in particular your guy is eating?'

'Sure. He told me that when he moors here he always grabs a bite to eat at John Dory's just along the wharf, there. You'll see him there. You can't miss him. Muscles, you know? They call him Big Red. Don't tell him, OK, but some of us also call him Red Rooster.'

They thanked him and drove down the wharf to the restaurant.


**19.25.**

The last panel van had left. Vic and Dirk sat in the kitchen, catching their breath. Dirk stretched out his bad leg and popped another tablet.

'*Yissus*, Vic. Big job.'

'Well done, Dirk. I won't forget this. I know you're in pain. I appreciate what you've done today.'

'No problem, Vic.'

'I can't understand what's happened to Tony. His last chance to get back in touch with me is at midnight. If he doesn't, Dirk, let me tell you something. There's more money coming your way. You did a lot of Tony's work today. And yesterday. I appreciate that.'

'Maybe they got Tony, Vic. It's not like him to just drop out.'

'I know, Dirk. That's what worries me. He would have called. He would have got hold of me somehow.'

'Do you think the cops got him, Vic?'

'I don't know, Dirk. Let me just think a moment, OK?'

'Sure thing, Vic.'

Vic played through the options. If the cops had got Tony then maybe they had turned him. Maybe there was a big bust planned for midnight. Only Tony knew what his plans were. Dirk knew he was going away for a bit, but as far as he was concerned, it was probably somewhere like Gauteng or the Cape. He had no idea that Vic was planning a much longer voyage. Maybe Tony would arrive at the last moment, having taken cover for a good reason. Dirk had seen the piles of cash. He knew how big this thing was. He didn't know about the other cash from the other deals that had been wrapped up. This was the big one, but there was at least this amount again from the other smaller deals that he and Tony had been sewing up over the last couple of weeks.

'OK, Dirk. We've got about four hours before I have to leave. We need to get counting. Get the laptop and the file, and let's get going.'

## 19.30.

There was a problem right at the outset. Ryder and Pillay almost collided with Big Red on their way into the restaurant. There was no mistaking him, after the brief description from the crew member. Ryder's eyes met Red's full on, because they were at almost the same level, Red being probably two inches taller. Pillay's eyes were at the level of his Adam's apple. No eye contact there.

The embarrassment was that just as their quarry passed them to walk away from the restaurant along the jetty, the two detectives were greeted warmly by the waitress who ushered them effusively toward a table. They were in the embarrassing position of immediately having to change their minds about sitting down for a meal.

'Welcome! Welcome to John Dory... I'm sorry, too drafty? Would you like a table further indoors?'

'Sorry,' said Pillay as Ryder turned to go, keeping his eyes on the departing Red. 'We suddenly realised... we hope to come back later...'

'Suit yourself, we're open late,' was the frosty reply.

They walked out swiftly, following their prey into the car park, and watched him get into a red Lamborghini LP700-4 Aventador. Ryder groaned as he realised that his Camry was going to have its work cut out against the V12 engine and carbon-fibre technology.

'Ever wonder how a bodybuilder captain of a boat can afford a Lamborghini, Jeremy?'

'Frequently, Navi. I admire these guys. They're always so ostentatious about their money.'

'I heard somewhere that those things get up to a hundred kilometres an hour in about three seconds.'

'About as fast as you can run, I heard somewhere.'

'Not quite.'

They had hastened their walk from a quick stroll to almost a canter, got into the Camry, and then watched in dismay as the Lamborghini sped away as if it was masquerading a small jet.

'Shit,' said Ryder. 'I think he saw us. Probably wondering why we turned back from the restaurant so quickly.'

They were favoured to some extent by traffic lights and stop signs, or maybe it was just that their quarry was watching them and keeping them in view. There was no way of telling. Even after the Toll Gate hill and the fairly open King Cetshwayo Highway leading up to Westville, where the Lamborghini could easily have roared away, the two cars remained within sight of each other.

They fell back, deliberately, as the Lamborghini swung off the exit and around onto the Rockdale Avenue bridge then onto Jan Hofmeyer road. They caught up again as the vehicle cruised past the Westville Police Station and then down past Westville Boys High School before turning suddenly left into Wandsbeck Road. The driver pulled up opposite the entrance to the school, outside a plush place with brick-paved driveway, manicured lawns, white walls and metal security gate overhung by a decorative plinth, all dressed with bougainvillea, jacaranda, and roses. The detectives drove past, around the corner into Nordene Road, up twenty metres, and switched off. They waited, craning their necks to enable them to look back through the foliage on the verge. The Lamborghini appeared to be idling outside the security gate of the house.

Eventually the gate opened and a man came out. He leaned in at the driver's window and then stepped back, opened the gate wider, and the

Lamborghini went in to the property. The detectives moved the car some twenty paces, then waited. The minutes ticked past.

'Looks like the tracks are being painted for the athletics season,' Pillay said, looking over at the school fields where the floodlights were on.

'Fancy a run, do you, Navi?'

'Nah. Look.'

'What?'

'Some kid has cracked 11.4 seconds for the hundred metres. Check it out. That sign there. *Barrington. School record. 11.4.* Or maybe it's just kids fooling around. Maybe it's not official.'

'Maybe it's Barrington himself that put that up, Navi. Looks more like graffiti than for real, otherwise the school would have put it up in proper printing or engraving, surely?'

'Must be unofficial. Maybe it's Mr Barrington's wishful thinking.'

'Probably.'

'11.4 seconds. Hmmmm.'

'Pretty good, Navi. Better than you?'

'Never. I'm way better.'

'I hear you still hold the record at your school.'

'Unofficial. Bastard timekeeper said there was too much wind. Talked shit.'

'So I heard.'

'Who told you? Didn't know it was the subject of discussion.'

'K and D were talking about it one day. Said you were bloody fast.'

'*Ja.*'

'Still?'

'Dunno. Haven't had to run a hundred metres for a while.'

'Not with that arm, anyway.'

'Who says? I don't run with my arms.'

'Well, they have to play some part in balance.'

'Suppose so.'

'OK, Navi. Long enough. Let's take a closer look.'

They stepped out of the Camry and made their way to the security gate. They peered through into the property, trying to ascertain whether there was some way of entering other than through the main entrance. Pillay checked around the side and came back. Ryder moved toward the intercom on the left of the driveway entrance.

'Might as well do this properly, Navi.'

'What are we going to say?'

*'Just checking, sir, we noticed you being followed by a suspicious looking character, and we decided to tail him, but he appears to have given us the slip. Everything OK with you?'*

'Sounds OK. Not good. Just OK.'

Ryder pressed the button and waited. He waited ten seconds, then the gate suddenly flew open and there was the big man. Along with his companion. Each of them with a Smith & Wesson .38 revolver. Each one pointed at a detective.

'Come in, please. Slowly. No funny stuff.'

'You're speaking to detectives...'

'Shut up and move. We'll do the talking.'

Ben giggled and thrust his weapon sharply into Pillay's back.

'This way, girlie. You first.'

Ryder and Pillay decided to play it their way for now, though Ryder had the momentary thought that the creep's comment to Pillay ran the risk of producing the first example he would ever see of spontaneous combustion.

Within a couple of minutes the four of them were inside the house. Ryder took in at a glance the Kandinsky original on the wall, the sumptuous carpets everywhere, the excessively ornate mock-gold-framed mirrors and numerous large solid brass objects, and the pile of plastic bags stacked in a cardboard box in one corner of the sitting room. The bags were without doubt stuffed with *nyaope*, and each contained an A-5 page sticky-taped to it.

'Saw you two at John Dory's a short while ago. Food not to your liking? As I understood it, you were just arriving as I was leaving. Don't like fish? I ask myself, why go to a fish restaurant if you don't like fish?'

Ben grinned at what he saw as his big companion's sharp wit, revealing only three or four teeth in his head. Then he responded with a high-pitched donkey hee-haw laugh as Red suddenly up-ended Pillay with a swift movement of his right foot, sweeping sideways and knocking her feet forward from underneath her. Ryder reacted instinctively and made a move toward him but found the big man's revolver pointed right at his forehead.

'Uh-uh! Hold it right there, mister. Ben, watch her. Sit on her if you have to. I want to talk to this guy.'

Pillay, struggling with only one arm, pulled herself into a seated position as Ben stood above her, his revolver pointed at her heart. He grinned.

'Got you, girlie. Don't try anything. No-one messes with me. Check it out.'

Pillay turned icy cold with fury as he giggled inanely and aimed the revolver at her, moving it from her heart to her head and back again.

'So tell, me, mister,' said Red. 'Why so interested in me? What makes you two want to tail me all the way out here?'

'It's like this, you see,' Ryder replied. 'I'm interested in how you, the captain of a little yacht moored at the Yacht Club, can come to own such a great car. I'm not a tax collector or anything, but a glance at this house adds to my interest. Princess Grace would like this place. Not the Monaco lady. I mean Grace Mugabe. She has just your kind of taste. Is that a genuine Kandinsky on the wall? Oh, wait, you probably wouldn't know your Kandinsky from your Stravinsky...'

'Oh, so we have a clever man amongst us, do we?'

'A real *lanie*, this *oke*, hey Red?' added Ben.

'But don't let me stop there, because the other thing I wonder about is how much you're being paid by the mystery passenger you're transporting early tomorrow morning.'

'What passenger?'

'You tell me. A very big man. Big in more ways than one, we hear. He must be paying you top dollar. Big muscle-headed guy like you...'

Ryder was ready for the impulsive move forward from Red, who was sufficiently riled by Ryder's comments that he misjudged for a moment and his anger produced a concentration lapse that gave Ryder a nano-second in which to act.

Ryder slapped the revolver upward at the same time as he brought his forehead smashing forward into the base of the big man's nose. Ryder had practiced the head butt as a teenager at school, and as a university student on one occasion he had brought it to near perfection in destroying four muggers who had set upon him in a cobbled back alley in Paris. On that occasion the young mugger in question spent four months in hospital with a fractured skull while his three companions suffered nothing worse than broken arms, wrists and, in one case, a multiple-fracture shin. Ryder had walked away from the police station with a tiny strip of Elastoplast on his forehead and some high-fives from the French cops. The attitude of the French cops on that occasion might even have been one of the reasons he first started thinking about a career in policing.

On this occasion there would be no need for the plaster strip. There was careful science in Ryder's split-second move. Tilt the head slightly downward, clench teeth, stiffen neck muscles, lean slightly backward, plan to use one inch above your own eyebrows, clench teeth, close mouth, use whole body weight. Good night.

The blow was as perfectly timed and aimed as Ryder had ever managed it, and the lights went out in Big Red's head even before Ryder followed through. Firstly with a massive powerhouse right that fractured the man's left eye socket. Secondly with a shattering left that smashed him just below the sternum. Game over, and Big Red melted to the floor with a pool of blood widening as it gushed from his nose, mouth, and left eye into the expensive long-hair Pakistan shag rug, ivory brown, that had once been advertised as one hundred percent natural wool at a bargain price and now covered more than half the surface area of the room. A rug that would now need some expensive cleaning.

Ben was stunned for a moment by the speed and power of Ryder's action and that gave Pillay the second she needed to kick out at his gun hand. The weapon went flying and Ben realised the game was up. He ran, even as Big Red was melting into the floor. He still held in his other hand the remote control that worked the security gate, so he was ahead of Pillay, who had to struggle to her feet without the aid of her left arm, hampered by the giant mass of inert muscle that Ryder had dropped almost into her lap. By the time Pillay was out of the door Ben was out of the gate and already running straight over the road into the school fields opposite.

Knowing that Big Red was down and out and safe for the moment, Ryder followed after Pillay. Ben hit the entrance to the floodlit field through the wide-open security gates where the workmen were still busy painting whitewash lines on the grass tracks. Pillay sprinted after him. By the time Ryder got to the top of the bank leading down to the field he realised that he was about to have a grandstand view of what could become a very entertaining event. One that he would be relating to friends time and again in the future.

Ben saw that his best chance of escape lay in trying to reach the opposite end of the field from where he had entered. There was a grassy bank there that led to some foliage that might give him a chance. He had no way of realising that he had just run onto the exact starting point of the hundred-metre track and was running in a straight line for the opposite bank, which took him all the way there perfectly in-lane. He was at the fifty metre mark by the time Pillay hit the ten metre mark. Ryder and the shocked workmen were then treated to the sight of Pillay gaining an extra metre for every metre that the terrified Ben took, pursued by *the tiniest beep-beep the roadrunner you ever saw*, as one of the workmen would describe it to his family over breakfast the next morning.

When he hit the sixty metre mark she was at thirty. When he got to seventy she was at fifty. He hit eighty and she was already at seventy. The workmen were cheering. Ben looked around in terror as he realised what was happening, and as a consequence hit a wobble. Which meant that she drew level with him even before he hit the ninety metre mark. She thrust out a leg, tapped his left foot behind his right, and he ploughed a long furrow with his nose, ending up five centimetres from the finishing line as she leaped over his body, her momentum taking her across the line. She stopped and turned to face him. To thunderous applause, whistles, and cheers from the spectators, Ryder cheering more loudly than any of them.

'OK *boykie*,' she said, standing in front of the downed man, and panting. 'What was that you were saying about *girlies* not messing with you?'

Ryder was on the phone to Dippenaar as Pillay brought the hapless Ben back down the track, to the jeers and jokes and sporadic applause of the workmen, who had been told briefly by Ryder, when they questioned him, that they were cops arresting a couple of no-goods.

Ben's face seemed to have turned arctic white on the sides – a combination of whitewash and terror – and it sported a deep and nasty graze that oozed blood from his hairline, straight down over the length of his nose and across his chin. Looks like the Cross of St. George, thought Ryder. A bit of a scar there, no question. He turned to face the guy, having closed the call with Dippenaar. The cleaners were on their way, and Koeks and Dipps would come with them to help Ryder and Pillay wrap up. Koeks would put in a call to the Westville Police Station to brief them.

The workmen crowded around Pillay as she arrived, and they didn't hold back on either the compliments to her or the jeers at her prisoner.

*'Well done, detective. Your fellow detective here tells us that you also do martial arts. Is that true?'*

*'Fantastic job, detective. You going to run in the Olympics?'*

*'Yissus, my china. You always get women to chase after you like that?'*

'*Why you paint your face red and white, boykie? You look like a blerrie Engelse rugby fan.*'

'*Is that what you call a one-arm bandit, chasing people down like that?*'

'*I tell you, Usain Bolt is going to poep himself for the next Olympics when he hears about her.*'

Pillay responded to the cheers and jeers and laughter and back-slapping with a mixture of irritation and gratitude. They all crossed the road back to the house with the fugitive, before the workmen eventually drifted away back to their tasks.

As they re-entered the house, Ryder began to have a closer look around. Pillay manacled her captive to the security gate on the front door, and undertook a quick inspection of Big Red before sitting down on the sofa, from where she continued the discussion with Ryder, who moved quickly through the rooms and called back down the passage to continue the dialogue.

'Looks like masses of *whoonga*, Navi. Have a look at the bags in the corner. Looks like Red Rooster makes his living from some interesting stuff.'

While they waited for the cleaners and the ambulance and the detectives, they managed to scare the terrified Ben sufficiently to elicit further information from him. Yes, Red dealt in *nyaope* and other drugs. Yes, he had been planning to take masses of the stuff back with him tonight to the boat. Yes, he was planning to sell the stuff abroad, because he had a commission to take some guy to sea so he thought why not use the opportunity to sell abroad. No, he wasn't sure where exactly it was but he thought from something Red had said that it was somewhere up the coast in another country. Maybe Zanzibar. Maybe Maputo. No, he himself wasn't part of the boat thing. He knew nothing about that, he said. He was just a friend of Red's and looked after his house for him while he was away on business. Yes, he had a licence for the gun. No, he hadn't used it before, except on a firing range.

Ryder searched quickly but thoroughly as they both threw out questions at Ben.

By the time the clean-up operation was taken over by the uniforms and the medics, with Dippenaar and Koekemoer being their normal helpful and efficient selves, Big Red had recovered consciousness. He was going to have one helluva headache, the medics reported. He was put in the ambulance under guard and taken off to be processed. Dippenaar handled the formalities and it was decided that the Westville Station would be the first port of call for him and his companion. But they would be dealt with separately, the big man obviously needing hospital.

'OK, guys,' said Ryder, finally. 'We need to get back to the unit and brief Nyawula, and make a few adjustments to the strategy for tonight. Now we know that we have the rooster and we know the ship won't be sailing, we'll re-think exactly how we prepare for Swanepoel.'

As they started winding things down, Ryder, Pillay, Dippenaar and Koekemoer laughed and joked their way across the street. Ryder held them back from going to the two cars for a moment, because he said he wanted to point out to K and D the school athletics track and give them a quick run-down of what had happened. He ignored Pillay's protest, and they all walked across to the floodlit field. Pillay made the initial sounds of protest, but she went along with it because, she would only partly admit to herself, she actually felt quite good about it. She hadn't run like that for a long time.

'I clocked you, you know, Navi?' said Ryder, as they surveyed the newly whitewashed tracks.

'What?'

'I clocked you doing the hundred metres with the guy pacing you.'

'Piss off, Jeremy.'

'Serious. I'm afraid, though, that young Mr Barrington still has the school record. I clocked you at only 11.5 seconds.'

'Rubbish man. There was a wind against me. I definitely did it in at least 11.2. And I was running one-handed, anyway. Barrington didn't have his arm in a sling. So make that a flat eleven seconds from me.'

'Sounds reasonable to me. Guys?'

Agreement from K and D. Laughter and teasing. And further insults.

'OK. Let's go, team,' said Ryder.


**20.50.**

The last panel van had left more than an hour ago. Maybe that had been it: maybe the final one. There hadn't been a gap of more than twenty minutes between any of the vans until now.

He had counted thirteen arrivals in total since the first one he had observed. How many there had been before that he couldn't know. They comprised a mixture of different shapes and sizes. A Mercedes Sprinter with what Thabethe estimated to be about a two-ton payload, a smaller

Volkswagen Caddy with about a half-ton payload, an Opel Movano with a carrying capacity of maybe one and a half tons, and other vehicles whose make and model he didn't know. The only thing they had in common was that they were all enclosed vans. Some of them had been the same van returning from an earlier visit, but each of them was handled in the same way. Arrive, door opens, into the garage, ten to fifteen minutes in there, then out again. Wait. Then the next one. A glance at the height of each vehicle above the brick-paved apron as it entered the garage told Thabethe, as it would any observer, that the vans all departed in a much heavier state than that in which they had arrived.

What had been of particular interest to Thabethe was something that occurred in only two of the instances. On about the fourth arrival he had observed, and again on or about the ninth or the tenth, the van had in each case been accompanied by a car, which had parked outside while the van went into the garage. In both these cases, when the van had emerged a man had come out onto the apron. Not the fat Afrikaner. This was a man who looked twice the weight of the Afrikaner. His extraordinary obesity was magnified by the fact that he was also incredibly short. And he waddled. On each of the two occasions he waddled over to the driver of the accompanying car, spoke briefly, and was handed a bag. In the first instance it was a brown paper bag. In the second it was a large manila envelope. On each occasion he looked over his shoulder, and up and down the street, tucked the received article under his arm, and walked back to the garage door as the cars pulled away, leading their respective vans, turned left into Sandile Thusi, and disappeared into the traffic.

'Cash,' thought Thabethe. 'Must be. Big one. Afrikaner boy said *they pulling big money*. Big man, big money. For Skhura.'

He assumed that in each of the other instances the driver of the van had handed over the cash, if it was indeed cash, inside the garage and away from possible observers. In the two instances in the street they had handled the transaction separately from the driver of the van, for whatever reason. Whether or not he was right about this, Thabethe was convinced that money had changed hands each time in the course of the afternoon's transactions.

It was time to check the house.

**21.50.**

Pillay, Koekemoer, and Dippenaar were being briefed by Ryder about the impending midnight raid on the yacht.

'Nyawula has been speaking to the commander at Point Road, guys, and the Harbour team are also set up for the raid at exactly midnight. He's also been talking to Durban North and they're providing a couple of plain-clothes along with a narcotics specialist. We'll have all their names soon.'

'Aren't you and Navi going to be there to harpoon the whale in person, Jeremy?'

'No, Koeks, not unless we get a call that he's actually evaded everyone and made it to the yacht without being spotted. In that case the Harbour guys will let us know the moment he arrives and Navi and I will drop everything and be there like a shot.'

'Jeremy knows that I want to be the one to read him his rights, Koeks,' said Pillay. 'That's something I'm looking forward to, big, big time.'

'We don't expect Swanepoel to make his move until a couple of hours after midnight. With Big Red already out of the picture and the boat not capable of sailing without him, Nyawula says there's no chance of Swanepoel slipping out to sea. So he doesn't want the four of us just sitting there waiting for the next four hours when something big could go down elsewhere. I think he's right. The vessel's scheduled for sailing at 4.00 am, and we assume Swanepoel's going to hide out until the very last moment before he arrives at the wharf. But by then the Harbour guys will have taken over the vessel, taken the crew in for questioning, and be set up in place for Swanepoel's arrival sometime an hour or two after midnight. Navi and I will get down there only after midnight, if nothing has happened before then, so that we can be in place to bust the Major when he arrives.'

'If Jeremy and I are wrong in our assumptions and he arrives earlier than the crew guy told us this evening,' Pillay added, 'the Harbour team have the go-ahead to call us immediately and wait for us to get there, but to secure the boat if there's any panic.'

'What do you want me and Koeks to do, Jeremy?'

'Thanks, Dipps. Captain says he'd like the two of you to be here, riding free like me and Navi, until whatever action goes down actually starts happening. I hope that's OK.'

K and D gave their 'no problem' assurances.

'It's only if Swanepoel evades being spotted by any of our guys in the next couple of hours and if he actually makes it to the wharf before midnight without any of us being alerted, that Navi and I will hit the gas and join the Harbour team.'

'So they're there really only to cover the base and nail him in case he slips through our fingers and arrives earlier than you expect him to?'

'That's it, Koeks. So, to recap, the Harbour team will hit the boat at midnight and take the crew into custody. Two plainclothes will be on hand to welcome Swanepoel if he arrives early, with another two in the shadows, and the bust will be videotaped in its entirety from two different cameras that are being set up as we speak.'

'Shit. It's hard sitting and waiting. I want to go whaling.'

'Patience, Navi. All good things come to those who wait,' said Koekemoer. 'Want some coffee?'

## 22.25.

Thabethe dropped silently from the tree onto the soft ground. After scouting around outside in the darkened garden, pausing for some time in the hydrangeas, checking in each window, and refraining from entering through the window with the damaged latch, he had chosen the tree. He had been up there for what seemed like a much longer time but was in reality only about an hour. He had sat immobile, straining every sense to identify how many people might be indoors.

He moved like a cat, light on his feet, and quickly opened the window. The latch was still loose. No-one had checked it. He slithered like an eel through the window and into the room, and stood, silent for a moment. He paused, listening, straining to hear even the slightest sound from either inside the house or outside in the street. Then he moved a couple of paces to the left of the window, and stood again for a moment, ears again straining to hear anything from the interior of the house.

He waited, as he had done the night before, for his eyes to adjust. Then he moved across the room, threading his way through the mixture of empty wooden crates and unpacked boxes lying open, discarded sheets of industrial plastic and shattered planks lying on the floor, bent nails and torn labels and discarded stickers strewn about, until he stood behind the door. He listened at the hinge of the door, and heard distant muffled voices. He slipped quickly into the passage and into the next room. The same. Empty crates and boxes and detritus. Probably the same in the kitchen and garage.

Then he heard the voices, distinctly nearer. They were coming out of the room at the end and about to enter the passage. Then the voices stopped. Nothing. Silence. He waited. And waited. Then he heard someone entering the passage and moving away from him, toward the kitchen. He heard the kitchen door close. Then nothing. He waited. Then in the distance he heard the outside door, leading from the kitchen into the back area and then to the garage. The back door appeared to have been slammed shut. He waited. Nothing. He moved slowly down the passage. He put his hand on the kitchen door handle. Before he could open it, he felt the rush of air behind him and stepped aside to his right just in time to avoid the worst of the crushing blow that had been aimed at his head.

Dirk smashed the heavy wooden stool onto Thabethe's left shoulder, screaming as he did so.

'Vic! I got him. Now, Vic!'

Swanepoel ripped open the kitchen door and barged back into the passage. But Thabethe was too quick for him. His left arm was useless, numbed from the blow to his shoulder, but he had the presence of mind to kick out at Dirk's damaged knee, eliciting a piercing scream and doubling his assailant over right into the path of the advancing Major. It brought him an extra two seconds as he scrambled up to his feet, and it allowed him time to draw the Z88 from the small of his back where it was tucked into his belt.

Dirk watched in horror as the enormous three-hundred-and-fifty-pound bulk of the Major engulfed Thabethe and they both fell to the floor, the Major's hands clutching at Thabethe's throat and Thabethe's left leg smashing horribly at a devastating angle against the upended stool, the calf muscle crushed under the weight of his adversary. But his gun hand was free and the massive abdomen of the Major was pressed directly against the Z88. Thabethe's wide-open staring coal-black eyes were two inches from those of the Major as he pulled the trigger once, twice, three times, four times, then paused, and as the Major stared at him in agonised horror Thabethe pulled the trigger again. And again. And again. His black eyes stared back in hatred at the fat man as the Major realised what was happening. Dirk stared, frozen in horror for a moment. Then, as Thabethe struggled to get out from under the mountain of flesh, Dirk, unable to get to his feet, scrambled backward arse-first into the room from which he had emerged, slammed the door behind him, reached up in agony for the bolt and slid it into place. Then scrambled away from the door in case Thabethe pumped bullets into it.

But Thabethe had another focus. He stood up, his left leg and left arm almost paralysed with pain. He stood over the Major and put an eighth bullet into his forehead. Then aimed at the fat man's throat and pulled the trigger. Click. Again. Click. Nothing. He looked at Dirk's door. Looked back at the corpse. Let the Z88 slip from his hand onto the floor. Then he hobbled in agony over Swanepoel's body, through the kitchen, and out the back door. He stumbled outside, through the garage, out into the road, and made his way to the white Ford Escort van.

**22.40.**

The calls came in from every source imaginable. iPhones, pagers, land-lines, car-phones were ringing all over. *Shots fired on Sandile Thusi.* Neighbours, passing cars, patrons from local restaurants. They were all on their phones tweeting and texting and calling.

Cars soon streamed down Margaret Mncadi, Pixley ka Seme, Stalwart Simelane Street, some came from Berea, some chose Umgeni Road and others rounded the Greyville Race Course. From all over they came. Detectives and uniforms, medics and private tow-cars. Word was out, and it was confusing. The messages ranged from fire to shooting to stabbing to theft to rape. They built on one another. One person said he had actually seen the shooting.

*Well, not actually seen, but, you know, it was like so, you know, there! Like right next to me. Over the wall there.*

His message was passed on, and elaborated in the passing on. *This is a big one. You should get over here.*

The crowds gathered. The sirens approached.

**22.45.**

Thabethe retrieved the key balanced on top of the rear right wheel. Fighting the waves of pain in both his left shoulder and his left leg, he unlocked the door to the Ford Escort. Dragged himself, in agony, behind the wheel, battled to find the ignition, started the vehicle, took off, and tore out of the parking spot and into the night. He careened across the inside lane on Sandile Thusi, flung the wheel over to the left, then lurched into the right lane. He could hear sirens in the distance behind him, and could see the faint glow of blue lights in the rear-view mirror. He was going to make it. He screamed in anger and frustration as he floored the pedal. He was convinced that the door behind which Dirk was hiding contained a stash of cash, and here he was running away from it. But at least he was not going to be caught. He was going to make it.

The car swung right and disappeared from view before the first blue lights appeared and the police vehicles then skidded to a halt, sirens wound down, and uniforms and plain-clothes alike swarmed into Tenth Avenue and then into the property.

Thabethe roared through two red lights and one green, turned, zigzagged, skidded through a stop street then another green light, cursing all the way. He eventually hit the M4, reaching maximum speed through

Durban North, flashing past the old Virginia aerodrome with his engine screaming as if it was a low-flying aircraft, then past Umhlanga, the car almost shaking apart with vibrations as he thundered through Hillhead, when he suddenly took his foot off the pedal, geared down, slammed on the brakes and screeched to a halt. He reversed, back toward the pantechnicon parked on the side of the road, engine idling. He could see the driver down the bank, in the bush, urinating. Thabethe grabbed the cell-phone from his pocket, and within seconds was talking to Mkhize.

'Spikes! You tell them now. You tell the cops. You tell them Skhura took the phone. Now. You phone the detectives. OK. OK. No, is all good. No problem. Yes, Spikes. You tell them. Tell the cops Skhura has got the phone. They can start the bug.'

He closed the call down and got out. He found the perfect spot on the enormous vehicle. He tucked the phone into the folds of the tarpaulin, ensured that it was safe and secured and not visible to passers-by, and then went back to the Escort. Then he went through the motions of urinating before greeting the driver as he returned to his vehicle. The driver shared some inanity with him about too much beer, which he only half-heard but understood, and carried on with his fake pee while the man got into the driver's cab and took off.

He watched the pantechnicon travel into the night. Hopefully toward KwaDukuza or further afield. Maybe Richards Bay. Maybe Maputo. Maybe Timbuktu. Idiot cops. There goes Skhura, into Africa.

He drove on, a little slower now, and turned right onto the M27 before slowing down for the ride past the beach. He pulled over at one point as he saw a car ahead.

He switched off the lights and waited for the vehicle to disappear into the darkness ahead of him. Not worth taking a chance. He could feel his heart pounding, His breath rasping in his chest. To be caught now would be to lose everything. He sat, tense, fingers as taut as guitar strings, his left leg throbbing in agony.

The car disappeared.

He waited, then started up and continued down South Beach road to the end.

**22.50.**

Ryder walked out of the Argyle house followed by Pillay, as Nyawula arrived and clambered out of his car.

'The Major's down, Captain, but his side-kick will talk,' said Ryder.

'Down?'

'And out, Captain. He's done. It's over. Looks like Thabethe's work. The Major's side-kick is already babbling like a baby. I think because he took one look at Navi, who knows him quite well. He's the Montpelier Road guy she put in hospital. He wants to talk. Will tell us everything, he says. As long as we don't leave him alone with Detective Pillay.'

'There's a laptop,' added Pillay, ignoring Ryder's comment, 'and huge amounts of cash, Captain. Really big piles of it. More than a million, we would say. There are four guys over it, counting and double-counting and triple-counting right now. We've called Piet to come in from home, to come in and help, especially with that side of it. He said he was happy to come in. Apparently the family dinner he had tonight was a bit of a disaster, so he said he would be thrilled to come in.'

'Looks like they were crunching numbers and deals and stuff when Thabethe surprised them,' said Ryder.

'And Thabethe?'

'He's escaped, Captain,' said Pillay. 'Gone. We lost him. Looks like he left us a present. Not just the Major. He also left us the last of the four Vektor Z88s. We'll check it out. But I can tell you already. It's one of ours. One of the four we lost with Thabethe. No question.'

'OK. OK. We'll pick him up, sooner or later. You've done well, both of you. Thank you, and to K and D, too. Thabethe is one of those thorns that stick in the flesh to make sure we don't ever stop with these guys. We'll get him. He can't last.'

'I've sent word to the Harbour team, captain. I've told them to bring the whole show forward by an hour. They should be going onto the yacht right now. I've told them pig number one won't be arriving, but that they should take in the whole lot of them for questioning. They might all be clean, of course. Swanepoel and his crony captain might have simply hired them as a professional crew for what they all saw as a straight sailing job. But we'll only know the details after each one of them has been through interrogation. They'll be taken by the Harbour team for questioning. And held overnight if necessary.'

'Thanks, Jeremy. That's good to know.'

Nyawula seemed exhausted as well as exhilarated, Ryder thought. His unit had cracked a big case. But the Captain had so badly wanted Thabethe. One of the most evil guys out there. If there was ever one thing he would want to do for Nyawula, it would be to get Thabethe's head on a platter for him.

The uniforms and the plain-clothes were milling about. Car radios were crackling and voices were issuing instructions. The medics were already at it. Cronje arrived, and was briefed by Pillay. K and D teased him about his dinner. He seemed in good humour and went in to help with the counting.

Nyawula barked instructions and people ran. Doors banged in the building. Pillay and Ryder walked over to Koekemoer and Dippenaar. The journos were arriving. Nyawula went into the house. Cameras were flashing. Backs were slapped. High fives were given. But there was a touch of gloom amid the festivity. Thabethe had escaped. Nyawula eventually came back out and walked over to the four detectives.

'OK, guys. That's about it. You can take off, this is all under control. Piet tells me that the money is just short of one and a half million.'

Whistles of surprise all around, with a couple of wise-cracks, before Nyawula continued.

'It will be bagged and recorded and witnessed. And, hopefully, tracked back to the purchasers. Looks like we'll have a few days follow-up on this. And who knows where they might find Thabethe. Meanwhile, forensics are on their way. They've had a rough night and are very short-staffed. But they're on the way. You guys can all pack it in. Sunday tomorrow. Tough day on Monday. Have a break. And thanks to all of you.'

They all murmured acknowledgements in their own way, and thanks back to him.

'Welcome to the team, Pillay.'

'Thanks, Captain.'

'I'm sure I speak for the others when I say that Monday's funeral is going to be a fraction easier for us. There'll be a gap without Ed, but I'm sure the men will agree with me when I say...'

'Thanks, Captain. I'll do my best.'

'I know you will. Thanks, Navi.'

As he walked away, the three detectives high-fived Pillay.

'Let's get a beer,' said Ryder.

**23.05.**

Thabethe came to a juddering halt in almost exactly the same spot where he had dragged the injured and handcuffed Dirk from the Honda Ballade two days ago. Then he remembered: got to move the car to a less conspicuous parking, otherwise someone will wonder and come prowling through the bush. He moved it a short stone's throw away and switched off. He locked the vehicle and limped his way stealthily and painfully into the bush.

He pushed his way into the dark and came to the same tree to which he had tied the Afrikaner, then collapsed, exhausted, leaning back in the same position as had his prisoner on Thursday.

He sat, recovering his breath, feeling his pulse returning to normal, letting the night settle back to its normal intricate tapestry of sound. A low buzz of crickets, beetles, mosquitoes and other insects, counter-pointed by the throaty syncopation of frogs and the distant crash of waves, smoothed his passage back to what he liked best. Darkness and solitude.

He pulled out a small piece of plastic wrapping and unfolded it. Within a minute he had drawn the toxic smoke and chemicals deep into his lungs. He felt them work their magic as he settled back into cold contemplation.

A glimmer of moonlight found its way through the topmost branches of the trees, and any observer from the thick foliage would have noted the tiny reflection of cold silver light in the two deep, dark wells of Thabethe's eyes, as they stared straight ahead into the darkness. Eyes that reflected deep and evil thoughts as he pondered over the action of the last few days, and pondered over what might have been. Pondered over how next time he would be more careful. Next time he would not make the same mistakes. Next time would be different.

His eyes stared, fixed on nothing except the dark foliage ahead of him. Eyes, some said, that sometimes made one feel that one was in the presence of the devil himself.

So they said.

# GLOSSARY

ag - ah, oh, well

aikona - no, no way, not there at all (see also haikona)

amaphoyisa - the police

amigo - friend (Spanish)

babelas - hangover

bakgat - great, excellent, fine, good

bantoe - corruption of bantu, associated with racist usage

blerrie - bloody

bliksem - hit, punch, strike

boere - (referring variously to) farmers, Afrikaners, policemen

boet - brother, male friend, dude

bok, bokke - buck, bucks (bokke as in Springboks)

boykie - boy: diminutive, little boy

bra, my bra - brother, my brother

braai, braaivleis - barbecue

breek - break

broer, bru - brother

bulala - kill

charra, charro - slang term for person of Indian ethnicity, often racist

china - friend, chum

chune - to tell someone

daarsy - there it is, there you are, that's it, dead right

deagle - Desert Eagle

dis reg - that's right

donner - hammer, hit, beat up

doos - box (lewd, meaning vagina), fool, idiot

dop - alcoholic drink

dronkgat - drunkard

dwaal - in a daze, lost

eekhoring - squirrel

eh-heh - yes, affirmative

eina - exclamation expressing pain

eish - interjection expressing disappointment, regret

ek sê - I say, I'm telling you

Engelsman - Englishman

fok - fuck

fokall - fuck-all, nothing

fokken - fucken, fucking

fokoff - fuck off

gatvol - fed up

geld - money

gemors - mess, disarray

gif - poison, marijuana

gogo - old woman, grandmother

hayi - no, no way (see also tchai)

hayibo - no, no way

haikona - no, no way, not there at all

hau - expression of surprise (what? hey? oh?)

heita - hello, howzit, how is it?

helluva - 'hell of a' (as in helluva long time)

hunnert - hundred

impimpi - sell-out, informer

ja - yes

ja'k stem saam - yes, I agree (ja, ek stem saam)

jeez - Jesus (exclamation of surprise or frustration)

jirra - exclamation of surprise derived from 'Here,' Afrikaans for 'God'

jislaaik - expression of astonishment (see also yissus)

jong - young man, friend

jou - your, you

jy - you

Kaatjie Kekkelbek - stereotypical cape 'coloured' stage character

kak - crap, shit

kêrels - guys, chaps, police

kif - great, cool, nice

klaar - finish

koeksister - (lit. cake sister) braided dough sweet delicacy

laaitie - lightie, young one

laduma! - score!, celebrating a goal scored in football

lanie - fancy, posh

lank - long, a lot, very

lekker - great, nice, tasty

madala - old man

mal - crazy, mad

mampara - fool, dolt, idiot

manne - men

mense - men, people

mina - me

mfowethu - brother

moer - murder, kill, beat up, also 'the moer in' ('fed up with')

moerse - large, big time, huge

moegoe - idiot

my bra - my brother

nè? - not so?

nee - no

nek - neck

nooit - never

nyaope - street drug (see also whoonga)

oke, ou, ouens - bloke, blokes

ouma - grandmother

ou toppie - old man, father, old person

pallie - diminutive for 'pal,' friend

poep - fart

praat - talk

reg - right

Seffrika - South Africa

shaddup, shuddup - shut up

sharp, sharp-sharp - ok, yes, quick-quick

shibobo - fancy footwork (sweet moves, like nutmeg) from football

shweet - sweet, cool

sies - sis, expression of disgust

skabenga - crook, criminal, no-good

skelm - thief, crook

skollie, skollies - crook, gangster (from the Greek skolios: crooked)

skrik vir niks - scared of nothing

slim jim – device for breaking into motor vehicles

snoeks - little fish, term of endearment

sommer - simply

soutie, soutpiel - derogatory term for English South African (salty penis)

spookgerook - (lit.) ghost-smoked, stoned to the point of paranoia

struesbob - as true as Bob

sug - care ('you think I sug/care?')

suss - to have suss - to be sharp or streetwise

swak - weak, broke

tchai - no, no way (see also hayi)

tjaila - time to go home

tjommie - chum, good friend

toppie - see ou toppie: old man, father, old person

trap - stairs, staircase

trek - pull, leave, exit

tronk - jail, prison

tsotsi - gangster

uclever - the clever one

uitlander - outlander, alien

umlungu - white one, white man (vocative: mlungu)

val - fall

vrek - die, dead

vrekked - died

vroeg - early

vuvuzela - plastic horn noisemaker, prominent at football matches

wat? - what?

weet - know (jy weet? - you know?)

wena - you

whatchamacallit - what you may call it, thing, object, what it might be

whoonga - slang for nyaope

yebo - yes

yissus - jesus (exclamation of surprise or frustration)

yislaaik - variation of yissus

# ABOUT THE AUTHOR

Ian Patrick writes full-time from his home in the United Kingdom. After working as an actor, director and teacher in theatre, film and television, he turned to an academic career and for some years published scholarly essays in a range of international academic journals.

'Not particularly page-turning stuff,' he says. 'Then one day the editor of a journal with a slightly more commercial and business-oriented focus, who had solicited an essay from me based on my scholarly research, asked me what my fee was. I had never considered the possibility that anyone might want to pay me for publishing anything I wrote, so I suggested that he pay me whatever he thought appropriate. He did so. After the resulting pleasant surprise I considered that there might be another dimension to writing.'

He believes that his years as an actor and director now play a modest part in his writing, as does his past experience in scholarly research. 'My fiction is based to the best of my ability on research and field work. I have to believe every word my fictive characters say, every action they undertake,' he says.

'I endeavour to make my fiction plausible and authentic. This requires exhaustive work and detailed research, and friends on occasion express surprise that it takes me at least a year of full-time work to write an eighty thousand word crime thriller. In my view, however, although it is clearly desirable to arrive at one's destination by bringing a work to publication, it is the *journey* that is the really exciting and enjoyable part of writing. I can only hope that readers will also enjoy the journey of discovering my characters and their foibles, their actions and their experiences. I hope, too, that they will inform me about and forgive me for any lapses in my work or any errors of detail.'

Made in the USA
Middletown, DE
24 June 2018